The Winemaker's Dinner
Entrée

Dr. Ivan Rusilko & Everly Drummond

OMNIFIC PUBLISHING
DALLAS

Omnific Publishing
10000 North Central Expressway, Dallas, TX 75231
www.omnificpublishing.com

First Omnific eBook edition, December 2012
First Omnific trade paperback edition, December 2012

The characters and events in this book are fictitious.
Any similarity to real persons, living or dead,
is coincidental and not intended by the author.

Library of Congress Cataloguing-in-Publication Data

Rusilko, Dr. Ivan; Drummond, Everly.
The Winemaker's Dinner: Entrée / Dr. Ivan Rusilko & Everly Drummond – 1st ed.
ISBN: 978-1-623420-06-2
1. Contemporary Romance — Fiction. 2. Erotica — Fiction.
3. Hollywood — Fiction. 4. Dr. Ivan Rusilko — Fiction. I. Title

10 9 8 7 6 5 4 3 2 1

Cover Design by Micha Stone and Amy Brokaw
Interior Book Design by Coreen Montagna
Photography by John Conroy (JohnConroyPhotography.com)
Cover Model: Dr. Ivan Rusilko and Adrianne Martinez

Printed in the United States of America

*This book is dedicated to the hopeless romantics
who believe that there is a love that exists in the depths of an unknown heart
that's just waiting for them to find it.
~ Dr. Ivan Rusilko*

*To Mags,
The best sister, friend, and confidant a girl could ever ask for.
~ Everly Drummond*

CHAPTER 1

"I Miss You"

"The trick to not overcooking tuna is to stick to the ninety-second rule," Jaden said confidently, smiling at the camera. "Make sure the oil is at the right temperature, add your fish, and sear for ninety seconds on each side." She looked down at the raw slab of sashimi-grade tuna hanging from the tongs and slowly lowered it into the oiled cast-iron frying pan, igniting a series of fierce sizzles and crackles. As a drop of oil splashed on the inside of her wrist, she held in a string of vulgarity and continued to smile pretty for the camera.

As the aroma of searing tuna wafted through the air and filled the studio, she could practically hear the rumbling stomachs of the surrounding crew members. They'd been at it for ten hours straight, taking only five-minute breaks here and there to use the washroom and have Kat touch up her hair and makeup. With the weekend fast approaching, everyone was eager to wrap up this episode, "Tuna: The Way To A Man's Heart," and enjoy the nice weather the weekend promised.

Jaden's smile widened at the thought of some time to herself. Lately her life had felt like one long rollercoaster ride. Fresh off a string of talk shows, guest appearances, and photo shoots, she was riding a high with no end in sight. She and Ivan had instituted a policy of never going more than two weeks without seeing each other, and it seemed to be the secret to their success. They'd been making things work despite the distance. She would fly to Miami once a month, and he'd come to LA. They'd negotiated their work schedules to allow for the long weekends. And oh, how she loved those long, lazy weekends of pure, unadulterated lovemaking. Okay, maybe it wasn't *only* the sex she loved so much. The time they spent together was amazing—but man, oh man, the sex was great. God! There was still a week to go before she could hightail it to Miami. Ivan would be waiting, flowers in hand, looking sexy as hell and ready to...*Fuck!* The tuna was about to burn.

In an instant, Jaden's attention returned to the semi-cooked piece of fish. With a flick of her wrist, she flipped it over and began to sear the other side, creating another wave of delicious aroma. She could have sworn someone in the back of the room sighed.

Through the bright lights and oil-slick haze the searing had created, Jaden noticed something out of the corner of her eye—something that stood apart from the standard five-man crew, hunched over from poor posture and oversized beer guts. No, it couldn't be! It was her turn to visit Miami, and that trip was still a week away. She tried to focus on finishing the segment, but her scrambled thoughts were suddenly invaded by a distraction of another, less-desirable sort.

How the hell could Kevin bring in some new co-host, especially when the show was doing so well? *One Hot Kitchen* was her baby, her show that she'd nurtured from the very first shoot. So why, all of a sudden, did she need a co-host—and worse than that, one who was only riding the coattails of his famous father, Chef François Gris? Granted, Jaden admired Chef Gris, but his son was still a threat to her show and a burden she wasn't in the mood to bear. Barely any experience to speak of and a womanizer to boot—no doubt he planned to *steal* his fifteen minutes of fame. And what if he wrecked the show in the process? Though she'd never even met him, Jaden was coming to loathe Damian Gris.

She cringed all over again at the thought of having to meet him at Kevin's welcoming party on Sunday. She'd have to wear some silly evening dress, drive all the way up to the Hollywood Hills, and plaster a fake smile across her face, just to meet some playboy masquerading as a chef. She was going to despise every agonizing minute of working with this dumbass. *Goddamnit!*

Once again, Jaden had let her mind wander almost too far, but she quickly snagged the perfectly seared tuna out of the pan. She regained her composure and continued talking without missing a beat. Turning toward another counter, where small bowls of ingredients had been laid out in a row, she gave step-by-step instructions for preparing a mint glaze, the very same glaze she'd created after being inspired by the Winemaker's Dinner last year. At Bianca it had become her signature dish.

"First," she began, picking up an empty bowl and a whisk. "Always make sure you combine your ingredients just before you glaze the tuna. Start by whisking together two tablespoons of sugar with three tablespoons of vinegar." Jaden added the ingredients to the empty bowl and demonstrated. "Next, always be sure your mint is fresh. You can determine its freshness by grinding one of the leaves between your fingers. By doing this, you will release the essential oils. The stronger the aroma, the fresher it is." She held the crushed mint leaf to her nose and inhaled. "I'd say this is pretty—"

She stopped midsentence, and her knees felt weak. Beyond the scent of fresh mint, there was something else in the air now, something overpowering and *very* familiar—something her mind translated as hair-pulling, lip-biting, mind-blowing, earth-shattering moments lost in Ivan's embrace. Her instructional banter came to a grinding halt, and her eyes zeroed in on the dark figure near the far door of the studio. "No, it couldn't be, could it?" Jaden whispered as she willed herself to not get her hopes up. Ivan had a medical conference in Washington, didn't he? He might be amazing, but being in two places at once was impossible.

As Jaden squinted against the bright lights, her eyes slowly made sense of the tall figure taking shape in front of her: wavy brown hair that brushed the collar of his pressed shirt, a bouquet of her favorite wildflowers, a blue suit that hugged every muscle of his body, and that all-too-familiar smile. Ivan.

All thoughts of the show and the crew and the tuna vanished as she dropped the sprig of mint and rushed toward him. "Take five!" she yelled as she ran across the studio floor, arms outstretched. Ivan tossed the flowers aside and caught her in midair. Their bodies melded into each other's as Jaden wrapped her legs around his waist, smiling against the soft contour of his lips. She grinned as she felt him cop a feel of her ass beneath the stiff kitchen whites, and they held each other tightly as their tongues dove deeper. This was no "Nice to see you" kiss. This was a passionate moment between two people desperately in love. Jaden trembled as she felt Ivan stiffen between her legs. She loved having this effect on him. She reciprocated by pressing herself into him and grinding. She could tell he needed this moment just as much as she did, and for a brief second there were no ogling cameramen, no hot spotlights beaming down on them, and no sexy-yet-annoying new co-host on the way. Just then there was only the two of them, and everything in the world seemed right and perfect.

Sensing that the others in the room likely didn't share their enthusiasm, no matter how romantic the gesture was, Jaden released her iron grip. She slid down the length of Ivan's body and gave him a long look, laced with love and lust, letting him know this little tryst was far from over.

"Great! That shot's ruined," a bearded man grumbled from behind the closest camera. "I don't have anything else to do tonight."

Though she felt badly, Jaden couldn't help but smile as the cameraman took off his ratty LA Kings hat and tossed it into the air, throwing a mini temper tantrum.

"Sorry about that, baby girl," Ivan whispered, squeezing her hand. He bent and picked up the bouquet of flowers. "I'll put these in your dressing room while you finish up."

"Yeah, I think that would be a smart idea," another cameraman mumbled from behind them.

Jaden glanced over and saw a hint of a smile on his face.

"Can we please wrap this up, Ms. Thorne?" he continued. "It's getting late, and we all have lives to get back to. I realize we're not as exciting as Prince Charming, but time is money."

"Of course," she said. "I just needed a moment there. Not sure what came over me." Though a bit embarrassed by her lapse in professionalism, Jaden couldn't stop smiling. Ivan was here, in LA, and that's all that mattered.

"*I'm* sure," said Kat, who stood nearby. She burst out laughing and was joined by at least a few on the production crew.

"I'll see you soon," Ivan said. He glanced down as he traced a sensual path along the neckline of Jaden's chef's jacket with the tip of his finger.

Standing on her tiptoes, Jaden placed one last kiss on his lips before returning to work. As she walked back to the set, she looked over her shoulder to watch Ivan disappear out the door. The heat of a blush rushed to her cheeks as she admired his muscular form. *Damn, the man looks just as good coming as he does going.*

Then, as if with the flip of a switch, Jaden snapped back into her role as Chef Thorne. "Next, always be sure your mint is fresh," she repeated, picking up where she'd left off. With her head back in the game, they'd be finished filming in no time flat. But her heart had already gone out the studio door with Ivan.

CHAPTER 2

"Wild Horses"

Okay, focus, Jaden thought. The promise of what was hidden beneath Ivan's clothes lay just beyond this next shot, and just out of her reach. Oh, how she'd enjoy torturously removing each item and wiping that cocky grin off his face. Not that he'd mind. Hell, he was probably waiting in her dressing room at this very moment, half naked and sprawled out on the sofa. But the sound of Brett hollering *Action!* snapped Jaden out of her revelry, and she went to work. Adding the last touch of minty flair to the plate, she held it up and waited the fifty years it seemed to take for the little red light on top of the camera to turn off. Five...four...three...two...one...

"That's a wrap!" Brett shouted, circling his finger in the air. There was a sudden flurry of activity on the studio floor as the crew hurried to store their equipment and start their weekend.

Rather than having all the food go to waste, Jaden usually set out the plates of finished dishes for the crew, but today she relinquished that duty to one of her sous chefs, whizzed through her customary thank yous, and headed for the door.

"Ms. Thorne, don't you want to see the final take?"

"Not today," Jaden replied as she hurried past Brett. She flung open the large glass double doors and raced down the corridor, past a group of onlookers watching her as if she were crazy, and to the door at the end of the hallway marked *Chef Jaden Thorne*. Her mind reeled and her heart beat so fast that she thought it might actually explode. *Is Ivan still here or did he go back to my place? God…I hope he's as horny as I am.*

"Well," she whispered to herself. "Let's see what's behind door number one."

She held her breath and opened the door. Much to her dismay, Ivan was nowhere to be seen. But in his place was a very shocked-looking Kat standing amidst what had to be at least sixteen dozen roses. Oversized bouquets of white, pink, and yellow blooms had been arranged on every available surface. The fragrance was so beautiful and powerful that it momentarily overwhelmed her, and she took a step back into the hall. How on earth had he managed to pull off something like this…again? And where *was* he? He was the real bouquet, a constant reminder that life is beautiful and precious. Walking carefully to the center of the room, Jaden looked around for some sort of note, something that might give her a clue about what the hell he was up to this time. And then she saw it: a small, white envelope attached to a black-and-gray bear that sat with the only red roses in the room. Jaden slipped the card from the envelope and began to read:

Your love has become the very definition of my smile—and I love to smile.

Say hello to BoBo! You helped create him. ;)

I'm running a few errands, but I'll see you soon!

~Ivan

As tears began to well in her eyes, Jaden glanced around the room again and sighed in exasperation. If only Ivan had stayed behind to share this with her. Grasping BoBo in her hands, she took in every detail of the patchwork bear. Suddenly she recognized the black velvet bag that Ivan's, and now her, favorite wine came in. As she turned the bear over, she identified strips of every piece of clothing she'd ripped from Ivan's body, spilled sauce on, or otherwise destroyed, and BoBo's eyes were the buttons from the infamous Perry Ellis suit jacket he'd been wearing the night they met. All of it reminded her of the romantic sprint they'd embarked on less than a year ago. It had taken both their hearts from zero to sixty in an instant.

The only thing that perplexed her was the red, silky material of BoBo's ears. She racked her brain but couldn't come up with any reasonable source. *I'll figure it out*, she mused and looked around the room again. How much had this little stunt cost? And how much trouble had he gone through to get all these flowers delivered to the studio? But she quickly dismissed the *how* of it all and focused on the fact that Ivan was really *here*. He was in LA, and in less than an hour she would feel the warmth of his arms as they wrapped around her and his sultry scent washed over her. A smile crept onto her face as she imagined all the ways she could reciprocate for this grand gesture—for him once again sweeping her off her feet.

Having forgotten that someone else was in the room, she jumped when Kat approached from behind.

"Need a hand?" Kat asked as she picked up a brush from the makeup table.

Jaden smiled. Despite Kat's crazy makeup and sometimes scary Goth girl appearance, she'd become more than a makeup artist and personal assistant. She was one of Jaden's only friends in LA. Tilting her head back, Jaden sank into the chair. "Make me look stunning."

"That's not very difficult." Kat chuckled and began to brush through Jaden's loose, ebony curls.

Jaden relaxed under Kat's expert touch. She loved having her hair brushed. Even as a child, she would sit for hours while her mom combed her hair and put it up in ringlets. She could feel her eyes growing heavy with sleep as Kat worked her magic, curling tendrils of her hair and pinning them together at the base of her neck. It wasn't until Kat began to speak that Jaden forced open her eyes.

"We're almost done," she said. Pinning the last tendril into place, Kat picked up a mirror and held it to give Jaden a view of the cluster of curls that gathered at her neck and cascaded down her back.

Jaden smiled. A sexy ponytail. It was perfect!

Kat put the finishing touches on Jaden's hair and gave it a spritz of hairspray, and a soft knock on the door caused both of them to look up.

"Come in," Jaden called.

The door opened and Stacey entered, carrying a clipboard in one hand and balancing a Styrofoam cup in the other as she tried to shut the door behind her.

"Jaden, I just wanted to ask you—" Stacey started, but stopped as she took notice of the ridiculously large display of roses. "Jesus, what are you now? A florist?"

Jaden laughed and waved Stacey forward as she stood up from the chair. "Would you mind getting my black dress from the closet?" she asked Kat before joining Stacey on the sofa.

"Let me guess! Ivan's in town for the weekend?" The words were out of Stacey's mouth before Jaden even had a chance to sit down.

Jaden nodded and both women giggled like little girls as they surveyed the myriad of flowers surrounding them. But despite Stacey's smile, Jaden wondered if deep down she was jealous. Stacey had clearly been fond of Ivan at The Winemaker's Dinner, and he could deny it until he was blue in the face, but Stacey had a crush on him. Who could blame her? Not too many men would go to such great lengths to woo a woman, and the garden of roses that encompassed them was proof that Ivan was in a league of his own.

"What do the two of you have planned for tonight?" Stacey inquired, plucking a yellow rose from a nearby vase and raising it to her nose.

"Oh, you know Ivan," Jaden replied. "I'm sure he has something special planned, but he had to take care of some business first."

"He's just full of surprises, isn't he?" Stacey said, shaking her head as she returned the rose to the vase. "Well, what the hell are you still doing here? Get your ass home!"

"That's the plan," Jaden replied, standing up. Then she realized Stacey must've come in to discuss something other than Ivan. "Was there something else you wanted to talk to me about?"

"Oh, I almost forgot," Stacey said with a laugh. "I wanted to be sure you were planning on coming to the dinner party Kevin's hosting for Damian. Sunday, six p.m. sharp!"

How the hell could I forget about that? "Don't worry. We'll be there," Jaden responded in the most enthusiastic tone she could muster. The corner of her mouth twitched as she forced a fake smile to her face. It hadn't seemed possible, but she was now looking forward to this party even less than before. Not only was the whole thing annoying, it would take her away from private time with Ivan. The only thing she wanted to do this weekend was Ivan. Literally.

"You know," Stacey said, pausing in the doorway. A lusty look spread over her face, brightening her features and making her look five years younger. "Kevin did well when he chose Damian. That boy is stunning. I wonder if he gives private cooking lessons."

Jaden laughed out loud. She could hear the roar of the cougar from across the room. Leave it to Stacey to set her sights on some blond-haired playboy. Not just a cougar, Stacey was an Alpha Cougar. Jaden, on the other hand, had no desire to even meet the guy. *One Hot Kitchen* was still kicking ass just like it had been, thank you very much, and as long as she had Ivan, she had everything she needed—and then some.

Once Stacey disappeared, Jaden turned to find Kat holding her dress. She slipped out of her kitchen whites and luxuriated in the satiny softness of the dress as she smoothed it over her shoulders and down the length of her body. After applying a fresh coat of pineapple lip gloss and a touch of perfume, she gathered her belongings and left the studio. The town car was parked in its usual spot in front of the building, but Adam, her personal driver, was standing beside a food cart with a hotdog in one hand and a soda on the other.

At the sound of her heels clacking against the pavement, Adam looked up. "Are you ready to go, Ms. Thorne?"

"Let's do it! And for the last time, Adam, it's Jaden, not Ms. Thorne."

"Yes, ma'am. It won't happen again."

Of course it would happen again. It happened every time. Adam was always professional, and no matter how many times she'd asked him to call her Jaden, he refused.

She often brought him a container full of whatever they'd cooked on the show, but in her haste this evening it had completely slipped her mind. She silently cursed herself—and Ivan's ability to scramble her brain. Over the past few months she and Adam had come to be good friends. He was as much protective older brother as studio-appointed driver.

As Adam finished off the last bites of his hotdog, she slipped into the backseat of the car and pulled the small, white envelope from her purse. She reread the card several times, grinning from ear to ear as she looked at BoBo and tried to piece together what sort of surprise Ivan had up his sleeve this time.

After a few moments Adam slid into the driver's seat. He lowered the glass partition. "Ms. Thorne, would you mind if we stopped at Chateau Marmot? I have to drop off a package for my sister, and she's already been waiting over half an hour."

Ivan had to have finished his errands by now and was probably waiting at her place, but Adam always went above and beyond. How could she say no? With a slight nod, Jaden replied, "Sure, as long as we can make it quick. I have plans tonight. Ivan's in town!"

"*Oh*," Adam replied, raising his eyebrows. "Of course, Ms. Thorne. It will just take a moment. Thank you."

Jaden sat back in the seat and watched as Sunset Boulevard passed by in a blur, and then it occurred to her: Why on earth would Adam's sister be at Chateau Marmot? As far as she could recall, his sister was an administrative assistant for some home renovation company. Chateau Marmot was more a luxurious playground for the Who's Who of Hollywood. Celebrities, not office workers, indulged in scandalous and secretive behavior deep within the walls of the hotel. Now Jaden was intrigued. She picked up her phone to text Ivan about this latest development.

> Hey, baby! We have to make a quick stop
> at Chateau Marmot. Be home soon.

As the car snaked along Sunset, the hotel suddenly came into view. She drew in a quick breath. After all these months in LA, she'd never seen the hotel firsthand. Its main spire rose above the tree line, and the windows glowed orange in the setting sun. The Chateau reminded her of a medieval castle nestled on a hillside in some remote European countryside. As they drove toward the main entrance, her eyes widened. *Is that...?* Jaden thought. *No, it couldn't be...But it is!* Celebrities were a dime a dozen in LA, but to see them up close still made her a little fangirl crazy. Jaden's country bumpkin side was oozing out, but safe in the back of the Town Car, she didn't mind one bit. She loved his movies.

The car pulled to a stop at the entrance, and Adam stepped out and opened her door. "Do you want to take a look around while I take this to my sister?" he asked, holding up a brown envelope.

"Yes, I'd love to," Jaden replied. "Are you sure it's okay?"

"I don't think they'll mind." Adam laughed and offered his hand, helping her from the car. As she stepped out, he pointed to a small garden off to one side of the hotel. "Supposedly that's the garden where one of the Blues Brothers had a bungalow. Right before...you know..."

Jaden couldn't get there fast enough. She supposed she was considered a celebrity in her own right, but she was easily starstruck. It was next to impossible for her to stand in line at the grocery store without picking up the latest trashy tabloid.

Forcing herself into a nonchalant walk, she strolled along the side of the building. Large Corinthian columns rose up beside her and archways loomed above her head. Looking through one of the windows, she saw rich mahogany trim and colonial furniture. She entered the garden and found it eerily familiar. This garden seemed similar to the garden in Sarasota where she'd first met Ivan, where they'd shared their first kiss...The flowers were different, but it somehow felt the same.

Even though she knew cameras were a no-no in a place like this, Jaden took out her phone and snapped a quick picture of the garden for Ivan. She typed a short message and attached the photo.

This place reminds me of our garden in Sarasota.
All I need now is some Sinatra and you.

She continued to reminisce as she wandered through the lilies and honeysuckle. Her phone buzzed, and when she opened the message, she was completely confused by what she saw. On the screen was a picture of her — standing in the very garden she was now touring.

"How on earth — " she began, and a low, masculine voice began to serenade her from behind. "The Way You Look Tonight" had never sounded so good.

That voice! It had been embedded in her very soul. Jaden's mind did back flips as she tried to process what was happening. How could she not have seen what was going on? The flowers, Adam having to make a stop at Chateau Marmot — it was all part of Ivan's romantic plan. She turned to face him, and without warning she jumped into his arms and crushed her mouth to his. Her lips parted, her tongue hungry for a taste as she took his bottom lip between her teeth and nibbled at it. Ivan returned her kiss, driving his tongue into her mouth and igniting a fire deep within that only he could extinguish. She smiled against Ivan's soft lips as his erection pressed into her thigh for a second time that day.

"What are you doing here?" she panted. "What's going on? And more than that why aren't you in Washington?"

Ivan adjusted his grip and lowered her to the ground. "As for Washington, I decided not to go. This sounded better. And as for here, I thought we'd spend the night before heading out in the morning: a mini vacation. I thought you might like this place, and I wanted to be the first one to experience it with you."

"Heading out in the morning? Where exactly are we going?" She held Ivan tighter and buried her head in his shoulder, trying to mask her excitement, but the scent of him almost caused her to come apart at the seams. It was familiar and soothing and made her long for him even more.

"You know, Ms. Thorne, sometimes you're too nosy for your own good."

"What's that supposed to mean?" Jaden slapped him on the shoulder.

"It means," he drawled, "that you'll just have to wait until morning to find out."

Just then she remembered Adam was waiting for her at the car. "I have to let Adam know I don't need a ride home." She slid out of Ivan's embrace.

He tried to hold back a laugh, but failed. "Adam's probably halfway home by now."

"Jesus, I really am slow." She felt a hot blush rise to her cheeks.

"Slow? No. Sexy? Most definitely." Still laughing, Ivan cupped her face, his thumb tracing her cheekbone as he placed a tender kiss on her lips. "Maybe we should go to the room."

Jaden might have taken a moment to figure out more about his surprise, but she knew the look that had appeared on his face — it was one usually reserved for behind closed doors. Pure lust. There was only one thought, shared between them: *Fuck. Me. Now.*

CHAPTER 3

"S&M"

*I*van watched as Jaden stood in the corner of the elevator, blushing, while an elderly woman looked at her as if to say "Been there. Done that." If not for the couple standing beside them, he'd have had her pinned to the glass wall with his dick in her hand faster than you could say Miami Heat, and the thought made his cock stiffen. A bell chimed, the doors to the elevator slid open, and the elderly couple exited. As the doors slid shut, he captured Jaden in his arms. A low groan emanated from deep within when she reached into his pocket and grasped his cock through the thin lining of his dress pants.

The doors opened again, and they tumbled haphazardly into the corridor of the fifth floor, entangled in an embrace. The scene was reminiscent of the first night they'd spent together in Sarasota — the garden, the kiss, the elevator — and Ivan could see a look of recognition flash across Jaden's face as well. He pulled her toward their room.

His voice, heated and needy, shook when he spoke. "No disappearing tricks tomorrow morning, okay?"

"Never again will I walk away from something so right," Jaden replied. She clung to him as he turned the key in the lock.

He kissed her again, and they burst through the door, locked in a passionate embrace, ravaging each other's mouths and necks as if coated in Tupelo honey. His erection pressed hard into her thigh as they danced across the floor and collapsed into the sofa. He tugged at the strap of her black dress, pulling it down just enough to expose her perfect, bare breasts. *Well, what do you know...No bra.* Holding her against the sofa, he trailed his fingertips across her skin until he found the bud of her nipple, firm with arousal. The feel of her skin made him harder and he ground into her, his hips thrusting as he took her breast in his mouth. Rolling her taut nipple between his teeth, he tasted and tormented her until she was writhing beneath him. And as her breathing increased, and her moans turned to pleas, he again took her in his mouth and began to suckle her firm, round breast.

Jaden widened her legs and looked into his eyes as she grabbed his face. "Fuck me hard, doctor," she demanded in a low growl.

He smiled wickedly at her and raised one cocky eyebrow. Jaden had transformed from a shy country girl into downright dirty erotic goddess, and he loved it. He loved when she talked dirty to him and wasn't afraid to make demands. A fire smoldered in his eyes, and his mood shifted to that of an animal ready to devour its prey. Jaden was fucked, in every sense of the word.

Wordlessly, he pulled her to her feet and bent her over the arm of the sofa. Lifting her dress above her waist, her grasped her pink thong and slid it down her long legs, grinning at how wet the thin strip of satin had become. The need to fuck her, to feel the warmth of her pussy engulf him, was overwhelming. Leaving her panties tangled around her ankles, he pressed his knee against the back of her legs, spreading them just enough to grant him entrance. But first he needed to ready her, to tease her into the same sexual frenzy that was driving him mad.

"Fuck me!" she screamed. She reached for his cock, but he stopped her.

"Not yet," he replied, his voice as hoarse and ragged as hers.

Rather than spending time admiring her perfect form or running his hand across the smooth planes of her ass as he usually did, he instead got to his knees behind her and buried his face between her legs, tasting and teasing every luscious inch of her sex and eliciting a deep moan of approval. He savored the taste of her, working his tongue back and forth, and sliding two fingers into her. His mouth and fingers moved rhythmically against her and in her, and still she cried for more. He could feel her body quiver as it neared orgasm, and a sense of electricity shot through him. He knew he could make her come at any instant with a simple touch of her clit. But only when her legs trembled and gave out did he take it between his teeth and roll it across his tongue. As she convulsed in orgasmic shudders, he encircled her waist with his hands and held her steady as she collapsed over the arm of the sofa.

Her breathing was heavy as she glanced over her shoulder to look imploringly in his eyes. As satisfied as she clearly was, she still was desperate for him. She lifted her hips and ground her ass against his erection.

"I want *you* inside of me—now!"

And this time he was more than willing to oblige.

Tearing at the zipper of his pants, he yanked them down as his cock sprang free, ready and aching for the feel of Jaden. Not bothering to remove his shirt or jacket, he ran his hands up her back, across her shoulders, and down her arms, capturing them in a vice like grip behind her back. She was at his mercy, and they both knew it.

He teased her with the plump head of his shaft, pressing it against her pussy and pushing the tip within, sliding it slowly between her slick folds. He loved the feel of her wetness against his bare dick, and he reveled in their commitment and trust—not to mention the pill—which made messy condoms a thing of the past. Inch by torturous inch he eased into her, only to pull out just as slowly. Her cries made him harder, and he slowed his pace even more.

"Ivan, please," she begged.

Finally the torture became too much for him to handle as well, and he thrust into her hard, sending shockwaves of pleasure up his spine. After a few strokes, hard and fast, he returned to his leisurely in and out.

"Goddamnit, don't stop!" she demanded. "Harder!"

How he loved when Jaden begged. Nothing made him harder than the sweet sound of her voice begging him to fuck her. Satisfied that he'd tormented her enough for one night, he unleashed a bout of commanding strokes that pinned her against the sofa as he fucked her hard and fast. The warmth of her pussy clenching his cock felt like heaven. Driving into her, he filled her completely, and the slapping sounds of flesh on flesh filled the room.

She struggled to free her hands, but he held them firm and pulled her arms taut behind her back, lifting her body off the arm of the couch. Harder and faster he invaded her, and yet she still moaned for more. He could sense that she was close, and as her pussy contracted around him, he gripped a fistful of long, black hair. Tugging her head back, he bent over to her ear and whispered, "You ready?"

"Y…E…S…" Jaden managed to reply.

A sense of supreme satisfaction and oblivion coursed through Ivan's veins like a powerful, wonderful drug, and with a groan, his hips surged forward. He buried himself balls deep in her warm depths. He released his grip on her hair and arms, reached around her body, and with the tip of his finger, circled her engorged clit. A touch was all it took to send her over the edge again, and he could feel her milking him as she came. With one final thrust, he pummeled into her, spilling himself deep inside her body.

As the aftershocks of climax began to ebb, he collapsed across her back, breathing heavily and dripping with sweat and satisfaction.

"Fuck me," Jaden sighed as they slid onto the couch.

"I thought I just did," he replied with a breathless laugh, wrapping his arms around her and pulling her close. He reveled in the sensation of still being inside her and feeling her body tremble in the wake of one of the best fucks he'd ever had.

"That wasn't a request, it was an expletive." She pushed herself up off the sofa.

He stood with her and reluctantly slipped himself free from her body. Running his hands across her smooth stomach, he nuzzled his nose in her hair. "Ay, ay, ay…"

She snickered as she headed for the bathroom. As he heard the shower turn on, Ivan found himself dazed and alone in the middle of the living room, and nearly in a sexual coma. He closed his eyes and smiled a very satisfied smile.

CHAPTER 4

"Into the Mystic"

*D*amp and refreshed, Jaden emerged from the bathroom wearing a white terrycloth robe with the hotel's logo embroidered in gold script on the lapel and a pair of matching white slippers. Classic rock streamed from the docking station where Ivan had plugged in his iPhone, but he was nowhere to be seen.

Wandering from the bedroom to the living room, she detected a faint trace of cigar smoke and noticed that the balcony door was ajar. There, leaning against the rail, his muscular physique illuminated by the setting sun, was Ivan. A cigar dangled from his mouth and his hand held a glass of wine. A simple white towel was the only thing he wore, and he appeared to be deep in thought. Bare feet, bare skin, and flowing brown hair that just reached the top of the tattoo inked across his back. The sight was almost perfect. *If only he'd lose the towel,* she thought. This man, a man she trusted implicitly and loved with every fiber of her being, a man who loved her back just as much, was a miracle. Finding what they now shared had been a once in a lifetime chance…and they'd been lucky to find it at all.

She watched him stand in silence, enjoying the fading blues, reds, and purples that painted the warm California sky. He pulled deep on his cigar, occasionally blowing a smoke ring. She could watch him for hours and be completely content, but she couldn't bear to waste a second of their precious time together, so Jaden cleared her throat and alerted him to her presence. When he turned and stared at her, his eyes full of love, she could tell he'd been thinking something along the same lines as she had only seconds before. As their gazes locked, she knew this was for real. Despite the distance—the thing Ivan had feared the most—they were making it work. And someday, when the time was right, they'd be able to close that distance between them.

"How ya doing?" he asked as she started toward him.

"Much better now." Jaden positioned herself on his lap as he slid into one of the chairs. "I think we both needed that. This distance thing is a bitch!"

"I think you're right." An impish grin curled the corner of his mouth, and his hand drifted across her thigh. He hugged her. "I do miss the feel of your skin."

After a pause in the music, "Into the Mystic" began to play, and Jaden hugged Ivan's arm as she sank into the warmth of his body. The sun set through the trees over an unseen horizon, and he stroked her leg. With each silent caress, she felt their love deepen.

When the last vestiges of the sun disappeared, Ivan cleared his throat. "Is everything okay at work?" he asked. "I hear you have a playmate coming to the kitchen."

"Are you *trying* to spoil this moment? Don't even get me started!" She kept her voice lighthearted, but inside she burned all over again. "The only reason Kevin hired Ken is to appeal to the young, female demographic. It's not as if he can actually cook!"

"Ken? I thought his name was Damian."

"Ken, as in Ken doll," she replied. "I think Kevin believes we'll reach a whole new viewership of teenage girls and desperate housewives."

"Well, aren't you the one attracting all the guys for a quick wank here and there? Doesn't that creep you out?"

She slapped him on the shoulder. "I do think there are a few people who watch the show for the *cooking*," she teased. "But not at all. That's what I have Adam for. He keeps the weirdos at bay."

"I find it funny that the girl every guy on the planet wants to sleep with loves to get downright dirty and nasty with *me*." Ivan slid his hand up her thigh and tickled her stomach. She giggled into his shoulder. "I feel like that geeky kid in high school who somehow managed to score a gorgeous girlfriend."

"Something tells me you were never the geeky kid, and you had your pick of girls."

He said nothing and just hugged her more tightly, leading Jaden to assume her suspicions were correct.

After a few moments he spoke again. "So are you happy with everything so far? With us, I mean. The distance, this lifestyle?"

"The only thing I would change is the distance," Jaden replied, puzzled by this new line of questioning. "Not being able to hold you, or smell you, or feel you every day is like a living hell. But I'm willing to bear it if that's what makes our lives possible right now. Saying goodbye to you at the airport almost breaks my heart, but knowing I'll see you again in two weeks keeps me going."

Ivan removed his hand from her stomach to pour her a glass of wine.

"How about you?" she asked, accepting her drink. "Are you okay with all of this? I know this whole long-distance thing was hard for you to accept." She took a sip and stared into his eyes. Only months ago she'd thought their relationship was over for good, but looking at him now, in the dim light of the moon, that felt like a lifetime ago.

"Everything is right as rain now, baby girl. That isn't what worries me, though. Love can withstand a lot of things for a little while. It's five or six months down the road when the distance becomes more of an obstacle that I'm worried about. When we get caught up in our careers and have to fight to find the time to spend together. When these weekend rendezvous turn into once-a-month meetups—that's when love will feel the true test of distance."

He took a long pull from his cigar and blew out a puff of smoke before he continued. "But right in this moment, I can tell you from the bottom of my heart that you are the destiny I'd risk everything for."

"You're a destiny I was born to fulfill," Jaden countered. "I love you, Ivan."

She leaned in to meet him and found what assurance she needed as their lips met in a kiss under the night sky. The heady scent of cigars and the sweet wine on her lips mingled to form a perfect union.

"Ohh! I almost forgot!" she burst out, pulling away from Ivan's kiss. "What is the red fabric on BoBo's ears? I know the other fabrics are…ummm…the clothes we mutually ruined."

He laughed. "Very good. I didn't know if you'd recognize my suits. Impressive! But mutually?"

"Okay, maybe seventy-five/twenty-five my doing?"

"That sounds about right. You can't place the red silk, huh?"

"No, I can't."

"Really?"

"No!"

"Besides a very sad man, what else did you leave behind in Sarasota?"

She thought for a moment about that hotel room after the Winemaker's Dinner. "Oh, you pervert!" she shouted. "My panties!"

"Bingo, baby!" Ivan announced in a terrible Austin Powers voice as he tickled her sides. "I am a man, after all."

"Ah, I love that bear even more now!" Jaden laughed, defending herself from his fingers. "Why is his name BoBo?"

"It was the name of my favorite childhood stuffed animal, so I felt it was fitting. I slept with that BoBo every night and cherished him, so I hope this BoBo will provide the same comfort for you when we're apart."

"Ahh…so sweet. Thank you," she said with a giggle. "But what about something for you?"

"I still have what's left of your panties for that." He gave her a creepy waggle of his eyebrows.

"Way to ruin a beautiful moment, Romeo."

"You laughed, so mission accomplished!"

After a good laugh, Jaden settled back in the chair with Ivan.

"Are you hungry?" he asked.

"I could eat."

"What are you in the mood for? And don't ask for a repeat performance just yet—but you can bet your sweet ass I'm not finished with you."

"You choose," Jaden replied.

"I'd hoped you'd say that, because I made reservations."

"So I just played right into your little plan, didn't I?"

"Yes, ma'am!" He nudged Jaden out of his lap and stood. "Now go put on a pretty dress, and be ready to go in ten minutes."

"You forgot one teeny little thing."

"I don't forget anything," Ivan said with a smug look on his face.

"I don't have a bag, much less a pretty dress."

"You *do* have a bag."

"No, I don't, I didn't—wait. You packed a bag for me?"

"It's in the closet in the bedroom."

"Amazing!" Jaden yelled as she raced toward the bedroom. She tossed the robe on the bed, grabbed the bag, and hurried into the bathroom to get ready.

CHAPTER 5

"Baby, I Love Your Way"

Ivan zipped up his pants, buttoned the last two buttons of his fitted white dress shirt, and cinched his tie around his neck. He attached a pair of turquoise links to his French cuffs and spritzed on a little Blue before he slipped into his loafers. After a final check to be sure his hair flowed properly down his collar, he headed for the living room. There he found a girl draped in the aura of a beauty queen wearing an all-too-perfect black and white ensemble that hugged her hips and didn't let go.

"Why was I not surprised to find a skirt that barely covers my ass in that little bag of tricks you packed?" Jaden asked with a raised eyebrow.

"What? That's your size, isn't it?"

"When I was in grade school!" she shot back. But then she gave him a sensual smile as she worked the fabrics that clung to her curves as if they were painted on.

He felt his breath catch. "If it were up to me, you'd wear that size all the time. God damn, you are delicious."

"How delicious?" she replied. She leaned in for a kiss and pressed her body against him.

"Can't you feel me?" he said, hinting at the erotic beast begging to be released. But reservations needed to be kept, he reminded himself. However, this didn't stop said beast from grinding its erect dick into her pussy, held firmly in place by his grip on her ass cheeks.

Jaden reached behind and detached his claws. "Didn't you say something about a reservation? We'd better get this show on the road!"

They rode the elevator to the lobby, and as they stepped out into the LA night, Ivan flagged a cab waiting close by. "Nine oh three North La Cienega Boulevard, please."

"Okay, you got it," the driver responded, giving them a look through the rearview mirror.

"Can you at least give me a clue?" Jaden asked.

"Absolutely not," Ivan replied. "Just relax."

Appearing to give in, she sank back in the seat. Ivan stroked her thigh, sneaking an occasional pinky under her dress and watching as LA passed by in a blur.

As the cab came to a stop less than a mile down the road in West Hollywood, Ivan appraised the crowd packing the restaurant's door. Lines were something they were no longer accustomed to standing in. "Thanks, boss," he called as he tossed the driver the fare.

Not wanting his girl, or his ego, to wait a second in the line, Ivan strolled to the front of the crowd to find a petite hostess with fire in her eyes and what seemed to be more piss than vinegar flowing through her veins.

"Hello, darling," he said in a playful way. "Reservations for two at eight-thirty. Rusilko."

"Yes, I see, but it's eight-forty-five now. Sorry. There will be a forty-five-minute wait."

Leaning a bit closer to the blonde blocking their entrance to fine dining and good vibrations, Ivan smiled his most charming smile. "You sure you don't want to check your clock again?"

Glancing back from some Hollywood friend of a friend who was bargaining and dropping likely fictionalized names, she gave him a withering look. "It's eight-forty-five. Sorry."

Ivan could feel the heat rising within him, but then he felt Jaden's hand on his arm. She slithered into the intense stare-down he'd started with the hostess.

"Baby, I really didn't want to eat here anyway. If their food is anything like their customer service…" She trailed off meaningfully. "Let me take you some place real, not manufactured."

He tilted his head to look in amazement at the woman who could melt his cares away and soothe his ego with a single word. "You're the boss." Without another thought, they made their way back to the plethora of yellow and black taxis waiting like bumblebees at the road side.

Dismissing his plans for a night of raw fish, saki-driven conversation, and an extremely long tab, he let his love lead the way as only she could. She slid into the car and spoke softly to the cab driver.

He seemed rather confused, but nonetheless pleased to be asked anything by a beautiful woman—particularly in such a secretive way. "*Yes*, ma'am!"

As they drove, Ivan noticed an increase in tourists—and the establishments they frequent. They were now surrounded by fast food restaurants, cheesy souvenir shops, and... "You've got to be fucking kidding me!"

Jaden began to laugh as they turned up the drive. Greeting them were glaring images of pirates, artificial waterfalls, and what seemed like hundreds of families playing miniature golf on a putt-putt course that must've cost a small fortune to construct.

He turned to find her grinning ear to ear. She might think this was funny, but he was going to have the last laugh. "Baby, I hope you know I'm a semi-pro mini golfer, and I have no intentions of letting you win. You're about to meet my competitive side."

"Is that so?" She raised her eyebrows. "And I'll have you know I won't go down without a fight."

"Twenty-five dollars," the cab driver shouted over the mounting competition in the backseat.

Ivan pulled money from his wallet and handed it to the cabbie. Once they'd exited, he noted a sly smile on Jaden's face.

"Here's the deal," she purred as they walked through the front gates. "If I win, I want a top-to-bottom full body massage...with a happy ending." She winked and motioned to her crotch.

"Funny, that's the same thing I was going to say."

"What? That you want me to have a happy ending?"

"Look who's being funny now," he replied. Giving Jaden a massage was one of his favorite pastimes, but if anyone was going to be getting a happy ending, it would be him. "Okay, smartass. If I win, I want a striptease to a song of my choice...with an even happier ending."

She slowed her pace and narrowed her eyes. "Deal! Big talk for a man who couldn't even get a seat at a restaurant. Speaking of which,

I'm still hungry! But don't worry," she added after a moment. "I'll take care of us." She turned her attention to a brightly colored hot dog stand in the parking lot outside the putt-putt course.

"Oh no you don't," he protested. "Let's go get something proper, and then we can come back. You know I don't eat that garbage."

"Well, tough shit," she shot back as she cozied up to the stand. "You should have done a better job charming that hostess."

"What'll it be, my lady?" asked a portly pirate behind the counter.

Ivan eyed the row of spinning pig lips and assholes behind the pirate and took another moment to mourn this evening's culinary tragedy.

"Hello, matey!" a giggling Jaden said in a wench voice with a Colorado accent. "Two dogs for me and me mate."

Ivan rolled his eyes. "You are unreal."

"I know, and that's why you love me, right?"

"I'm starting to wonder."

She drew him in like a tractor beam, and they shared a warm kiss, which was interrupted by a salty voice.

"Your dogs, miss."

The pirate handed the ketchup-coated coronaries to Jaden with a lingering gaze, and Ivan stifled a laugh. He loved that he'd just caught the pirate eye-fucking his date.

Smiling, she handed him his dog and toasted the situation. "To the man who promises a five-star dinner and delivers something better."

Taking a deep breath, Ivan smiled, shared her toast, and took a gigantic bite of his dog.

"That will be eighteen dollars," the pirate announced.

"Seriously? When did hotdogs become so expensive? But you are so worth it, darling," Ivan added with a flourish as he paid the man.

"Oh, thanks!" Jaden smiled as she finished off her hot dog and grabbed his hand, leading him back to their challenge.

As the overdressed pair approached the front counter to pick up their clubs, he realized they'd become more of a spectacle than the ten-foot octopus and one legged pirates that decorated the course. Teenagers on dates and parents with their children gawked as they approached the pimple-faced employee sitting on a stool collecting the entrance fee. A man dressed in a suit and a tall, leggy vixen in stilettos were not your typical Friday night putt-putt golfers.

"Can I help you, sir?" the boy asked, appearing confused by the sight before him.

"Yes, a table for two—preferably a window seat, please," Jaden said.

"What?" the boy asked, looking even more confused.

Ivan leaned over and spoke in hushed tones. "Don't mind her. She's a little slow. The doctor says it's only temporary, but I'm not holding my breath."

"So do you want to play mini golf or not?" The boy looked from one to the other and then to the wad of money Ivan now held in front of him.

"We might as well play a round since we're here." Ivan shrugged as he held back a laugh.

"That'll be thirty-five dollars, please."

Ivan waggled his eyebrows as he peeled off two twenties.

Jaden bolted ahead and snagged a bright yellow ball as she headed to the course. Without looking back, she disappeared toward the first hole.

Ivan ignored the boy, who was waving a five-dollar bill at him, and grabbed a ball as he rushed to catch up. *Of course it's pink*, he thought as he glanced at it. *Damn, she must really want that massage… or maybe just the happy ending.*

"You ready?" She stood tapping her foot.

"All right, so here's the deal," he said, skidding to a stop on the green. "Massage for you if you win, and striptease for me if I win. Either way, one of us is getting a happy ending."

Jaden just smiled and drew near. The tip of her tongue traced a trail of fire as she licked her way up his neck to whisper in his ear. "Don't worry, baby. One of us is gonna get fucked good tonight."

His cock sprung to attention. He had to give her credit—her tactics were working. Mini golf was the last thing on his mind as he watched her position herself on the green and hike up her skirt. "So that's how you wanna play, huh?"

A crack echoed through the night as the metal club connected with the ball, and the match was underway. The first four holes went by without a hitch, a hole in one here and a six-shot there. But

Ivan was surprised at how seriously Jaden was taking their match. An intense look decorated her face as she stood over the fifth hole, sizing up her shot. It wasn't about the sex or the massage. It was all about the competition, and Ivan could see now that Jaden was fierce.

How could he not find that sexy? The little cocktease was working him into a sexual frenzy as a means to win. Watching her bend over to examine the position of her ball and bounce down the green to chase after it drove him wild. As they rounded the corner to the seventh hole, they found themselves in a secluded portion of the course. To one side was a tall waterfall and on the other, a pirate ship ornamented with skeletons and a golden treasure chest. Not able to bear it any longer, he grabbed her by the waist and pinned her against the coarse faux stones of the waterfall.

She inhaled as he grasped the hem of her dress and began to lift. "Not here," she panted, though her eyes burned with lust.

"Yes, here." He reached beneath her dress, fumbling with her panties.

Just then a burly voice behind them yelled, "Hey! What the hell do you think you're doing?"

Ivan turned around and came face to face with a monstrosity of a man wearing a black T-shirt with SECURITY printed across the front. "Oh shit," he whispered and grabbed Jaden by the hand.

As the man took a step toward them, they dropped their clubs and began to run toward the exit, hopping over ponds, sidestepping a screaming child, and almost running head first into a garbage can as they burst through the front gates and into the parking lot. The sound of their laughter floated through the night air, and they walked hand in hand back down the drive.

"So it's a draw?" she asked.

"No, I think you were ahead, babe." He smiled and squeezed her hand.

CHAPTER 6

"Girl, You'll Be a Woman Soon"

Even with the blinds shut and the drapes pulled across the windows, a sliver of light managed to seep through, warming Jaden's naked form and alerting her to the start of another day. Stretching beneath the covers, she noticed how her muscles flexed with ease and her body felt refreshed. Then she remembered the feel of Ivan's strong, skillful hands roving and massaging her body as she fell into a peaceful slumber. It wasn't exactly how she'd planned on spending her evening in bed with Ivan, but damn did she feel good. And what felt even better was his erection, now pressing into the small of her back. Remembering their deal from the night before, she grinned and pressed her ass against him, grinding her hips against his stiff cock. He owed her a happy ending, and she was ready to collect.

"Good morning, sleepyhead." She wiggled the cheeks of her ass once more for good measure.

"Morning, baby girl. Did you sleep well last night?" He groaned and pressed into her, his erection twitching and eager to start the day.

"I did, but I would've slept better if a certain someone had held up his end of the bargain."

"Is that so? I'm pretty sure someone fell asleep halfway through her massage," he replied, his voice still groggy with sleep.

"Mm-hmmm…" Jaden reached beneath the covers and grasped his cock, leisurely working it up and down as she guided it between her legs.

Ivan nuzzled his face into the crook of her neck and let out a low, guttural moan. He slid into the warmth of her sex, working his way deeper with each thrust.

His slow movements were excruciating. Jaden moved her hips, trying to pick up the pace, but Ivan's strong arm encircled her and held her against his body. His hot breath tickled her skin and his deep morning voice sent shivers up her spine when he spoke.

"Stay still." He held her tighter.

Jaden lay perfectly still as he took her from behind. There was something arousing about his commanding tone and forceful grip, and her body trembled and inched closer to climax. She could feel him tensing behind her and knew he too was getting close. His grip on her loosened, and she felt his palm trace a heated path along her arm to her hand. Taking her hand in his, he guided it between her legs.

"Touch yourself," he whispered fiercely. He spread her labia, revealing her swollen clit. "I want you to feel yourself come."

"Ivan…" she protested, but she could tell by the tone of his voice that this was turning him on. She began to circle her clit with the tip of her finger. With each motion, his pace quickened, driving them both hard and fast toward climax. With each thrust, his cocked filled her, stretching her to the limits.

"Come for me."

His hoarse voice reverberated across her skin and drove her over the edge. With one final stroke of her clit, she exploded around him, her muscles constricting around his cock. She could feel her clit pulsing beneath the tips of her fingers as shockwaves of pleasure rippled through her body. And before long, Ivan found his own release, moaning out her name as he spilled himself within her.

They lay in each other's embrace as the climax ebbed. Jaden could feel the blush that still heated her cheeks. She'd never touched herself in front of Ivan before, but he obviously enjoyed it. And truth be told, she enjoyed it too.

"That was—"

"Quick?" Ivan laughed.

"I was going to say intense, but quick works too."

"That's what you get for catching me off guard at—" Ivan raised his head and peeked over her shoulder at the alarm clock on the bedside table. "Seven a.m."

"Is it that early?" Jaden moaned and buried her face in the down pillow. "Ugh. Weekends are meant for sleeping in."

"Not today, baby. It's good that we're up. We have a full agenda." And with that, Ivan placed a kiss on her neck, tossed back the covers, and slid out of bed.

Hand in hand, Ivan and Jaden walked beneath the grand archway that led to the restaurant at Chateau Marmot. As they waited for a table, Ivan grabbed a copy of *USA Today* from the counter, and soon they followed a waitress to the back of the lounge. They sat in companionable silence as they ate, Ivan reading the paper and sipping at his iced coffee, and Jaden checking her emails and nibbling an egg white omelet, famished after last night's mini golf incident and the early-morning interlude.

"Are you ready for your day, young lady?" Ivan asked, looking up from his paper, his voice deeper than usual.

She watched as his eyes roamed her body. Even dressed in yoga pants and a T-shirt, and no doubt looking a little worse for wear from the stress of her job, she loved that Ivan looked at her as if she were the most beautiful woman on earth. "I don't know if I can ever be ready for one of your surprises. What's the plan?"

"If I told you, then it wouldn't be a surprise, would it? But I can tell you this: if we don't hurry, we're going to miss our plane." Ivan folded the newspaper and placed it on the table, then offered her his outstretched hand. "Shall we?"

What the hell was he up to this time? Jaden had become accustomed to Ivan's spontaneity and lavish surprises, but after the ridiculous display of affection in her dressing room yesterday, not to mention their sumptuous evening's accommodations, she had a feeling this adventure was going to take the cake.

He snagged the check and led her to the front desk, where it seemed he'd already checked out. He handed the bellman the ticket for their luggage, and moments later his suitcase appeared.

Jaden smiled and interlocked her fingers with his as they took one last look at the elegant lobby and headed outside to hail yet another cab.

"LAX, please," Ivan directed as they slid inside.

As the driver pulled away from the curb, her curiosity bubbled over. She shifted sideways on the seat to face Ivan. "Okay, I can't take it anymore. Where are we going?"

He tried to keep a poker face, but the corner of his mouth turned up into a sly smile. "Take a load off and relax. I'm giving you exactly what you need: some stress-free pampering."

"Are you sure you packed everything I need —"

He cut her off with a glare.

"Never mind," she sang quietly as she sank back into the seat. It didn't matter whether he'd packed her bag well or not. A trip with Ivan might very well mean staying in bed, so they wouldn't need clothes at all...which she could totally get behind.

"That's my girl," he said with a wink. He picked up her foot and put it in his lap, continuing with the massage from the night before.

The cab pulled to a stop in front of Alaskan Airlines, and she could feel her anticipation mount. Alaska? Putting her shoe back on, she slid out of the taxi behind Ivan and followed him to the near-vacant check-in counter. He handed the woman his ID.

"Good morning, Dr. Rusilko. Your flight to Santa Rosa is on time. And this is Ms. Jaden Thorne, I presume?" the attendant asked.

Jaden silently gave thanks for her oversized purse that contained everything but the kitchen sink as she handed the woman her passport. Then she began to bounce up and down on the balls of her feet, bursting with excitement.

Ivan shrugged as if admitting defeat. "Well, I got tired of waiting for the next Winemaker's Dinner, so I figured we'd have our own wine-infused celebration. There's no place like Napa for that."

"Ivan." Jaden wrapped her arms around his neck and pressed her lips to his cheek. "How did I ever get so lucky?"

"I'm the lucky one," he whispered as he turned to find her lips.

After a moment, the attendant cleared her throat, and they returned to focus on the task at hand. As they headed for the gate, Jaden continued to bounce, and with each step counted her blessings for having found Ivan. They traversed the crowded airport and arrived to find their flight already boarding. Before her relationship with Ivan she would've been nervous about flying on such a small plane, but having visited his family in Pennsylvania, and now flying back and forth constantly between LA and Miami, airplanes had become second nature.

Settling in their seats, they each prepared for the almost two-hour flight: Jaden with a book and Ivan with his iPod. While the flight attendant delivered her lecture about seatbelts and exits, Jaden reached across the seat and plucked the earbud from Ivan's ear. "Thank you, baby."

He smiled sleepily, and she wondered when he'd had the time to organize this little excursion. But she could tell now was no time to ask, and sure enough, he was snoring before they left the runway. He scarcely moved until the screeching wheels and jolt of their landing roused him from his nap.

"Sleep well?" Jaden nudged his shoulder.

"Yes, yes, I did," he replied with a yawn.

"That must've been one hell of a dream. You mumbled through the entire flight."

"Oh, you know," he replied. "Vineyards, fine wine, and a whole lotta lovin'."

"Hmm... *That's* something I could get used to."

"So could I," he said. "But I promised Stacey I'd have you back in time for the dinner on Sunday."

Jaden tilted her head back and sighed. Having a new co-host was inevitable, but having the guy invade her time with Ivan was unacceptable. With a phony pout, she turned toward him. "Do we really have to go? Couldn't we just buy a small vineyard and live in Napa? As long as you didn't tell anyone where we were going, no one would ever find us."

Ivan laughed as they shuffled forward with the flow of passengers waiting to exit the plane. "Babe, I would love nothing more than to stay holed up in some vineyard for the rest of our lives, but I'd be depriving the rest of the world of the most beautiful and talented chef on the face of the earth."

Jaden smiled, silently thanking him for everything — most of all for his unwavering support. What would she do without him?

Once off the plane, they scurried through the Santa Rosa airport and into their rental car. She watched as vineyard after vineyard passed in a blur of sinewy vines. Dinner on Sunday or not, she felt lighter than she had in weeks.

CHAPTER 7
"Inside of Love"

Ivan eased the rental car into the turn lane and continued on as the pavement gave way to a dirt road. Pebbles crunched beneath the tires, and a haze of dust swirled through the air, leaving a faint film on the hood of the car. Majestic blue oaks grew at regular intervals alongside the road, their branches hanging over clusters of wildflowers below.

"Where are we?" Jaden asked as she surveyed the scene. Ivan just smiled as he zig-zagged his way up the hill, following the curves in the road as it wound gracefully through the trees. After a few more minutes, the trees began to thin out, and the sky opened above them as they emerged from the shade of the blue oaks and into an old, abandoned vineyard now overgrown with weeds.

"What is this place?" Jaden leaned forward in her seat. A large house, reminiscent of an old English cottage, materialized in front of them. Leafy green ivy clung to the fieldstone walls, weaving itself around the aging structure, and Palladian windows on either side of the double front doors glinted in the California sun. Above them, a stone terrace hung from the second floor, supported by two Corinthian columns. He pulled the car to a stop, and she slid out. "Is this where we're staying?"

He soon joined her at the front of the car, wrapping his arm around her waist and pulling her close. "Do you like it?"

"Do I like it?" she scoffed. "Are you kidding me? This place is fantastic."

Brilliant purple and red flowers occupied the well-manicured beds, and three identical black SUVs parked side by side in front of a garage that resembled the sublime architecture of the main house. But Ivan soon tore his eyes from the scene to take in the best view of all. Nothing made him happier than seeing Jaden so full of joy. If given the chance, he would spend every day of the rest of his life ensuring that she wore the dazzling smile she did at this very moment. Squeezing her tighter, he closed the sliver of space between them. He pressed his lips to her temple, whispering against her skin: "A castle for my princess."

She said nothing, but tilted her head back and brought her lips to meet his. She traced his bottom lip with the tip of her tongue. When at last their lips parted, she leaned back on the hood of the rental car, seeming a bit breathless. Her gaze dropped to the growing bulge in Ivan's pants and an impish grin appeared on her face. "So, you never did answer my question. What is this place?"

"Well…" Ivan took a moment to adjust his pants. "It used to be a winery, and for a short period of time was a bed and breakfast."

"And now?"

"Now it's a private getaway for family and friends of an associate I've done some work for. He's spent years trying to restore the estate to its former glory."

Jaden glanced over her shoulder at the abandoned vineyard behind them. "Looks like your friend still has a lot of work ahead of him."

"Ah, but looks can be deceiving, Ms. Thorne." Ivan laughed. He relinquished his grip on her waist and fished in his pocket until he found what he was looking for: a solitary brass key on a silver key ring. "Shall we?"

She sighed and took his proffered hand.

They walked in silence to the back of the car, collected their bags from the trunk, and walked together toward the house, taking in the view once again. He smiled at her again and felt a shot of butterflies ripple through him. Perhaps her excitement was infectious. As they approached the front door, he lifted the key to the lock, but the door swung open, revealing a rather robust woman on the other side of the threshold. Wild, curly black hair hung around her face, and a peasant skirt and floral blouse covered her abundant form.

"You must be Dr. Rusilko!" the woman all but shouted, her voice thick with enthusiasm and a heavy Spanish accent. Stepping aside, she waved them into the house. "Señor Shok said I should be expecting you this afternoon. Please, let me take your bags."

Ivan released Jaden's hand and twisted sideways, thwarting the woman's attempts. "Thank you, but I can manage, Mrs....?"

"*Miss* Marta," she replied, not so subtly giving him the onceover.

He heard Jaden stifle a laugh, and she blushed crimson as a chuckle escaped her lips.

"Señor Shok failed to inform me that there would be other guests joining us this evening," he said kindly, ignoring Jaden's fit of giggles.

"Oh no, Dr. Rusilko, I am only here to see you to your room and ensure that you're settled in," Marta assured him. "You will have the house to yourselves this evening, but I'll prepare your supper before I leave. Now, come. I'll show you to your room."

"Thank you, Marta." Ivan took Jaden by the hand.

Floorboards creaked underfoot as they moved through the house. Despite the modern amenities, it had a certain old world charm. Cherry hardwood floors stretched out in every direction, and mahogany panels lined the walls, adding character and ambiance to the sparsely furnished space. They reached a small kitchen at the back of the house and Marta began climbing a small stairwell off to one side.

This wasn't the type of lodging Ivan had grown accustomed to in South Beach. No marble floors, no heated swimming pools, and no grand staircases. This place reminded him of the simple cabin in Pennsylvania he and Jaden had shared not long ago—the place where they'd declared their love for each other again and again. The memories of that night brought a smile to his face, and he could feel the stirring of arousal as well. Squeezing Jaden's hand in his, he turned to her and smiled. He could see all the love and lust and adoration on his face reflected in her emerald green eyes.

One-by-one they inched up the stairs to the second-floor landing, and Miss Marta's commanding voice echoed in the hallway, breaking the quiet that had settled among them.

"This is your room." She produced a key ring with dozens of keys of various shapes and sizes. She selected one and opened the door. "The bathroom has been upgraded. There are fresh towels in the closet, and the hairdryer is beneath the sink."

"This is lovely," Jaden said, looking toward their accommodations.

"Will there be anything else, sir?"

"No. Thank you, Marta."

"Very well. Dinner will be ready in a bit. I'll be in the kitchen if you need anything."

He nodded politely, and Marta took her leave, closing the door behind her. He placed the suitcases on the floor at the foot of the bed and surveyed the room while Jaden flitted from window to window like a butterfly, once again radiating pure joy. He couldn't help but smile, but he also felt a tingle race up his spine. This was it, wasn't it? All he truly needed. His love for Jaden threatened to overwhelm him for a moment. Bending down, he busied himself with unzipping his suitcase and retrieving a small leather bag of toiletries.

"Going somewhere?" Jaden's voice was smooth and seductive as she joined him at the foot of the bed.

"Just thought I'd freshen up before dinner," he said, taking a deep breath.

She raised her hand and cupped his face. "Is everything okay, babe?"

"Couldn't be better." He smiled.

"You know you can talk to me about anything, right?"

Damn! This weekend was supposed to help Jaden relax, not make her worry. He rested his cheek in her palm, then kissed her hand, luxuriating in the softness of her skin. Oh, what he would do for her — the love of his life, the gatekeeper of his soul.

"Jaden, I would never keep secrets from you. I swear." Taking a step back, he cocked his head to one side and offered a mischievous smile. "Well, maybe one."

"Ooh! You and your surprises!" She tackled him, bowling him backward onto the bed. She eyed him from above for a moment, then draped herself over him, snuggling in for a full-body hug.

"You like it so far?" he asked.

"Yes, I love it. I'm the happiest I've ever been, and you're the reason," she said, sitting up to look in his eyes.

Only the sound of Marta calling to them from the bottom of the stairs saved them from working up an even bigger appetite. But there'd be plenty of time for that later. Eyes twinkling, Ivan led Jaden downstairs to the feast awaiting them.

CHAPTER 8

"I Wanna Know What Love Is"

"Kudos to the chef, Marta," Ivan said as their hostess passed by the door. She nodded appreciatively.

Jaden smiled as Ivan sank back in the chair, seeming contentedly full and perhaps a little tipsy. They'd polished off a bottle and a half of wine with dinner. She stood and began to clear the plates from the table, thinking again of work despite her attempts to relax, but Marta reappeared to stop her in her tracks.

"Please, miss, leave the dishes. I'll tidy up before I go home."

"Really, it's okay, Marta," Jaden assured her, but with her mind preoccupied by an impending co-host, she didn't notice the small rug on the floor by the fireplace. As she stepped past Marta, her toe caught on the rug's corner and she fell ass over end, the plates smashing into white ceramic shards.

"Oh! Miss!" Marta gasped.

Ivan rushed to Jaden's side. "Are you okay?"

With Ivan's hand on her shoulder, she regained her composure.

"Has someone had a little too much to drink?" he asked, helping her to her feet. He looked her up and down, examining her body for any signs of injury.

"No, someone has *not* had too much to drink. I just didn't see the rug." She playfully smacked Ivan's hand away. She could feel his eyes on her, assessing her, and she tried to change the subject. "It's a beautiful evening. Why don't we go for a walk?"

Giving her one final look, he agreed. "Sure, but let me get your jacket. It's chilly out."

Jaden brushed herself off and continued to the sink to help finish the dishes.

"Please, ma'am," Marta implored. "The dishes are my job, and I don't wish to anger Señor Shok. I'll get to them right after I clean up this mess."

"Don't worry, it'll be our little secret." Jaden smiled. "It's the least I can do since I *made* the mess!" She took a pot from the dish rack and began to dry it. As she rubbed the towel over its surface, her thoughts again returned to *One Hot Kitchen*...and one ridiculous playboy.

"Are you ready to go?"

Jaden jumped at the sound of Ivan's voice, almost dropping yet another plate. She turned to find him staring at her, grinning with a bag slung over his shoulder. She'd know that look anywhere: a wicked grin to match his wicked thoughts. At that moment she knew what the night had in store, and a familiar warmth spread through her body. Her heart beat in anticipation. She smiled at Marta, dried her hands on the dish towel, and joined Ivan at the door, all thoughts gone except for the promise of what this evening would bring. Would she ever tire of him—of the feel of his hands as they caressed her and the touch of his lips as his mouth claimed her? No, never.

Taking her jacket from him, she shrugged it on and matched his devilish grin. With a goodbye and thank you to Marta, they stepped out into the vast expanse of the vineyard. After just a few minutes, they were lost among the overgrown vines, strolling hand in hand and deep in conversation.

"I'm looking forward to moving to an independent medical practice. I can't believe it's about to happen. Just a few more weeks. It's a big change, but I'll really be able to provide customized, concierge service—something my clients demand."

"I know you'll do great. I'm so proud that you're taking a chance and doing this." She squeezed his hand. "It will totally pay off!"

"Thanks, babe. And don't worry—I'm also doing a photo shoot here and there for shits and giggles, and working with a few charity events. I do manage to have a little fun. Your old restaurant just opened a night club underneath it, by the way, and it's amazing. We'll have to check it out next time you're in Miami."

"I know! Tasha tells me she's there all the time. She and Micky love it."

"Yeah, I see them there sometimes, crazy in love as ever. They're getting pretty serious. I think you'll see Tasha trade in nightclubs for diapers and baby strollers in the near future." Ivan looked at her pointedly, as if trying to gauge her reaction to this declaration, but she just smiled.

They continued walking, talking about the latest goings on with Micky and Tasha, when they came upon a small clearing in the vines. Jaden paused to drink in the scene before her. Clusters of purple grapes clung to the vines, glowing in the setting sun, and Ivan glowed as well, the sun glinting in his hair. The silence was beautiful, accented only by an occasional bird chirping or leaf rustling. The smell of clean country air mixing with Ivan's amazing scent created a memory she would call upon soon enough. They'd have to say goodbye again, and she'd be without him. Jaden silently cursed the dreaded and all-too-frequent goodbyes. Ivan said they were "see you laters," but calling them something else didn't make them any easier.

But tonight was breathtaking, and memories like this helped ease the loneliness, so she collected as many as she could.

"Do you want to stop here?" Ivan's voice was barely above a whisper.

She nodded, and as she did, he handed her two flutes, which he'd produced, along with a champagne bottle, from his bag.

Pop! The sound of a fine bottle birthing a cork echoed through the vineyard, startling a flock of birds and accenting the tranquil sound of the breeze that ruffled the leaves. He poured two glasses. After a delicate clink, they each took a long sip of the bubbly, their eyes locked over the rims of the glasses.

A few quiet moments passed as they leaned against a pair of posts, and Jaden realized she'd slipped into some kind of daze. She shook her head to clear away the trance and returned to the earlier conversation about their friends. "So…uh…Tasha and Micky…" she stammered and took another long drink of wine. "You're right—she seems more and more sure about settling down every time I talk to her. It's scary."

"Scary? Why is it scary?" Ivan asked.

"Well—"

"I can see why it might be scary," he suddenly continued. "But when two things fit so perfectly together, it's almost a crime not to unite them, right?"

"Well, I do think they're great together but…I don't know. It's been so fast, and they've had a few fights here and there over stupid little things…But I know she loves him, and he loves her. So I guess it wouldn't be too scary, now that I think of it. But babies? Yikes! That *is* scary—for Tasha, I mean. She forgets to breathe sometimes," Jaden said with a laugh.

"Fair enough. So, I'm curious…" Ivan continued after a moment.

She turned to look at him, and he took a sudden healthy sip of his wine before finishing his sentence.

"Would it be scary for you?" he asked. "Hypothetically speaking, if I were to ask you to be my one and only, to spend the rest of your life by my side, what would you say?" He waited for a beat and offered up a few potential responses: "Too soon? Maybe? All in?"

A resounding *yes!* screamed in her brain and nearly burst out of her mouth. But instead, Jaden lifted her eyes to meet his gaze and looked deep into his soul as she responded. "Hypothetically speaking…if you were to ask me such a question, I would be the happiest girl in the world."

"Even if it meant giving up your dream and moving back to Miami?"

She stilled. This question served up an unwelcome dose of reality. Could she let go of everything she'd worked so hard to achieve? There had been a wild glint in his eyes only a moment ago, but now she recognized love, admiration, and something else…fear. His face held so much hope, but at the same time he was clearly treading water and, without a doubt, nervous. Though she too felt a pang of fear deep within, Jaden's heart warmed. In that precious, vulnerable moment, she knew how she had to answer his question—hypothetical or not.

"Ivan, there's nothing that could keep me away from you—not three thousand miles and definitely not some job. I'm all in." She watched the smile bloom across his face, and she couldn't hide a sly smile of her own. "Hypothetically, of course."

She wrapped her arms around his waist and as she pressed her forehead to his, she could feel moisture. He *had* been nervous. He buried his face in the nape of her neck and held her tight. Ghosting tender kisses down her neck, he whispered, "Jaden, in a world filled with heartache, pain, and uncertainty...your love is the mountain I needed to climb, the song I needed to sing, and the chance I needed to take. I wanted to know what love could be, and I found the answer in you. You're everything to me."

Jaden's heart leaped in admiration of the man who held her. He would give her his world, and equally, hers was his for the taking. It just had to be. No matter where life took her, she knew she'd always remember this perfect moment. They stood in their own little universe: a rugged landscape with a cool breeze caressing them, birds singing in the distance, the setting sun painting a masterpiece across the sky, and their hearts beating as one. Their souls had fused for an instant, but an instant was all they needed. It was right, and it was hers forever. *He* was hers forever.

"Thank you," he whispered.

"I should be thanking you."

Some say sex is the physical manifestation of love, but Jaden knew what she'd just experienced was much more. Something she'd never felt before. Ivan's soul had penetrated hers. She now understood what fairy tales promised and why so many were desperate to find this. This was a spiritual manifestation of love—something no word, touch, or expression could define. Something only those who've experienced it could ever understand. It was beautiful.

They walked back to the house in silence, sensing that something had changed, something that would forever alter the course of their relationship. After their "hypothetical" conversation, Jaden couldn't help but wonder if Ivan intended to propose to her. Why else would he have brought it up? She longed to savor the perfection of the evening, but her thoughts continued on to his other question, a question that had been nagging her since the moment he'd asked it: *Even if it meant giving up your dreams?* If marrying Ivan meant giving up the show and everything she'd spent the past year working for, she'd be ready to do it...right?

Returning to the house, they slipped inside, whispering and tiptoeing as if there were someone they might disturb. But everything was in its place, and Marta had left for the evening. They found another bottle of wine chilling in a sterling silver bucket and a plate of fresh fruit on the counter. Releasing Jaden's hand, Ivan dropped off their empty bottle from the vineyard and pulled the chilled wine from the bucket. But not once did his gaze stray from the most beautiful woman he'd ever seen. Long, slender legs, tanned skin, toned stomach—a stomach that might one day carry his children—and willowy fingers that would wear a ring as a symbol of their love for each other. He sighed, and the realization hit him like a ton of bricks: whether Jaden moved back to Miami or he transplanted to LA, he'd found his place in the world. It was at her side.

Only logistics stood in his way. He needed the perfect ring and the perfect setting for his proposal. As much as he wanted to get down on one knee right here in the middle of the kitchen, this was going to require some thought and planning. It was going to be fun.

Jaden picked up two fresh wine glasses and took his hand. As she turned to go up the stairs, he followed along behind her, admiring the view. Before she reached the top, he'd swept her into his arms. He was surprised when she didn't resist or squeal or giggle, but simply wrapped her arms around his neck and kissed him full on his lips. He staggered down the hallway, absorbed by Jaden's kiss as he carried her to their bed.

He placed her on the comforter, set the bottle on the nightstand, and moved to hover above her, his hands pressed into the soft mattress on either side of her body. Lowering himself, he traced the tip of his nose along the length of her neck as she arched her back in pleasure and ran her thigh between his legs and against his erection. He moaned at his maddening desire for her. Only her.

He ran his tongue along the shell of her ear, exploring every curve and tonguing the silver hoop earring that pierced it. "I love you," he breathed.

"And I you," she responded, writhing in sensual delight. She ran her hands across his shoulders and chest and down his ribs, then gathered the tail of his shirt and in a single motion pulled it over his head. She then removed hers, and there were no barriers to the warmth that had been building between them.

Her eyes locked on his, she pushed him onto his back and kneeled next to him. Her hair draped around her as she bent to place tender kisses on his stomach. She deftly managed the button and zipper on his jeans as he ran his hands through her hair. He inhaled as she ran her tongue along the exposed length of him, and in an instant, her fingers slipped inside his waistband, tugged his pants from his body, and tossed them to the floor.

He pulled her onto his naked body. Her legs parted to straddle him, and they fit together perfectly, as if made for one another. Their lips explored with delicious kisses, tasting and teasing until they were lost in each other. The kisses grew deeper and more passionate as the friction of their slow and sensuous grind began to build.

Without breaking their kiss or the bond between them, Ivan reached to remove Jaden's shorts. She shifted to help him as he smoothed them past her tight ass, down her taut legs, and on to the floor with the rest of the discarded clothes. Then she draped her body back over his. As they melted into each other, the feel of her smooth pussy meeting his cock was nearly unbearable. Ivan felt her smile of anticipation as she kissed him, and she moaned as he nipped her bottom lip between his teeth.

He pressed his hips back against the mattress, and they moved as two parts of the same whole. Sharing an exhale, Jaden lowered herself as Ivan pushed up, his cock sliding into her. Her warmth and wetness surrounded him. The feeling of complete bliss grew with every stroke, and the emotions he'd felt in the vineyard welled to the surface once again.

Their bodies worked in unison as he gripped her hips and pumped himself in and out of her. She matched him thrust for thrust, taking as much of him as she could and calling for more.

Without missing a stroke, he maneuvered her to her back and took control. He had to see her, to watch this beauty find her rapture. He positioned himself for optimum penetration and slid in and out, back and forth, as they neared a powerful precipice. Together they gasped and groaned as every nerve in his body fired and cried out *yes!* Their bodies reached the breaking point simultaneously and succumbed to the delicious torments of genuine lovemaking. Ivan thrust hard and true, spilling all that he was into her emotionally, spiritually, and physically. Her head thrown back in ecstasy, Jaden was gorgeous. And she was forever his. Wave after wave thrummed through them as they climaxed together as one.

When there was nothing more to give or receive, they collapsed in an exhausted lover's embrace. He rested his head on her breast and listened to her heart beat as she stroked her fingers through his hair. The world had never been more perfect.

CHAPTER 9

"Dance Naked"

*I*t didn't matter who was visiting whom, Jaden's west coast time clock always out-slept Ivan's east coast setting. And one of his secret pleasures was to wake and find his love fast asleep. He loved these quiet, uninterrupted moments when he could indulge in her raw and unguarded beauty, memorizing every freckle and feature. He brushed her hair away from her face, slowly so as not to wake her.

Jaden lay on her side with her hands clasped under her chin. The white sheet was draped low over her hip, revealing the feminine slope of her body. He loved the way her long, dark eyelashes were such a contrast to the delicate skin just above her cheekbones and how the heart-shaped curve of her lip formed the most perfect pout when she slept. Her ribcage rose and fell with every whisper of breath.

Ivan ghosted a single finger across her shoulder, along her stomach, up the slope of her hips, and back again. Her eyebrows twitched, and she began to stir. She nuzzled her head against the pillow and a slow smile spread across her lips. "Hmmm…Morning."

He added a bit of pressure to the patterns he traced on her skin. "Good morning. Did you sleep okay?"

"I did." She wriggled closer to him on the bed. "I wish we could fall asleep together every night."

"One day soon," he replied, his voice full of hope and unspoken promises. He kissed to the top of her head, inhaling her sweet scent—a scent that evoked a flood of memories from the evening before. "Big night tonight. We get to meet that pretty little co-host of yours."

"Please, don't remind me," she shot back with a growl. "At least I'll have you there to keep him at bay."

"Damn right I'll keep him at bay. I may need to mark my territory, so if I pee on your leg during the party, think nothing of it."

Her eyes opened, and she giggled. "You're such a freak!"

He wrapped his arms around her, gripped her ass with both hands, and pulled her against him. "And you love it!"

"I sure do." She snuggled into him and wrapped one leg over his hips as he began to grind his erection against her. "How much time do we have before we have to leave for the airport?"

"Enough."

"Ohhhh, no. I'm not falling for that. Remember the last time we had a pre-flight quickie? You had to bribe the cabbie, and we sprinted all the way to the gate."

He nestled his head in the crook of her neck and began kissing and nibbling just below her ear. "It was totally worth it."

"Yes, ahh…yes, it was…" she said. "Ivan…"

He smiled against her warm skin and kept up the teasing, hoping he could coax her into the same groove.

"Stop, babe," she pleaded with a laugh. "I need to shower."

"I'll go with you."

"No." She wedged both her hands between them and pushed against his chest, forcing him away so she could look at him. "I've got a better idea."

He raised an inquisitive eyebrow. "Better than showering together?"

"Yes." She smiled a wicked smile and matched his raised eyebrows. Then she looked toward the bathroom and back to him. "But you have to do as I say."

He smiled at her, loosened his grip, and then submitted to the sexy fantasies that filled his lustful mind. "All right."

She slinked out of his arms and untangled her legs from his. She sat up next to him. "You stay here."

"Yes ma'am." He sat up against the headboard, adjusted the covers, and laced his fingers behind his head. When Jaden failed to move from the edge of the bed—momentary jitters?—he cleared his throat expectantly.

She stifled a laugh and turned away from him, gathering the sheet around her and taking it with her as she went. She walked to the bathroom, the damn sheet hiding her full glory. She was covered up, but he was lying naked on a stripped bed, fully exposed and hard as hell. His dick grew harder by the second in anticipation of what was to come.

As she disappeared behind the door, the sound of water streaming onto a hard marble floor filled the air. A moment later the door flew back open, and the shower's light blinked on. Then, in his mind, two and two became four. This was way better than what he'd had in mind. All he needed was popcorn.

A beautiful bare leg came into view from behind the door, and he marveled at its perfection. The leg was followed by a bare hip, beautiful pelvis, and toned stomach. And then—with one slow but intentional step—every glorious, naked inch of her was revealed. He'd admired her body before, of course, but never every curve of her naked skin in such a voyeuristic way.

As she stepped into the glass-walled shower, things got a whole lot hotter. He shifted on the bed and groaned. He couldn't take his eyes off this peep show. He watched as she dropped her head back under the flowing water. He watched as she ran her fingers through her slick black hair. The water formed rivulets that ran down her face, slinked past her tits, and skated over her sculptured abdomen and smooth pussy. He was desperate to be with her, but he couldn't bring himself to look away, let alone move, except for the hand that now reached for his dick.

A thin vapor of steam wisped out of the bathroom, and drops of water pattered against the glass as Jaden hummed the first song they'd ever danced to: "The Way You Look Tonight." Something about the way she moved, the way her hands roamed her body as she touched herself, was so…uninhibited. She caressed her breasts, working the soap into a lather. Thousands of tiny bubbles adorned her taut, wet nipples. He longed to suck them, to take her into his mouth and taste the salt of her skin. His cock was so hard in his hand that it had its own goddamn heartbeat.

He watched in astonishment as she again tilted her head back into the flow of water. Ribbons of bubbles ran down the length of her body and into the drain below. She lowered her head and opened her eyes, casting him a sidelong glance, but she carried on as if no one was watching. Her hand dipped between her legs and he watched, his eyes fixated on the juncture between her thighs, as she massaged. She arched her back against the wall and her body quivered as she began to peak. He stroked himself in time to her rhythmic movements, each pass of his hand sending jolts of ecstasy along the length of his spine and curling his toes.

He felt awkward, embarrassed, and invigorated all at once as he continued to enjoy both the show and himself, and Jaden continued to do the same. It was as if there were no walls between them anymore.

When she screamed out her climax and collapsed against the shower wall, Ivan found the ability to move. With purposeful strides, he marched to the bathroom with only one thought on his mind: *Mine. Now.* Throwing open the shower door, he joined her under the hot water. He grabbed her by the arms, spun her around, and pinned her to the shower wall. His cock pulsed as he pressed up against her, his erection nestling between the cheeks of her ass.

"Do you have any idea how sexy you are?" He groaned and took her earlobe between his lips, nibbling and biting, and he smiled when she writhed beneath him.

"Did you enjoy watching?" she murmured. Grasping his cock, she began to stroke it up and down.

He took a fistful of her hair, pulling her head to the side and exposing her neck. He bit her shoulder softly. "You have very skillful hands, baby. I've often wondered how you used them when I wasn't there."

"Let me go, and I'll show you what other tricks I have up my sleeve."

Instead he pressed into her and pinned her more firmly to the cool, wet wall. Using his foot, he spread her legs farther apart. "Hmm, I'm gonna hold you to that, but right now I need to feel you." He reached down and replaced her hand with his, positioning himself between her legs, and pushed.

Jaden stiffened, her body going rigid as she gasped.

He stilled. "What's wrong?"

"Umm, baby? I think you have the wrong hole."

He tried to stifle a laugh but failed, and they both launched into hysterics. "One of these days, I'll take you there too."

Her laughter immediately faded, and she turned to look at him. "Are you serious?"

"Sure, why not? I'll take you any way I can get you," he replied, his voice sultry.

He studied her reaction. Had he gone too far, crossed some invisible barrier just when he thought they'd shared everything? But the look on her face told him no, he hadn't. And the look of desire that flashed across her delicate features next made his cock stiffen even more.

"I'm going to hold you to that promise." She stood on her tiptoes for him.

He adjusted his position and entered her swiftly. They groaned as their bodies settled around and in each other. He hooked his arm under the back of her knee and brought her leg high in the air. Then he worked deeper into her core, and the sound of flesh on flesh drowned out the echo of the water splashing on the tile floor. Sweat mixed with the water running over their bodies as he took her from behind, his thrusts pushing her into the wall with each stroke of his cock.

She tilted her head back and screamed, pushing her hips down against his. "Oh, God!"

"What is it? What do you want?" He gripped a handful of her ebony locks and pulled her head back, his lips meeting hers and quieting her cries. Their tongues mated feverishly, their lips crushing together.

Jaden pulled back, breaking the kiss. "Please, let me come!"

Ivan loved it when she begged. It was like an aphrodisiac. "Your wish is my command."

He reached around her body, finding her clit, and rubbed it not so gently with his thumb. He could feel her body tremble, her muscles clamping down on his cock as she convulsed around him, but his own release seemed just out of reach. He picked up his pace, thrusting into her harder and deeper, and he could feel another climax building within her, nudging him closer to his own release.

"Oh fuck, yes!" Her body flung forward into the wall. "Again!" she roared.

That was all the coaxing he needed. With one final thrust he slammed into her, deeper than ever before. Hot jets of semen poured into her, filling her with everything he had.

Exhausted and sated, he lowered them to the floor, sliding out of her warmth, and they sprawled on the tile. When their breathing had returned to normal, he reached up and took the bottle of body wash from the shelf. He squirted it into his hand and, with steady motions, drew circles over Jaden's skin with his palm, working up a rich lather. Neither spoke as they took turns washing each other.

When at last the hot water began to run cold, Jaden spoke. "Maybe we should get out now. I'm turning into a prune."

He took her hand and raised it to his mouth, kissing the tips of her fingers. "No, you taste too sweet to be a prune."

She placed her head on his chest and ran her fingers through his long, wet hair. "You're too good to be true. How did I ever get so lucky?"

"Babe, I'm the lucky one."

"How do you figure?" She raised her head to look at him.

"You said yes."

"After that ridiculous display at Bianca, I thought Geoff was going to fire me for sure. I had to say yes just to get you out of the restaurant before all hell broke loose."

He laughed as he remembered that day: the "business" lunch, chasing her into the kitchen, spilling sauce on the ridiculously expensive suit he'd worn to impress her, and finally, asking her out. Laughing, they untangled their limbs and stood. Ivan turned off the water while Jaden retrieved two towels from a nearby shelf.

"You know," he said, tossing his towel aside moments later and rummaging through his suitcase for clean clothes. "I think—"

Billy Idol's "With a Rebel Yell" blasted from his phone, interrupting him and startling Jaden.

"What the hell?" she squeaked.

"That's our wake-up call," Ivan explained as he pulled on a pair of jeans. He held up the phone and showed her the time. "Two hours until our flight. Ha! Told you we had enough time."

CHAPTER 10

"It's a Beautiful Morning"

As she gathered her belongings and repacked her suitcase, Jaden's heart sank. It was the same lethargic feeling she always got when one of their weekends was coming to an end. She didn't know how much more of this she could take. She needed Ivan like she needed air to breathe. Tears stung her eyes, and she quickly wiped them away with the back of her hand. Instead of pondering the "what ifs," she busied herself with cleaning the room. She stripped the bed of its soiled linens before collecting all their belongings. She didn't find a sweater in her suitcase, so she rifled through Ivan's and pulled on his old Mercyhurst College sweatshirt. She held it to her nose and inhaled. It smelled of sand and sun, cigars and cologne. It smelled exactly like Ivan.

When everything had been packed, he took her hand and led her down to the front door. She looked around one last time before her eyes settled on his, and they both smiled. Something different, something life-altering had taken place over the weekend in this romantic cottage in the middle of the Northern Californian wine country. Whatever *it* was, both of them knew, but neither said anything more about it.

As they sped back to the airport, she fished her phone from her purse and checked the emails she'd been neglecting all weekend. Skimming through various work updates and spam, she smiled when she saw a note from Tasha. God, she missed that crazy girl. But then the next message, from her mom, caught her eye. Tapping the screen, she opened it and began to read:

Honey,

Just wanted to send you a quick reminder about the retirement party we're throwing for your father in August. I know that's three months away, but you're a big Hollywood celebrity now, and I'm sure you need time to plan. Don't forget us simple folk!

Anyhow, your father also wants you to bring that boyfriend of yours so he can see who's been occupying all of his baby's time. He says Ivan is getting off easy with only chatting on the phone. You know your father and how he's set in his ways, so if Ivan is free that weekend, please invite him. We would love to finally meet him in person.

Your brother and sister say hi and that they love you. Call them. They miss you, and so do we.

Love,

Mom xoxoxo

A knot tightened in Jaden's chest. What would Ivan think of her family? What would they think of him? They'd done pretty well on the phone so far, but was it really a good idea to have her father, a park ranger sceptical of hunting enthusiasts, and her boyfriend, who considered hunting a fantastic family activity, in the same room together? Particularly with copious amounts of liquor involved?

She grimaced as she recalled Ivan's first conversation with her dad. Last Christmas had been their first together as a couple. He'd been bogged down at work, and she'd had only a one-week hiatus from the show, so they'd decided to have a low-key Christmas together in Miami. When she'd called her family to wish them Merry Christmas that morning, her dad had requested to speak with Ivan, then lectured him about the importance of family being together over the holidays. Once Ivan had finally assured him he was not trying to keep her away, the two men had found some common ground, and they'd spoken several times since.

But this was different. At the retirement party, all her kooky relatives would be there. Her dad's family didn't exactly hail from the Upper West Side, but damn, they were fun to be around. Actually they were a lot like—*quite* a lot like—Ivan's family in Meadville.

Jaden smiled. If they could get past the awkward introductions, Ivan would fit in just fine with her crazy, awesome family. At heart, they were all a bunch of rednecks.

Turning to Ivan, who was singing horribly as usual, she fiddled with the buckle of her seatbelt and readied herself to ask the question. "Hey, I umm…I have something I need to ask you."

Glancing over, he sat up and turned down the music. "What's up, toots?"

"Well, my dad is retiring in August and—"

"He is?" Ivan raised an eyebrow. "He's never mentioned that to me. Is everything okay?"

"Yeah, everything's fine, and it doesn't surprise me that he never mentioned it. He's not too happy about the idea, but mom thinks it's time. She wants to do some traveling while they're still young enough to enjoy it."

"Are they throwing a party for him?"

Nerves crept up Jaden's spine. "Yes, the second weekend of the month, and I was wondering if you could come with me to Colorado. My family wants to meet you in person."

"Damn, that's a pretty busy time, babe."

She looked up at him, and for the second time that day, her heart sank.

He reached across the seat and cupped her face in the palm of his hand, his thumb caressing her cheekbone. "It's a shame my patients will have to deal with it."

She laughed and swatted his shoulder. "Damn right they can deal with it. I don't know if I can handle *that* many of my insane relatives on my own."

"Of course, baby girl. I would love to meet everyone. I wouldn't miss it for the world. Thank you for inviting me."

A blanket of relief covered her and warmed her to the core. She placed her hand on his and squeezed. "Thank you."

They rolled to a stop in front of the car rental, dropped off the car, and began the trek to the gate for their flight back to LAX—and to the party she'd been dreading. But suddenly she didn't mind as much. Her new co-host was likely an ass, and she had to deal with him whether she wanted to or not, but her stress about Damian had been replaced with pleasant thoughts of Ivan and her family. She began compiling a mental list of things she wanted to do with him in Colorado. While they waited at the gate, she opened her email and began to tap out a response to her mom:

Hi, Mom!

Of course I remember. I can't wait! And you ALL better be on your best behavior. because Ivan's coming with me!!! So no anti-hunting talk from Dad or craziness from anyone else. ;)

I love and miss you more. And yes, I'll call Magan and Justin sometime this week.

PS...They have phones too!

Love you lots,

Jaden

Slipping the phone back into her pocket, Jaden smiled at Ivan and waited for the plane to take them home. China, Alaska, Colorado — she didn't care as long as he was by her side. After their weekend, she felt happier than she had in a long time, and she owed it all to him. He'd succeeded in making her the luckiest girl in the world...yet again.

CHAPTER 11

"God's Gonna Cut You Down"

The night air was cool and crisp against Jaden's skin. The smell of citronella infused the air, but it sparked a sick feeling in the pit of her stomach. She and Ivan walked hand in hand past the row of tiki torches lighting the walkway of Kevin Gibbs' fabulous Hollywood backyard. What had been billed as a small, informal dinner had turned out to be a lavish affair complete with open bar, DJ, and a pig on a spit roasting over an open fire. The man had spared no expense. There had to be at least a hundred guests at this "informal" dinner.

The tiki light cast an iridescent glow against the shimmering fabric of her emerald green dress, a color that matched her eyes. The dress was simple but elegant, and she'd selected it because it hugged her curves in all the right places and accentuated her *assets*. She knew Ivan loved the dress, because on more than one occasion she'd caught him gawking at her backside while she was wearing it. But tonight was not about Ivan's attention. It was about making a statement that said, "Back off, boy toy. This is my show!" Damian Gris was nothing more than a pretty kitchen utensil, she reminded herself.

As if he could sense her stress, Ivan squeezed her hand. "Don't worry," he whispered. "This guy doesn't stand a chance against you."

She looked up into his soulful brown eyes. How did he always know exactly what to say? She was thrilled to be clinging to his arm as she made her grand entrance. With him by her side, she felt on top of the world. Of course it didn't hurt that he was, as far as she was concerned, the most stunning man at the party. He'd leave Damian in the dust. His ruffled brown hair hung at his shoulders. His shirt, black as the midnight sky, fit him flawlessly, as did his tailored dress pants of the same color.

A goofy grin lit up her face as she remembered the events of the past hour. Upon returning from a beauty session with Kat, she'd walked into the house to find him ready and waiting for her in the living room, looking impossibly handsome. God, how she loved him.

"Just a quickie," she'd begged, but he'd warded off her advances.

"Baby, we don't have time for this. The party starts in forty-five minutes."

"Screw the party," she'd scoffed. "We'll be fashionably late." She'd grabbed the bulge in his pants and felt him stiffen under her touch.

"Jesus, Jaden, you're gonna be the death of me."

"Well, maybe not the death of you, but certainly your undoing. Just one taste, please?" she'd asked as she got to her knees in front of him.

Reminding herself where she was—Kevin's backyard with a hundred other people—she cleared her throat and forced her thoughts back to the present. Ivan had been right. They were twenty minutes late, and the updo Kat had carefully crafted was now nothing more than a mass of jet black curls hanging down her back. But the taste of him still lingered in her throat. Delicious.

"Are you ready? It's show time." Ivan gave her hand another reassuring squeeze and kissed the top of her head.

"As ready as I'll ever be. Let's do it!"

Side by side, they made their entrance. She gripped his hand, inadvertently digging her nails into his flesh.

"Ow!" he whispered. "Relax, babe."

She took a deep breath and forced herself to smile at everyone she passed. Thankfully she did not see Damian—though she hoped he'd seen her.

"Well, I'm guessing you wanted to make a statement," Ivan said once they'd joined the party. "And I'd say you succeeded. You look good enough to eat."

"I think we both do." She laughed and felt some of the pent-up stress drain from her shoulders. Unlike the first event she and Ivan had attended in Miami, back when he was teaching her South Beach party etiquette, they now worked the crowd in tandem like the power couple they were. As they danced their way into the party, their usual light-hearted banter began to flow.

Stacey, with her over-the-top makeup and predatory gaze, slid from a bar stool and came over to greet them. "Hey, guys! How was your weekend? Was Napa everything you'd hoped it would be?"

Jaden felt a flash of irritation. Why would Ivan tell Stacey, of all people, Ms. Cougar herself, where they were going? She tried to brush off the unsettling feeling, but God, the woman irked her sometimes. She'd better not have her sights set on Ivan. Then she stopped herself and took a deep breath. *Stacey is not the enemy. She is a friend. The friend who gave you your amazing job,* she chanted silently, willing it to be true.

"It was magical," Ivan finally responded, seeming to realize Jaden was not going to.

"I'm so glad you had such a wonderful time." Stacey stumbled forward, and she raised her glass to wave it at a passing waiter. Then she turned her attention to Jaden. "Are you ready to meet your new partner?"

Partner? Partner?? *Screw that! He's not my partner,* Jaden mentally screamed. But feeling Ivan's hand on her shoulder, she drew strength from him and forced a smile to her face. "Yes, of course," she replied.

Just then the crowd erupted in applause as Network President Kevin Gibbs made his way through the throngs of people to the front of the tent. Standing in the shadows behind him, Jaden could see the ominous outline of her new co-host.

"Oh my God, he's here. He's here!" Stacey squealed.

Jaden whispered in Ivan's ear. "I don't think I've ever gotten that worked up over someone I work with."

"Ladies and gentlemen," Kevin's voice boomed over the speakers. "Thank you all for joining me here tonight. Now I know Sundays aren't the best day of the week to be holding a party, but judging by the look of things, we're doing just fine."

The crowd burst into another round of cheers.

He raised his hands and motioned for them to hold their applause. "Tonight is a special night for the cast and crew of *One Hot*

Kitchen, for tonight we embark on a new journey and welcome a new cast member to the program: a new co-host for the lovely and talented Chef Jaden Thorne."

Jaden slunk back against Ivan as every set of eyes turned to her. Onstage Kevin raised his hand, waving to her over the heads of the crowd. She scowled to herself, but returned his wave.

"Now let's all put our hands together for the man of the hour, the son of world-renowned Chef François Gris, and the new co-host of *One Hot Kitchen*...I give you Damian Gris!"

The crowd once more produced thunderous cheers, but Jaden stood silently as the shadowy figure crept forward into the orange glow of the lights. Damian's all-too-perfect jaw line and bright blue eyes were topped with a mass of streaked blond hair that curled and fell into his eyes. His T-shirt and jeans left him wildly underdressed. The man didn't have the decency to dress up for his own fucking party?

Though she'd suspected all along, Jaden now clearly understood why Kevin had brought Damian to join the show: more women viewers. Yes, the show would get a boost and yes, the ratings would go up, but she had a sinking feeling about the quality of her work environment. He had an air about him—one of cockiness, entitlement, and greed. She shivered at the thought of spending grueling hours working with this guy. Most women would die to be in her place, but she didn't care. Damian Gris was trouble.

Tossing back his hair, he took the podium and began to speak. "I want to thank each and every one of you for coming tonight to welcome me to *One Hot Kitchen*. It's an honor and a privilege to be here, and I am especially looking forward to working very, *very* closely with my co-host, Jade."

Before she could even formulate a response to Damian's fake familiarity and use of the name Jade—one she hated almost as much as she now hated the name Damian—she felt Ivan's body go rigid. His fake laugh and half-cocked smile signaled his fury over Damian's comment.

Somehow Ivan's anger made her feel better. She stood tall and proud. "I'm not exactly sure what your definition of *close* is, Damian," she called. "But welcome to the team."

The crowd burst into cheers again—they'd cheer for anything, it seemed—and drowned out the last of her new co-host's speech.

Returning to the podium, Kevin wrapped things up. "Be sure to say hello to Damian and introduce yourselves," he told the audience. "We have a busy few months ahead of us, so let's make this season even better than the last."

"That was interesting," Ivan snorted.

"What an ass! Jade? Really? I've never even met the guy, and he's acting like we're best friends. This is *not* going to be fun."

Ivan turned her to look at him, and for a moment everything else faded away. He brought her lips to his for a furious, pineapple-flavored kiss. His breath was warm and heady as he whispered against her lips. "Baby, you're a rock star. Never forget that. There's nothing—"

"Jaden, I'd like to personally introduce you to Damian," a voice behind them announced.

She broke the kiss and took a deep breath. Then together, she and Ivan turned to face Kevin and Damian.

As the lion observes the gazelle before it pounces, Damian studied her for a moment, his eyes bright with intent and mischief. "Wow! You're even more stunning in person."

"Umm…thanks?" She suppressed a laugh. This guy oozed cockiness. Biting her tongue and willing herself not to say something she'd regret, she shook his hand. "It's nice to meet you."

"We're going to have a lot of fun getting to know each other," he continued with a smile. He seemed unaware of the fact that Ivan stood beside her, and he placed a hand on her arm as he leaned in. "We should grab a drink sometime soon and *really* get to know each other."

"Thank you, but no," she said quickly. She dared a glance at Ivan and could tell he was beyond furious. Trying to defuse the situation, she jumped right in to the introductions.

"Damian, I'd like to introduce you to my boyfriend, *Dr.* Ivan Rusilko."

His smile faltered for just a moment as he extended his hand to Ivan. "Sorry about that, man. I didn't see a ring, so I figured the little lady was single. No hard feelings, right?"

Little lady? Is it 1957 or something?

"Yeah, I know, I should probably take care of that soon—the ring, that is," Ivan countered, his voice smooth and even. "With a girl this special there's always going to be some pretty boy waiting to scoop her up. But I'm not worried. I mean, pretty boys are a dime a dozen…"

He paused to smile at Damian, then turned to Jaden and planted a firm kiss square on her lips, lingering perhaps a bit longer than he otherwise would have in a professional situation. She was thankful for him all over again.

"Well," he announced, giving her a warm smile. "I'm going to grab us a drink. I'll let the three of you get acquainted."

With one final glance over his shoulder, he winked and disappeared into the crowd. Damian now looked decidedly less cocky, and Kevin looked dumbfounded and slightly perturbed. Jaden took a moment to compose herself, swallowing her laughter. This had been quite an introduction. Perhaps she could handle this guy after all. Without missing a beat, she jumped into conversation. "So, Damian, how do you like California so far?"

"Umm…" He seemed unsure how to respond. "It's okay, I guess."

She smirked. *Yeah, you just got handed your ass on a silver platter, didn't you?*

Then, thankfully, Kevin took over. They began a discussion of the changes the show needed to make in order to accommodate a co-host. Of course Jaden would have to sacrifice time on camera, but there was the potential for a huge jump in ratings, so she swallowed her pride and accepted the fact that this was a done deal. Damian was now an integral part of the show. At some point Ivan returned with the drinks he'd promised and stood close by, not once saying a word.

As they talked, her gaze wandered from Kevin to Ivan and then to Damian. If she were being honest with herself, she could see why women flocked to him. His aqua blue eyes contrasted with his sun-kissed hair and deep brown tan, and his angular jaw line emphasized boyishly handsome features. She could also tell that beneath his rumpled clothing was a well-toned body — and not the type of body you get by spending hours at the gym. It was more the physique you get spending your days in the ocean. But the fact that Damian managed to manipulate every conversation to revolve around him made her blood boil. *Confidence is sexy, cockiness isn't.* He would *not* be fun to manage on camera.

The wind shifted and a pungent aroma wafted through the air, causing her to sneeze. It took her just a moment to realize the sickly sweet smell was Damian's cologne. *Good God, I hope he doesn't wear that every day.*

Out of the corner of her eye, she could see her blond former nemesis stalking the crowd, her eyes trained not on Ivan, but Damian. For the first time that night, Jaden was glad for Damian's presence. If Stacey had her sights set on him, then maybe Jaden could stop worrying about her carrying a torch for Ivan. The crowd parted as Stacey headed toward them, seeming intent on joining the conversation. "Kevin, darling, do you really think it's fair to keep this fine young man all to yourself?" she screeched with a too-loud laugh. "There are others waiting to meet our newest up-and-coming star."

"You're absolutely right, my dear, but we've been discussing the new plans for the show. Damian was just telling me he may be able to get his father to join us as a guest host." Kevin's face beamed with excitement and…something else, something Jaden couldn't quite put her—ah! *Greed.* Kevin saw Damian and his father as a meal ticket. Of course! How could she not have seen it before? Having Damian on the show would not only boost ratings, it could also mean millions of dollars in sponsorships. This epiphany, fueled by several glasses of wine, was almost too much for her to process. This show she loved was just a business at the end of the day. She took this as her cue to excuse herself. She'd come to the party and met Damian, and now it was time to go home and enjoy her last evening with Ivan before he had to leave for Miami.

"I hate to interrupt," she said, not paying much attention to whose conversation she was interrupting. "But Ivan and I have to get home. He has to work tomorrow, and his flight leaves first thing in the morning."

A small smile crept over Damian's face. "Oh, the two of you don't live together?"

"Ivan lives in Miami," she said, her voice like ice.

"Wow! That must be difficult. A guy like him living alone in Miami while his girlfriend is on the opposite side of the country? What did you say he was? Some sort of doctor, right?"

She knew the picture Damian was trying to paint, and she wasn't about to help him. "It is tough, but when you love someone as much as Ivan and I love each other, you do everything in your power to make it work." Taking her own turn at being overly familiar, she leaned in. "Every girl should date a doctor who specializes in women's sexual health. The sex is fucking amazing."

With that she turned and gave Ivan a little pat on the butt, startling him out of his conversation nearby. "Are you ready to go home?"

"I'm ready if you are," he replied. "Kevin, next time I'm in LA, we'll have to squeeze in that game of golf. And, Stacey, it was great seeing you again. Give me a call the next time you're in Miami. I have a few business associates I'd like to introduce you to. Damian, the pleasure was all mine. Love the jeans."

Hand in hand, Jaden and Ivan bid the group farewell and moved quickly to the exit, hoping to escape any delay from the rest of the party guests. With this huge burden off her shoulders, she could now focus her full attention on the night ahead. This fantastic weekend needed to be capped off with a bang. She'd give Ivan a going-away gift to keep him going for quite some time.

CHAPTER 12

"Stereo Love"

"I keep meaning to ask you—when did you get this?" Ivan screamed from the driver's seat over the roar of the wind.

"It's a loaner," Jaden yelled back. "Kevin had it sent over the day after he told me the studio was hiring a co-host for the show. Coincidence, huh?" She sank into the black leather seat of the silver Mercedes Roadster and cranked up the stereo. The sultry sounds of synthesizers blared through the speakers, the beat reverberating through her body like an erotic symphony.

With slow, purposeful movements, she reached across the seat and traced the inseam of Ivan's pants, outlining his growing erection with the tip of her finger. It still amazed her that he was so receptive to her touch, that this alone was enough to make him rock hard. "Oops! Did I do that?" she teased. She toyed with the button on his pants. "Do you want me to take care of that for you?"

A devilish look flashed across his face, and she could tell he was wondering just how far she was willing to go. *All the way, baby, all the way.* She began to undo his zipper, but stopped halfway when he grabbed her by the back of the neck and pulled her toward him. Bringing his mouth to hers, he delivered a passionate kiss, fueled by a fire that had been ignited hours ago.

The car lurched a bit and, passion or no, she remembered they were screaming down Mulholland Drive and approaching Dead Man's Outlook, one of the most notoriously deadly curves in the

Hollywood Hills. She wriggled out of his grasp, breaking the kiss. "Maybe you should keep your eyes on the road, baby."

"Good Lord, Jaden." He reached down and unzipped his pants the rest of the way. "You can be such a cocktease sometimes, you know it?"

She shifted on the seat to face him, licking her bottom lip. Her tongue scraped across her teeth, and she could feel herself getting wetter. This game of cat and mouse was about to come to an end. It was time the mouse got a little taste of the cheese.

She paused as Ivan maneuvered the car around Dead Man's Outlook, but once they were safely around the bend, she unbuckled her seatbelt and got to her knees on the black leather seat. The music continued to flow through her body like a rhythmic aphrodisiac, and her pussy thrummed with the beat. With one hand, she steadied herself on the dashboard, and with the other, she hiked up her dress, giving her more freedom to move and exposing the bare cheeks of her ass.

"Maybe we should wait until we get back to your place." Ivan sounded tortured, his words dripping with need and anticipation.

"You take care of the driving, and I'll take care of you," she said, bending over his lap.

With her mouth inches from his cock, she looked up at him, silently asking for permission. The look on his face told her all she needed to know. His needs were as great as her own. With the flick of a lever, he tilted the steering wheel and readjusted himself in the seat. He knotted his fingers through her hair, but this time he didn't try to kiss her. He guided her head to his lap. She opened her mouth, and her lips surrounded his throbbing cock, taking him into her mouth and down her throat, every luscious inch of him.

The rhythm of the music, the vibrating of the car, and her sucking as she swallowed Ivan drove her just about over the top. Her hand stroked the base of his cock, and her tongue flicked the tip. Each of her movements made him harder and wilder, and he began to thrust himself into her mouth. She could feel his hand riding up her thigh. The cool flow of air from the air conditioner blew between her legs, a welcome relief from the heat coursing through her. His hand now rested at the sweet spot just below the cheeks of her ass, and his fingers toyed with the fabric between her legs. Pulling it aside, he slid his middle finger into her core and stroked it back and forth in sync with each pull she took on his cock.

She moaned and cried out, releasing his dick from her mouth, only to take it back in a second later even deeper than she had before.

"Fuck me!" Ivan groaned and grabbed the back of her head, guiding her movements and pushing himself farther down her throat.

He thrust forward and at the same time hit the accelerator, causing the car to lurch again. He jerked it hard to the right, and the inertia forced Jaden's head deeper into his lap.

She sat up on her knees, gasping and coughing for air. "I'm back to thinking we'd better wait until we get home. My gag reflexes can't take another hit like that. Deep throating is one thing, but I think you were in my stomach."

"Ooh, sorry, babe," he managed before bursting out laughing. After a moment he wiped tears from his face. "I think you may be right."

He looked over and she scowled, which set him off laughing again, and this time she joined him. He took her hand and squeezed. She smiled and settled into her seat to enjoy the rush of speed. Ivan's laughter hadn't slowed him down any. Road signs passed by in a blur, and just as she was about to mention their exit, he veered hard to the right and they sped over to the off ramp. The next two miles flew by. Speed limits were shattered, and stop signs were merely suggestions. They both knew what was on the menu for this evening, and it seems they were famished. Gratification was just around the corner…

The Roadster screeched to a halt. Barefoot and dishevelled, she ran to the door and fumbled with the keys. Ivan was right on her heels with fire in his eyes. The front door to her townhouse burst open, and they tumbled into the hall. Before she could turn to face him, his hands were on her shoulders, holding her against the wall. His teeth scraped the skin just below her ear, and his tongue trailed fire across her flesh. Goose bumps rose on her forearms. With a twist she freed herself from his grasp and ran toward the stairs.

"Catch me if you can!"

"Two can play this game," he yelled after her as he began to run.

She took the stairs two at a time, and she could hear him drawing near. As she reached the top, her toe caught on the step. Red-hot pain shot through her knee as it skimmed the carpet, but that faded in an instant as Ivan wrapped his hands around her ankle and pulled. She slid down the stairs, and he captured her in his arms.

He rested his hands on either side of her head, steadying himself on the stairs, and hovered inches above her. "You didn't really think you were going to outrun me, did you?"

"You haven't caught me yet, doc," she squealed, backing up the stairs. A glint sparkled in Ivan's eye. The tables had been turned. He was the cat and she was the mouse. He was the hunter. She was the prey. In a final attempt at escape, she twisted her body and propelled herself up the steps.

She could feel him behind her, his hot breath tickling the back of her neck. They raced into the bedroom, and his arms wrapped around her waist. They collapsed onto the bed, succumbing to a fit of giggles. All around them were mounds of dresses that hadn't made the cut, and they now provided an extra layer of cushioning. Jaden struggled to rid herself of the emerald green dress she wore while Ivan tossed around on the bed beside her, making quick work of his pants and shirt. This was the last time they'd see each other for weeks, so there was no time for pleasantries.

He rolled onto his back and disposed of his briefs. His erection sprung free and stood at full attention: hard, throbbing, and demanding to be touched. Following his lead, she stripped out of her bra and panties and tossed them to the floor. She straddled his legs and felt him tense beneath her. Leaning over, she opened her mouth and enveloped him, picking up where they'd left off in the car. Her mouth moved languidly down his shaft, and she felt him twitch as the head of his cock hit the back of her throat.

"Stop!" Ivan's hands circled her forearms, and he pulled her up the length of his body. "If you keep that up, I'm a goner, and I'm nowhere near finished with you yet."

"Hmm…" she breathed. "I like the sound of that." Her body slid against his as she positioned herself above him. She reached between them and grasped his cock, positioning it at the entrance to her sex, she began to lower herself onto him. At that moment he raised his hips from the bed and thrust into her, filling every inch.

"Agh!" she cried, and he stilled within her.

"Are you okay?"

"I'm fine," she assured him. "That was just a little…unexpected."

He eased out of her and relaxed his hips on the bed, letting her take the lead. She rocked back and forth, slowly at first, but her tempo increased with every downward thrust. He snaked his hands around her waist, his fingers biting into her flesh as she surrendered herself to him. God, how she loved the feel of him in her, filling her, the touch of his hands searing her already heated skin.

Suddenly he flung her onto her back and plunged into her. Her moans morphed into screams as his cock drove deep into her pussy. She wanted to beg, to plead for release, but she was lost to his touch. Ivan stroked into her, and his cock brushed the bundle of nerves buried deep within. Her legs began to tremble. She was on the cusp of a monumental orgasm that had begun at the party, but just as she was about to spill over the edge, to find sweet release, he withdrew.

"Get on your knees," he demanded before she could utter a word of protest.

She smiled. She loved it when dominant Ivan came out to play, so she complied. She'd barely registered what was happening before he slammed into her from behind, once again bringing her hard and fast to the brink of orgasm. His chest pressed against her back as he laid a trail of fiery kisses from one shoulder to the other. His breath felt warm as he whispered hoarsely against her skin.

"Do you trust me?" His voice was raspy, his breathing uneven.

She glanced over her shoulder, puzzled. "Of course I trust you, but—"

"Shh…" He pressed a finger to her lips, silencing her.

She closed her eyes. The feel of his fingers caressing her clit as he took her from behind was nothing new, but she did not expect to feel his fingers trailing along the crevice of her ass to circle the tight bud of her anus.

"Ivan…" She began to object, but she did trust him…

He slowed to a stop as the tip of his finger breeched the taut ring of muscles, and she let out an audible gasp. "Are you okay? Do you want me to stop?"

"Yes." She nodded. "I mean no. Don't stop." Being touched in such an intimate spot had her senses reeling and made it impossible to form a coherent thought. This was more pleasurable than she could've imagined, and she found herself pressing back against his finger, burying it deeper. When at last her muscles relaxed enough to allow him complete entry, he eased a second finger into her.

Jaden had never felt so full in her life, and never had she dreamed that being taken in such a way would make her feel so sated. As her body became accustomed to the sensation, she started to move her hips, thrusting back against him, taking more of him into her. She tilted her hips and pushed against him, and with one final backward thrust, she came. Waves of pleasure radiated everywhere in her body, washing over her like a tidal wave. Her mind was hazy as her stomach coiled and another climax began to build. Not trusting her legs to hold her, Jaden bent over and placed her elbows on the bed for support. She felt a biting sting as Ivan withdrew his fingers from her ass, and the sensation caused her to explode around him and left her wanting more.

As if sensing this, he thrust into her at a maddening speed. He wrapped his arm around her stomach and pulled her up into his chest. His cock twitched inside her, and he pulled out to come on the small of her back. Sucking and licking the base of her neck, Ivan continued to grind against her ass, prolonging the bliss until he'd emptied himself.

She collapsed on the bed, taking him with her, and quivered as remnants of the monumental orgasm she'd just experienced flitted through her body. "That was amazing," she whispered. "You're amazing."

"No," he responded, kissing her forehead. "*We're* amazing."

They lay, naked and lazy in each other's embrace, for what felt like hours. Moonlight streamed through the window, and the fluid on her back began to cool. With great reluctance, she extricated herself from Ivan's arms and stood. "I think it's time for a shower."

"Agreed," he said. He grabbed his shirt from the floor and wiped away the cream that smeared his thighs.

She could feel his gaze on her with every step she took. With deliberate movements, she entered the bathroom and bent over to turn on the shower, exposing everything she had to him. She felt a blush warm her cheeks, but she smiled. The mattress squeaked, and she knew he was coming to join her. Somehow, they'd managed to maintain the perfect balance of love and lust, despite the nearly three thousand miles between them.

CHAPTER 13

"Listen to Her Heart"

"Hey, sweets!"

Jaden gripped the countertop in the studio kitchen, took a deep, calming breath, and counted down from ten. This was her new reality, and she needed to find a way to manage it. She'd been pleasantly surprised by Damian's on-camera personality during the first few shows they'd taped together. He'd been focused, attentive to her instructions, and professional to the crew. But in the ensuing months, he seemed to believe he'd mastered everything, and he was increasingly difficult and cocky. When her count reached one, she placed a smile on her face and turned around—only to discover just how close behind her he'd been standing. Raising a finger, she warned, "If you call me that one more time, I swear to God I'll rip your tongue out."

"Oh, feisty! I like that." He seemed about to add another snappy remark, but instead raised his arms and took a step back. "I was joking around," he said. "You know, trying to lighten the mood. I promise to behave now."

"No, you weren't, and no, you won't. It seems you don't know how to behave, Damian," she retorted. "This is a professional workplace, and you've *met* my boyfriend, so please stop with the sleazy antics."

"Listen, Jade…"

Sweets? Jade? Was it too much to ask that he call her by her proper name?

"I really am sorry," he added. "I'm not trying to step on your boyfriend's toes. I just want us to have some fun together. If my sense of humor offended you, I'm sorry. For the sake of the show, can we at least try to be cordial to each other?"

She couldn't make heads or tails of this guy. His mischievous look did not at all match the sincere tone of his voice. But for a moment he seemed almost…vulnerable? *No,* a voice in Jaden's head warned. There wasn't a sincere bone in Damian's body.

However, because of the show, and to spare her fading patience, she nodded and gave him the benefit of the doubt. "Apology accepted. Now, can we please finish this shot so we can go home?" *Filming has taken* extra *long today because you can't seem to figure out how to read your lines and not talk over mine,* she added silently.

"Sure thing, boss," he replied. With a spring in his step, he returned to the back of the kitchen and the task at hand.

Five minutes passed, and then ten—without so much as a peep from Damian. Jaden busied herself with putting the final touches on the plate of steamed clams, and the camera crew readied themselves for the final segment.

Bang! She turned to find her favorite serving platter shattered into a million shards and scattered across the tile floor of the set. Damian stood beside the stove, his hands now empty. He looked at the mess, but instead of bending down to pick it up, he just shrugged and turned away as if nothing had happened. *It's not my platter, it's the network's,* she reminded herself, but deep breaths were of little use now. She'd had just about enough of Damian and his entitled attitude.

"All right, boys and girls. Let's wrap it up and call it a day. Everyone take your places," the cameraman called as the crew finished cleaning up the set.

Damian looked down at Jaden, smugness oozing from every pore in his body, and winked. "I have a date with Cathy from editing tonight," he whispered. "Let me know if you'd like to join us." He raised his eyebrows meaningfully, then turned toward the camera and began to speak. "So with your seafood feast prepared…"

Jaden swallowed her shock and composed herself as quickly as she could, but not before Damian had taken the liberty of describing the clams *she'd* prepared. *Poor Cathy,* she thought. *And poor me.*

The next twenty minutes felt like the longest of her life. When the cameraman finally yelled, "Cut!" she hightailed it to the closest exit, not bothering with a final review or even a change out of her kitchen whites.

She hurried around the corner to the spot where Adam parked. She didn't have the patience to text him and wait for him to pull around to the front of the building.

As she slipped into the backseat, he looked up from his newspaper, surprised. "You're in a hurry, Ms. Thorne!"

"It was a long day." She laughed half-heartedly. "I'm ready to be somewhere else."

"Straight home tonight?" he asked.

"Yes, please."

She sank into the black leather seat and was thankful when he raised the partition between them. Somehow he always seemed to know when she needed time to herself. As the studio disappeared behind them, she fished her cell phone from her purse. As she suspected, not a single message from Ivan. He'd been consumed with his new practice and busy supporting various local charities. *Mostly by attending their cocktail events*, she thought bitterly. And now he was out of town on some trip. She didn't even know this time where he was… There was, however, a text from Tasha. It was short and to the point:

Call me…NOW!

Jaden calculated the time difference between LA and Miami…a little past eleven pm on the east coast. With any luck Tasha would be asleep and she could postpone the inevitable tongue lashing she was sure to get from her best friend. They didn't talk nearly often enough.

"Hello?" Tasha answered, her voice heavy with sleep, after a few rings.

"Hey, it's me," Jaden whispered. "You sound tired. Why don't I call you back tomorrow?"

"Oh no you don't! I've been waiting to talk to you."

After some chatter about the weather, Tasha seemed awake. And she jumped right in, as blunt as ever. "So, how are things working out with Ken?"

"You mean Damian?" Jaden spat, the day's frustrations coming back in a rush.

"Yeah, pretty boy. Who else would I be talking about?"

But talking about Damian was the last thing she wanted to do. "Can we please talk about something else?"

"Sure!" Tasha said much too agreeably. "Do you want to tell me why, in all the weeks since you went to Napa — what was that? Almost two months ago? — you haven't mentioned that Ivan dropped the M-bomb during your trip?"

"What? Wait…how do you even know about that?" *Ivan had been talking about their weekend?* "Never mind. I got it: Micky."

"Yes, Micky. It certainly wasn't my best friend."

"Tasha, I'm sorry. Things have been so hectic since Damian showed up, and Ivan's been so busy…Well, that just seems like a million years ago. I can hardly believe it happened. And it's not like he proposed or anything. He mentioned it hypothetically."

"And did you hypothetically say yes?" Tasha asked.

"Of course I did!" Jaden filled her in on the vineyard conversation, hoping that would satisfy her. But as she knew it would, the conversation found its way back to Damian.

"Now, do you want to tell me what's bothering you?" Tasha asked. "I can tell there's something, and you haven't called me in a week."

Jaden proceeded to give Tasha a full account of the past week, including all of Damian's blunders. "So not only did he break my favorite serving platter, he also set fire to the stove. He's hit on every single female on the crew — successfully, I might add — insulted my makeup artist…Oh, and today he invited me to be in a three-way with him *just* as the camera started rolling."

"Seriously? That guy has some balls. But he can't be all bad, can he? I mean, just look at him. He's sex on a stick. Those blond curls and — my God, girl — his ass! How can you not stare at that all day? He has to be good for the ratings."

"Yes, I think his boost to the ratings might be his most endearing quality at this point. Every once in a while I catch a glimpse of a real person in there — someone who isn't putting on a show for everyone," Jaden conceded. "But for the most part he's just unbearable. *And,* by the way, *of course* I've noticed how he looks. I may be dating Ivan, but I'm not dead. Truly, I think that makes him *more* annoying."

"Ah, just relax. He may be a bit of a man whore, but he's one fine piece of man candy too. Just focus on the ratings and forget about the rest. You're not having any fun, and you've worked too hard to have some Ken doll take that away from you."

"Maybe you're right."

"I'm always right," Tasha joked. "Besides, if he messes up enough, I doubt the studio will keep him around. By this time next year you'll have your show back, and Damian will be licking his wounds on the beach in Maui."

"Hmmm...I like that idea," Jaden said with a laugh. "But enough of this. Tell me about you. How's the real estate biz? How's Micky?"

As Tasha launched into an animated story, Jaden closed her eyes. Though she loved catching up, she always felt homesick talking to Tasha. As they said their goodbyes, she swallowed a lump in her throat. She missed Ivan, she missed Miami, and she missed gossiping over lunch with her best friend.

CHAPTER 14

"Time of the Season"

Two more weeks. Two more weeks. Two more weeks. The mantra repeated in Jaden's head like a Gregorian chant. Just two more weeks until her trip to Colorado to see her family. She needed all the stress-relieving and anger-reducing help she could muster to continue handling her co-host's endless line stealing and inappropriate flirting. Also not helping was the fact that she and Ivan's usual two-week rendezvous had been postponed because he'd been called away on business to New York. So he'd be going there, rather than coming to LA this weekend. He'd told her it was something of great importance and would explain everything to her when the time was right. *When the time was right? What the hell did that mean?* He'd been overly busy and constantly on the phone the last few times they *had* managed to be together, which made her even more anxious. Despite these unsettling feelings, she comforted herself with the knowledge that her dad's retirement party was right around the corner. Ivan had sworn he could still make that trip. Knowing she'd see both him *and* her family soon was the one positive she could come up with in her otherwise dark and dreary mood. *Two more weeks. Two more weeks. Two more weeks.* The mantra continued.

"So, Jade, are you going to the network gala tonight?" Damian asked in his too-familiar way, sidling up next to her. "I can only imagine how stunning you'll look—a pretty little thing like you all done up."

His fake French accent sounded like nails on a chalkboard. What kind of question was that? Of course she was going tonight. The annual gala was the network's largest and most public gathering, and she'd been planning on it for weeks. Yet another thing Ivan was missing, but still, it was an important event, and she was determined to have a good time. Taking a deep, calming breath, she responded. "Yes, Damian, of course I'm going. And again, my name is Jaden, not Jade. Please don't call me that."

"Oh, someone's getting a bit testy. Haven't gotten laid in a while, I assume?" He let the question linger just long enough to exasperate her, then switched into professional mode. Well, as professional as he got. "I'll just do a little prep for the next show now. Excuse me," he said with a smile that almost seemed sincere.

"Damian," she sighed. It was the only response she could muster. Over the past few months she'd built up a certain tolerance to his inappropriate comments, and despite herself, she had to admit he was occasionally entertaining. Though he was always a challenge on the set, he did spice up the show. And, as Tasha liked to point out, he was nice to look at. She was a woman with needs, after all, and Damian was, well…gorgeous. Women would give their left arms to be in her shoes—to have a man like Damian lust after them. *But those women don't have Ivan*, she reminded herself. However, the fact that she didn't often give Damian the time of day had made him more intent on getting into her pants. *God, men are so easy…*

But with his last ridiculous comment, Damian had actually been right, which irritated her even more. The buzzing bunny that kept her company during occasional dirty phone calls with Ivan was growing old and boring. She longed to feel him in her and on her, his scent surrounding her. The sex they shared—when they shared it—was full of raw and unbridled passion, which built up to impossible levels during their time apart. She loved their journey into experimentation and exploration, testing the limits of how far the other was willing to go. God, she was horny all the time these days. A pull of her hair, a bite on her neck, the feeling of him working his way deep inside her inch by inch—*Fuck!* How had she become such a nympho? Ivan had made her some sort of sexual diva. And a frustrated one at that.

"Oh, but, Jaden?" Damian called from the set. "If you need a ride—in the car that is—I'd be happy to pick you up."

His voice snapped her out of her daydream. "No, it's okay. I'll have Adam take me. But thank you for the offer."

"Okay," he replied with a shrug. "Just call me if you need a lift."

Good God, you've made your point! she shouted silently. "What a pain in the ass," she mumbled under her breath.

And yet she found herself staring at him as he arranged cookware on the set. He wasn't the type she'd go for, and he was nothing like Ivan, but she couldn't help but admire the back of him. Dressed in khakis and a surfer boy short-sleeved shirt, he did remind her of a Ken doll. *I just need to get laid,* she told herself. *By Ivan! Two more weeks...*

Jaden looked at her watch and sighed. She was expected at the party in a few short hours. As she started out of the studio and toward the dressing room to meet Kat and get ready, she fished her phone from her purse. The message on the screen informed her that she had several missed texts, all of them from Ivan. The first one read:

> I hope you have a great time tonight, baby girl.
> Wish I could be with you.

A smile spread across her face as she read the second message.

> So excited for Colorado!
> Could you plan on being gone a few extra days?
> I have a surprise for you! ;)

Surprise? It had been too long since she was treated to one of Ivan's amazing surprises. Praying there was nothing major coming up on the schedule, Jaden whipped out her phone and checked her calendar. Perfect—they didn't start filming again until midweek after she came back. Feeling excitement course through her, she read the third and final message.

> My love for you runs through my veins like a fine wine.
> You intoxicate me.

With a wide smile, she typed a quick message back:

> I can take a few extra days—anything
> for one of your surprises!
> Gotta run to the gala. Xoxo

As she put her phone away, Jaden pulled the tiger eye rosary from her purse—the one Ivan had made as a teenager and she'd selected from among his mother's jewelry creations. She drew comfort from it whenever they were apart. Smiling, she tucked it back into the inside pocket where it had been since the day Marie gave it to her.

Inside her dressing room, she found Kat ready and waiting, dressed from head to toe in black and wearing a million-dollar smile.

"Hey, girl, are you ready to be made up? I have a new eye shadow I picked up just for tonight. I think you're gonna love it!"

"Yes, darling, make me purrrrty," Jaden replied in the thickest hillbilly accent she could manage.

"Did you see the dress the studio sent over for you to wear?" Kat asked, motioning to the closet door.

Jaden turned to look and gawked in surprise. "Pink? Really? Wow, they're really trying to girl me up, aren't they?"

"I'm guessing they're dressing Damian in blue so the two of you can be the Barbie and Ken of the party: One Hot Couple from *One Hot Kitchen.*"

"That boy is a perfect Ken," Jaden remarked. "Thankfully I'm not Barbie, and Ken is *soooo* not my type."

"What, no bad boy fetish?" Kat mused. She gestured for Jaden to sit and began brushing her hair.

"I never understood the whole bad boy, cocky attitude thing that appeals to some women," Jaden admitted. "I'm more of an old-school gal. I go for compliments and chivalry — the whole jackets over puddles deal. Thinking your shit doesn't stink does nothing for me. Damian needs a bit of an attitude adjustment. He's one hot piece of real estate, but he's just not for me."

"I'd do him in a heartbeat," Kat countered.

Jaden burst into laughter. "I'm sure all you have to do is ask him! No doubt he'd be a hell of a lay. I'd be lying if I said I hadn't Googled him and admired a picture or two, but I have everything I need with Ivan." She sank back in the chair while Kat went to work on her hair and makeup, giggling at her crazy stories.

"How are things with Ivan?" Kat asked when the conversation had steered itself back in that direction.

"Things are okay, I guess. But it's getting harder. The distance makes it difficult. But he's still as romantic as ever. There was the Napa trip a couple months ago, and now he's planning some other surprise when we go to visit my folks in Colorado in a couple weeks. He's trying to make things as easy as possible, but it's still hard."

"He's meeting your family?"

"Yes." Jaden smiled. "My mom invited Ivan to my dad's retirement party."

"Hmmm," was all Kat said as she continued her inquisition. "Do you trust him? I mean, he's a doctor, a model, and has all the right connections. I'd be worried he was dipping his pen in the proverbial Miami ink."

Jaden sighed, trying to sound dismissive. What was it with people always suggesting Ivan was unfaithful? She trusted him, and he trusted her. That's why they had such an amazing relationship. Without trust, it would've collapsed ages ago.

"All I know," Kat continued, "is with his good looks and charm, I'd keep him under lock and key."

"Ah, well…" Jaden managed, this time not feeling as certain. Her mind began to spin in every direction. He had been distant…and so busy…But that's just what happens sometimes, right? Then, clear as a bell, a conversation that did not actually include her began to play in her head:

Is he being faithful so far away?

> *Yes, of course. He would never*
> *do anything like that.*

Wouldn't he? How much does she
know of his past?

> *She knows of his present, the promises*
> *he's made, and that's what matters.*

She's only known him for so long.
Is there history she doesn't know
about?

> *Why does there have to be history?*

Doctor, model, entrepreneur
…come on, really?

> *Those things don't mean*
> *he's destined to be a playboy.*

How stupid are you?

> *Trust builds relationships that last.*

Doesn't trust afford the opportunity
to cheat?

> *She's happy now. There's no need
> to question it.*

Question it? What if she's missing
the time of her life?

> *Hasn't she had amazing moments
> with him the past year?*

Yes, but what has she missed?

> *Nothing of consequence
> because he's the One.*

How do you know he's the One?

> *Because of the way they fit together,
> the commitment they've made.*

But she needs to make sure,
doesn't she?

> *No, there's no need to risk anything.
> She just needs to be strong.*

Better to know now than later, I say.
She needs to get laid…

Was Ivan being unfaithful? Is that why he'd found reasons to change their plans? Was she missing opportunities because she'd become so focused on him? What was passing her by? She shook her head to clear her thoughts and earned a disapproving glare in the mirror from Kat.

"Okay, you're done," Kat announced a few minutes later, pinning the last of the curls to the top of Jaden's head. "Let's get you into that dress."

Jaden stood and stripped down to her panties and bra. With Kat's help, she slid the oh-so-pink dress over her head. *Damn!* As much as she avoided pink, the dress highlighted Kat's subtle makeup job and warmed the natural tone of her skin. She did a complete turn, earning a nod of approval.

"Girl, if I was into women, you'd be in some serious trouble," Kat said. "You look stunning."

Blushing, Jaden admired herself in the mirror. Excitement began to rise in her chest. She'd been looking forward to this evening for months, and even though Ivan wasn't there to share it, she was going to have some fun.

The clock on the wall told her it was much later than she expected. Adam had been waiting outside for quite a while now. She hurried to collect her belongings and stopped to give Kat a quick kiss on the cheek. "Thanks for everything. You did an amazing job as usual."

Kat's voice echoed down the hallway as Jaden headed for the car. "Have fun tonight, and don't do anything I wouldn't do."

The sound of her high heels clicking against the polished marble floor echoed off the walls as she dashed toward the door. And as expected, Adam stood beside the car waiting patiently.

"Ms. Thorne, you look absolutely stunning tonight."

"I bet you say that to all the women." She smiled and tucked herself into the backseat of the town car. As they dipped around corners and down hills, her stomach began to flutter. Tonight promised to be several fun-filled hours of drinks with the hosts of the other network shows — people she'd befriended since moving to LA, but never got to see enough of.

Her phone buzzed, announcing a text message, and she fished it out of her purse. This time it was from Tasha.

> I miss you, girl. Big party tonight, right? You're probably just on the way, and I'm going to bed! Hope you're doing great, and I hope to see you soon. Love you!

> Miss you too, girl! Yes, big party so wish me luck. I'd rather have pizza and beer with you.

> Yeah, sure. Stay safe, and don't do anything I wouldn't do!

Jaden rolled her eyes. The thought of what Tasha *would* do was both frightening and hilarious.

Oh shit, Ivan! Texting with Tasha reminded her she hadn't really acknowledged his messages from earlier — other than the quick calendar check. But now Adam was pulling the car into the parking lot of the hotel hosting the evening's event. Tucking the phone back into her purse, she promised herself that no matter how late she got home, she'd email Ivan to tell him all about the night.

"We're here, Ms. Thorne," Adam called from the front seat.

She took one last deep breath, then opened the door and stepped out into the night. *Here we go!*

"Have fun this evening. I'll be waiting for you."

"Thank you, Adam." Before she started across the parking lot to the check-in area, she grabbed him a Rusilko bear hug. Judging by the shocked expression on his face, she'd caught him off guard. She laughed, feeling buoyant as she walked toward the crowd and added a little strut to her step. Stacey cleared a path for her between the photographers and climbers who were clamoring for a chance to attend the hot-ticket event.

"Stunning as usual," Stacey said as Jaden pushed her way through the throngs of people.

"Thanks. You look great too. How is everything in there?" Jaden motioned toward the door where a line had started to form.

"It's insane. That's why they've got me out here on door duty." Stacey scowled and rolled her eyes. "I'll be in a minute to join you. Work that red carpet, girl. And wait until you see what Damian's wearing. Wardrobe went all out on that boy."

For reasons unbeknown to her, Jaden smiled at the thought of seeing Damian all dressed up. *No jeans and T-shirt this time, eh?* She giggled to herself.

The not-so-helpful voice piped up:

Mmmm-hmmmm....

CHAPTER 15

"Rootless Tree"

The hotel lobby was pure decadence. The venue had been made all the more popular by its recent appearance in a national architectural magazine, and Jaden could now see what all the fuss was about. A ten-foot waterfall anchored the open space, surrounded by plush white leather couches and shiny glass tables. The smell of eucalyptus wafted through the air and mingled with the rumblings of a party getting underway.

With every step she took, Jaden grew more confident. Though not what she would have picked for herself, the soft pink gown hugged her curves and her silver four-inch heels shimmered against the white marble floors and ruby red carpet. Jaden drew closer to the party's entrance and saw a sea of reporters and photographers awaiting her arrival as if she were some celebrity. Wait, is that what she was? A celebrity? Despite all the fanfare that had recently surrounded her, Jaden still had a hard time wrapping her head around her sudden fame. *Yeah, maybe a G-list celebrity.* She laughed to herself.

A reporter for the six o'clock news began speaking into her microphone as Jaden approached. This alerted the other press sharks, who joined the media frenzy. Within seconds, thirty or so photographers and cameramen had their lenses trained on her as she strode past them, escorted by a young woman dressed head to toe in black. The girl deposited her near a large *One Hot Kitchen* logo that stood beside the entrance to the ballroom.

"Oh my. She looks gorgeous," a woman wearing an *LA Times* press pass gushed to the man beside her.

With the logo behind her, Jaden smiled. Cameras began to click and a hundred flashes lit up the room. Confidence welled within her. She knew she looked good, and the buzz she heard over the clicking of cameras confirmed it. Ivan had taught her so much, and posing for the media was no problem now. But hell, this was a far cry from Miami, let alone Estes Park.

The flashing of cameras stopped just as quickly as it had started, and she paused mid-pose. The media's attention now turned to the next celebrity to grace the red carpet. *Well, if that was my fifteen minutes of fame, I'll take it,* she chortled to herself. She turned to enter the party, but the woman in black seized her arm.

"Would you mind posing for a few more shots?" she asked.

"Yeah, we'd love to get a few shots of you and your co-host together," a photographer at the front of the media circus added. He jerked his head toward the back of the room, where the person who'd stolen her show—and now her red carpet moment—had just entered.

Strutting down the red carpet as only he could was Damian, larger than life and sporting his ever-popular I-don't-give-a-fuck attitude. Despite this, she couldn't help but stare. His usual surfer boy jeans and T-shirt had been replaced by tailored pants that hung from his hips and poured over his black pointed dress shoes. And his black suit jacket covered a crisp, patterned white shirt, accented by a cobalt blue skinny tie. He had a smile for everyone he passed and worked the media like a pro, as if truly in his element. His chiseled jaw appeared even more defined than usual, and his eyes, blue and sparkling in the flash of the cameras, were fixed on…her? Looking the way he did, how could she not be impressed?

"Hello, Jade," he said with a drawl. "Don't you look delicious tonight?" Snatching her hand in his, he kissed it, posing for the cameras and giving the media what they salivated for.

Not quite able to conjure up the anger to scold him for calling her Jade, she simply replied, "Thanks. So do you." Wait…*Did I just tell Damian Gris he looked delicious? Fuck!*

"Let's take some pictures and give them what they want. Shall we?" He smiled and took her hand as they stood side by side in front of the show's logo.

When Damian wrapped his hands around her waist and pulled her to him, she noticed the whispers that began to spread through the crowd. She tried to distance herself from him, put some space between their bodies, but the flashes once more began to pop.

When the media's enthusiasm dwindled after a few moments and the photographers turned their attention to the next person on the red carpet, she was thankful for the reprieve. She needed a minute to collect her thoughts and stepped away from Damian. She hated him, didn't she? He was supposed to be the enemy, but she found herself softening toward him. He was here tonight, working hard and promoting the show just like she was. That had to count for something…She felt him lean over and his voice, soft and just the right amount of friendly for once, whispered in her ear.

"Let's grab a drink."

Yesterday she would've said no to his request, but tonight, she nodded in agreement. The two made their way through the throngs of people in the ballroom. Crowds milled around, talking in hushed tones, but their whispers quickly transformed into chatty gossip and blatant stares. *Where's the goddamn bar?* Jaden searched the room. *Bingo!* There wasn't just one bar, there were several.

"Be a doll and grab me a cranberry and vodka. I have to ask Stacey a question," Damian announced. "I'll only be a minute." And without a backward glance, he disappeared into the sea of people.

Did he just call me doll *and make me his waitress?* For a moment, she'd allowed herself to look at Damian as her equal, not some pretty boy trying to ruin her life, but he'd just reminded her how annoying he was. He was a womanizer who only thought of himself. Ivan had *never* sent her to the bar. The people in Damian's life were there as long as he deemed them useful, she suspected. When they'd exhausted their usefulness, he'd discard them like yesterday's trash.

"One dirty martini and one vodka cranberry, please," she told the man behind the bar. As he went to work, she sighed. She'd been looking forward to this night for months, so how was it that ten minutes with Damian had her wanting to run for the hills? She leaned against the brass rail of the bar.

"How does your boyfriend want his martini?"

"He's not my boyfriend. He's my co-worker," she snapped, startling the man. "I'll have *my* martini straight up, and I'm guessing he wants his vodka cran on the rocks."

"Sorry, ma'am," the bartender replied and went back to making the drinks.

A moment later, one dirty martini and one vodka cran sat on the bar in front of her. "Thank you." She picked up the drinks and merged back into the mess of media and industry people.

Weaving her way through the crowd, she joined Damian, Stacey, and a third man she didn't know. She handed Damian his drink, then stood and watched. He spoke with great energy, demanding attention from everyone around him, and Stacey clung to his every word. Hell, if she drooled any more, the woman would need a bib. After a few more moments of nonsensical conversation, Jaden jumped in just to change the subject.

"Hi, there, I'm Jaden Thorne," she bellowed, conveying her mood and startling the others. She offered the unknown man her hand.

"Hello, Jaden. I'm Gary Pallaria," he replied in a thick Boston accent as he shook her hand. "It's a pleasure to finally meet you. I love your show."

"Thank you. And what is it you do?"

"I manage an exclusive venue and event planning company in—"

"Ladies and gentleman," Kevin's voice boomed over the PA system. The lights grew even more dim, and their conversation ceased as he took the stage.

"Please excuse me," Gary whispered. "It was nice to meet you, Ms. Thorne. You are all that and more." He disappeared, leaving her with Damian and Stacey.

"I want to welcome you all here tonight," Kevin continued. "It's such an honor to have everyone under one roof—and not working! Tonight is our thank you for all your hard work. So grab a guy, grab a gal, grab a drink, and let's enjoy the evening."

The crowd erupted in cheers, the spotlight lifted, and the grand chandelier in the ballroom once again came to life. Both Damian and Stacey seemed confused to find just Jaden standing beside them.

"He excused himself, and so will I," she said. "I'll let you two chat." Without waiting for a response, she slipped away. Halfway across the dance floor, she dared a glance over her shoulder and caught Damian eyeing her. A jolt of adrenaline left her feeling like a giddy high school girl. It was the same look Ivan flashed when he was feeling frisky, and she made a beeline for the closest bar. God, how she missed Ivan. If only he were here.

After another martini and a visit to the ladies room, she found her way to a group of people standing by yet another bar. She didn't recognize them all, but she spotted a few familiar faces among the eclectic mix of other stars from the network, as well as PR gurus and the fashionistas who consulted with wardrobe. Many of them seemed eager to talk with her, and it was a change to be the one sought out rather than the one doing the seeking.

"Excuse me, miss."

Jaden turned to find a waiter at her elbow.

"Compliments of Mr. Gris," he added, handing her another martini. *That's more like it,* she thought, her mind a bit fuzzy. *That's the way you treat a lady. Maybe there's some hope for him after all.*

Is someone feeling a little sassy?

No, someone is feeling drunk.

Quelling the voices and turning back to her entourage, she continued to field questions about her show, her dress, and, of course, her hot co-host. As she chatted and laughed — it was a relief to speak with others in the business, those who really understood the pressures and demands of television — martini after martini found its way past her lips, each one tasting better than the last, though she wasn't always certain where they came from. From time to time Damian caught her eye from across the room, and she couldn't stop herself from smiling in return. He was taking such good care of her. What was Ivan doing right now? Who even knew. He said he was working, but she was smart enough to know there were no guarantees.

Suddenly Jaden's thoughts surprised her, and she needed to clear her head. She excused herself from the circle of conversation and retreated to an empty table in the shadows. Oh, how she missed Ivan — his touch, his smell, the way he brushed her hair aside to look into her eyes as she woke in the morning. She pulled out her cell phone and stared at it for a moment. She needed to hear his voice, but it was the middle of the night on the east coast. What if she called and he didn't answer? She'd only feel worse. *You don't need Ivan right now. You're perfectly capable of handling yourself. Be confident!* She returned her phone to her purse, and another martini appeared on the table in front of her — attached to the end of a very tan arm. Sparkling blue eyes bore down on her.

"Mind if I join you?"

"Why not," she said, throwing her hands in the air as Damian took a seat across from her. Then he scooted the chair around. Even in her inebriated state, she knew this scenario had "bad idea" written all over it. But how could she resist such a cute puppy dog face? She held the glass in the air and examined the viscous liquid through heavy eyes. "I don't know if I should drink this. I've had far too many of these little suckers already. Maybe I should just find Kevin and go home."

"Is Kevin driving you home? I thought you had a driver."

"He isn't. I mean, I do, but I'm not sure." The words she slurred sounded confusing even to her. She'd had far too much to drink, but it would be a shame to waste the martini in front of her. Jaden raised it to her lips and downed it in one gulp before slamming the glass onto the table. "What I meant was no, Kevin is not driving me home, and yes, I do have a driver waiting for me outside. So perhaps I should go."

"What? It's ten thirty on a Friday night, and you're already calling it quits? I thought this was the time of night you Californians *started* the party."

"Well, I'm not from California," she countered.

He offered her the puppy dog look again.

"Fuck it! To a good time and a great night," she announced, raising her glass to his.

Now sporting a victorious smile, he clinked his glass with hers. "That a girl."

Her glass was empty, so Jaden flagged a passing waiter and secured yet another dirty martini. How many was that now — seven or eight? Maybe more…Friendly banter transformed into open flirtation. Damian was always overly familiar, but now she could see his charm. Perhaps she'd misjudged him. They sipped their drinks, throwing each other seductive smiles and risqué glances. Jaden knew she should just stand up and walk away before she said or did something stupid, but Damian's infectious smile kept her glued to her chair.

"So how are things with the boyfriend? Ivan, isn't it?" he asked. And before she could formulate an answer he continued. "Are you happy with the show? With me?"

She was caught off guard. He really seemed to want to know. His fake façade was nowhere to be found, and she could see him for who he was: a handsome, successful, charming overachiever who was doing his best to make her feel at ease. Feeling courageous, she decided to be candid. "At first I wasn't happy with the idea of you being on the show, but I think you're kind of growing on me. Granted, you're gorgeous, but it was my show, my baby that I'd worked so hard for."

Damian's smile spread across his face. "I'm gorgeous, am I?"

"You know what I mean," she slurred, slapping him on the shoulder. "Of course you're good looking. That's the reason Kevin hired you."

"Ouch. Now *that* stings."

The smile on his face belied the hurt in his voice, and Jaden felt a tinge of guilt. "Sorry. I didn't mean it that way."

"Yes, you did," he cooed as if he didn't mind a bit. He took her hand in his. "But you still didn't answer my first question. How are things with you and Ivan?"

She knew she should withdraw her hand. Something about this was wrong. But they were *talking* about Ivan. He knew she had a boyfriend. And his skin was warm, welcoming. Squeezing his hand, she stammered her response. "Things are great. He was supposed to be here this weekend, but he was called away on business. The distance can be tough, but we're working through it. It's just been way too long since…" She stopped talking, as if her mind had switched off in an emergency.

"It's been too long since what?"

Was that his hand on her knee? *Damn!* Her mouth sprang back into action, and she was unable to prevent herself from finishing the sentence. The time for thinking rationally seemed to have passed. "It's hard, you know? He's in Miami, and I'm in LA. When we're together the sex is great, but when we're apart…Well, let's just say I've replaced the batteries in my silver bullet more times than I care to count. And I suppose the same is true for him…"

"Jaden, you're young. I still don't understand why such a beautiful woman has limited herself to one man. You should be out there experimenting and experiencing new things, not waiting for a boyfriend who may or may not be out with another woman at this very minute."

"I don't know." She sighed and shifted forward in the chair, her knees now touching Damian's. "I don't think Ivan would cheat on me. He's not the type."

He eyed her for a moment, then sprang into action. "Come on," he said, as if making an important decision. "Let me drive you home. We can talk on the way."

"I don't know if that's a good idea." She looked around the tilting room, hoping to catch someone's eye. Someone else needed to be part of this conversation. Where was Stacey?

"Please? I'd feel bad letting you go home alone." His fingers brushed her leg, causing her to shiver.

Worried about a missed opportunity?

No, she's just curious.
There's a difference.

No, no, no. If curiosity is piqued
that implies doubt, right?

No, not necessarily.

No stone unturned...

"Are you sure?"

"I wouldn't have it any other way," Damian assured her. He picked up her purse. "Let me take you home and put you to bed."

"Okay?" Jaden conceded, standing unsteadily and still unsure what to do.

Next thing she knew, Damian was leading her by the hand to the back exit of the hotel, through the parking lot, and to a waiting black Mercedes Roadster, the twin of the one the network had provided for her. Her heart pleaded with her as she slid into the front seat, but her mind—drunk on martinis and well-placed words—ignored the requests. After ensuring she was buckled in, Damian slid into the driver's seat. With a flick of the key, the Roadster roared to life and eased out of the parking space, leaving Stacey, Kevin, the party, and her last shred of dignity behind.

The car screamed down the highway toward...her place? Damian's? He wasn't asking for directions, and she couldn't tell. Her lazy mind decided not to care. His hand found its way to her thigh, smoothing her skin with long strokes and every so often sneaking beneath her dress. She relished the feel of his cool hand against her heated flesh, and the world outside the car began to disappear. With every twist of the road and turn of the steering wheel, her mind became more and more consumed with Damian. His hand crept farther up her leg, then retreated, as if he were working up his courage, testing the waters. He was intimidated by her! She smiled to herself. He was like a nervous high school boy. How sweet—and hot...

The car slowed and came to a stop in front of a house Jaden didn't recognize. It must be his. *I need this*, she told herself, taking a deep, unsteady breath. *I want this.* What if Ivan was out with some other girl? What if the distance had become too much for him? What if it was too much for her?

She needs this.

She isn't missing anything.
She has everything.

She doesn't want any regrets.

Maybe Damian was right. Maybe she needed to experience more before she settled down with one man for the rest of her life. Now the battling voices in her head seemed to be saying the same thing.

If she sleeps with Damian, she'll know.

She's doing this to know for sure.

She needed this. It was justified. And it might be nothing Ivan wasn't already doing. Without warning, Jaden leaned across the seat and crushed her lips to Damian's, tasting every inch of his greedy mouth. She could feel him grin against her lips and increase the fierceness of the kiss. Then suddenly his door was open, and he disappeared, only to reappear moments later and open her door. Supporting her weight, he claimed her in a lusty embrace.

Her mind had shut down, no more voices of any kind, and she was now running on pure instinct. Live in the moment. They headed up the path to Damian's townhouse, laughing and tripping over each other's feet as they clung together. The front door unlatched and a spine-tingling gush of cold air flooded out of the darkness. Jaden felt her body shiver, although she couldn't tell if it was Damian or the cold air causing it. The door slammed shut behind them, and he once again took her hand to lead her inside.

There was nothing but the sound of a lock sliding into place and the giggling of a girl about to leave no stone unturned.

CHAPTER 16

"Criminal"

The banging of her heart echoed in her ears. Her temples felt as if a vice was tightening around her head. Darkness, utter pitch black darkness, surrounded her because she literally could not open her eyes. The air that filled her lungs carried with it a cloying aroma. Far from her favorite in a cobalt blue bottle, this was too sweet, too much. Her stomach rolled as she struggled to place the scent, to grasp its meaning. Then her conscience reminded her of its source.

Oh fuck! A jolt of disdain, the likes of which she'd never known before, resonated through every cell in her body. Her hangover was shoved aside by a desperate feeling that spread through her body. How could she forget? That same sickening scent had accompanied him to every taping of the show this year. It belonged to the man who stood beside her every day, preening in her spotlight and contributing minimally to the actual cooking. It was Damian's cologne, and it clung to her like a parasite.

Oh my God, what has she done?

She did it. She needed to.

No, she didn't. It was a horrible mistake.

Jaden forced her eyes open to find an empty bed and an even emptier feeling. The evening was a blank—a hazy, throbbing blank—in her memory, but she didn't have to lift the covers to know her clothing was missing. She lay under the down comforter wearing only her bra and panties. The pink dress she'd worn the night before now lay on the floor, a wrinkled mass of silk, satin, and regret. She grasped the beads of her tiger-eye rosary, both comforted and horrified to find them around her neck, and tried to force the tears from her body. She was incapable of producing them. Her chest constricted. All her body would allow was an occasional gasp of air. Guilt coursed through her veins and pressed down on her chest. Seconds turned to minutes as she lay paralyzed, not knowing what to say or do. *What have I done?*

Finally a sound outside the door diverted her attention. Then there was a clang that sounded like a pot or pan. *What do I do? What do I do?* If she grabbed her clothes and made a run for the door, where would she go? She didn't have a car, nor did she know where she was. Praying that her phone was close by, she slid out from beneath the covers and tiptoed over to the dresser to search for her purse. *Shit! Not there.* Glancing around the room, she saw the shiny strap peeking out from underneath the bed. *Thank God!*

She ignored the throbbing pain in her head and bent over to pick up her purse, emptying the contents onto the bed. Wallet…check. Keys…check. Phone…check. She slid her finger across the touch screen and punched in her password, unlocking it. Two notifications appeared, both text messages. The first was from Ivan and the second from Adam. She could not yet begin to deal with the pain of thinking about Ivan, so she opened Adam's first. It was not just one message, but a string of messages sent one after the other. Jaden cringed as she began reading.

Ms. Thorne, I'm outside waiting for you.
Most of the guests have left.
Please text me and let me know
if you need assistance getting to the car.

Ms. Thorne, I've searched the building twice.
Security has not seen you, nor do they know
your whereabouts. Please message me back
as soon as you get this.

Jaden, I've been driving around looking for you for hours.
Please let me know you're safe.
I'll come get you wherever you may be.

God, I love that man, she thought, and her fingers snapped into action.

Adam, I'm so sorry. I'm at Damian's house.
Can you please pick me up as soon as possible.
Do you know where he lives?

*I hope he replies soon, it's only...*Jaden scanned the room for an alarm clock. *10:30? My God, how long did I sleep?*

Within seconds, her phone beeped with Adam's response.

I'll be there in five minutes.

She texted back immediately.

I'll meet you out front.

A wave of relief washed over her. At lightning speed, she slid on her dress and gathered the contents of her purse from the bed. *Now, where are my shoes?* Scanning the floor, she spotted two silver heels next to the closet. She walked over to the double doors and bent down to pick them up. What she saw next to them took her breath away. A crumpled condom wrapper taunted her and murdered her last shred of self worth. Anger grew like poison inside her, and it focused not on Damian, but on herself. It wasn't Damian's fault she'd ended up in his bed. Well, maybe a bit, but she'd known from day one that he was a womanizer and wanted to get in her pants. By the looks of it, he'd now succeeded. She was furious at her weakness, her insecurity, her stupid drunken self with no judgment whatsoever. With a single reckless act—which she'd been too wasted to remember—she'd risked losing Ivan forever.

Thoroughly disgusted, she hung her head and opened the bedroom door. She turned the corner to find Damian at the granite kitchen island wearing a white shirt and soccer shorts. He munched a bowl of cereal while watching Sports Center. He turned to look at her, and satisfied smile that screamed "I Win" spread across his face.

"Sleep well, Jade?" he asked, but his eyes returned to the replay of last night's hockey game.

"What happened last night?" she demanded.

Nearly spitting out his mouthful of Cheerios, he scoffed, "You're kidding, right? Please don't tell me you can't remember. I never would've thought…" He managed to look at her for a moment. "You're quite the sexual kitten. I thought having some bigwig doctor boyfriend from South Beach would make you a stuck-up bitch. But, man, was I ever wrong."

Jaden felt horrified as his eyes bore down on her. She was lost, with no idea how to react to his words, how to function, how to work. She swallowed hard to prevent herself from vomiting all over the floor and then just got the hell out of there. "I gotta go!" she yelled over her shoulder.

All she heard as she scurried down the hall in her high heels, pink dress, and smudged makeup was Damian's riotous laughter.

"What?" he called. "Was it something I said?"

She slammed the door behind her, but not before Damian left her with one more thought: "I'll see you at work on Monday, sweets!"

Once outside, all she could think to do was run—run as far and as fast from this house as possible. But just then a black sedan rounded the corner and pulled to a stop in front her. Adam sprang from the driver's side and rushed to her side.

"Ms. Thorne, are you okay?"

"Yes, yes, I'm fine," she replied, horribly embarrassed. "Let's just get out of here." She made a beeline for the passenger door, but Adam stepped in front of her and got his hand on the handle first.

He looked her over before opening it. "You're sure there's nothing I need to…take care of?" he asked, glancing back toward the house.

"Adam, I'm fine. Honestly. Thank you for coming to pick me up on such short notice. Can we please just go home now?"

He nodded and closed her door.

When the network had assigned him as her personal driver, she'd gained a friend. What had she done to deserve so many honorable men in her life? The answer to that question came easily: nothing. She didn't deserve their love or respect. Jaden curled into a ball on the backseat.

As the car began to move, she began to process. Guilt evolved into panic, which hit like a wrecking ball to her stomach. What had she done? Would she ever know? How could she explain this to Ivan without breaking his heart? In a few weeks they were supposed to visit her family in Colorado. What lie would explain his absence?

"Adam?" she called. "I'd appreciate it if you didn't mention this to anyone. It's just that—" Before she could finish her sentence, Adam had pulled the car to the side of the road and stopped. He turned so he could look at her.

"Of course, Ms. Thorne," he said. "But may I also say I've been a driver for almost twenty-five years, and I've met a lot of people. Some are not nearly as genuine as you seem to me, but all have made mistakes. You are not alone. You just have to decide what happens next. No matter what, remember that your destiny is yours to create, not anyone else's. When the time is right, I know you'll know what to do."

She burst into tears. "But what about Ivan? What kind of person does that to someone they love? He's going to hate me. *I* hate me. I wish I'd never gone to that stupid gala in the first place."

When she'd cried herself silent, Adam spoke again. "Do you love him?"

She wiped away tears with the back of her hand. "More than anything."

"Does he love you?"

"Yes."

"Then, Ms. Thorne, I think you have your answer. If you love him, you'll tell him what happened, and if he loves you, he'll respect your honesty. What happens from there, I can't guess. You may lose your relationship, or it may grow, but you'll have acted with integrity."

Lose the relationship? She felt another wave of nausea.

"If you don't tell him, I fear you'll suffer for it, and you'll lose him for sure should he ever find out. Whatever you decide, you'll have to live with your choices, Ms. Thorne. And I want you to be able to live."

"Thank you, Adam. Thank you for everything."

"Of course, Ms. Thorne."

He turned and eased the town car back into the flow of traffic. Jaden sat in silence for the remainder of the ride, twiddling the cross that hung from the rosary she wore. She reminisced about sea turtles and torn clothes and the scents tattooed into the depths of her mind. No matter what Damian had said, or what she'd convinced herself to worry about in the moment, she knew Ivan would never do what it appeared she'd just done to him. What was she going to do? Could she ever gather the courage to tell him?

The car pulled up at her house, and Adam stepped out into the bright LA sunlight. When her door opened, she stepped out and joined him on the curb. "Thank you," she said again, and forced a smile to her face.

"Of course, Ms. Thorne. I am happy to be of service. You're sure there's nothing you need?"

She shook her head again, and feeling him watch her like a hawk, she made her way to the front door. He pulled away once she'd unlocked and opened the door, and she immediately felt alone—alone with her thoughts and her conscience. There was no Damian to taunt her or Adam to offer her words of wisdom. There was simply Jaden, someone she had no desire to be around at the moment. The silence was deafening.

Wanting to wash away all traces of the previous night, she slid out of her dress and pulled off her bra and panties, tossing them into the clothes hamper. She set the water to scalding and stepped into the steamy stream, hoping to wash away the biggest regret of her life, which ironically, she could remember nothing about. *Fuck, Jaden. How could you let yourself get so goddamn drunk? What were you thinking? How could you be so stupid?*

Tears pressed against the back of her eyes again and soon mixed with the flowing water. After showering, her body felt clean, but her mind was still stained with regret. With a towel cinched around her, Jaden stood facing the mirror, but she couldn't recognize the woman staring back. She studied her, trying to grasp what the hell she'd done and why, but found no answers. She slid to the tile floor, not because she wanted to, but because her legs could no longer support her. She cried and cried until her throat grew sore. And only when she'd cried herself dry did she stand and look into the mirror once more, finding a broken girl.

She shut off the bathroom light and stumbled over to her bed. Her purse sat open on her night table, and the corner of her phone stuck out, taunting her just as clearly as Damian's words had when she left his house. Using the last of her energy, she retrieved it. She couldn't put off the inevitable any longer. Ivan had been texting her, and the least she could do was return his messages. She opened the first of two unread texts that had arrived in the wee hours of the morning.

**I heard from a little birdie that you looked stunning.
I hope you had a blast. Love is beautiful, and so are you.
I love you with all my heart.**

She lay back on the bed and clutched her side, trying to catch a breath that would not come. Remorse and utter disgust washed over her. She had to choose, and she had to choose now. Did she want to save their relationship? Her mind and soul struggled with the answer while her conscience screamed. The voices had returned.

She'll never do it again.

It was an accident. And she doesn't even know what she did.

Now she knows she loves him.

She always knew that.

Can she bury this mistake?

She won't be able to.

It happens to everyone.
He doesn't need to know.

Love is about trust. He needs to know.

She will lose him if she tells him.

She will lose him if she doesn't.

Tell him.

She'll hurt him if she does.

She'll hurt him if she doesn't.

She'll lose him if she does.

Jaden inhaled and exhaled slowly. Her fingers quivered and lingered over the keyboard. With a heavy heart, she typed her response.

Hey! Sorry but my phone died.
Party was fine. I'll call you tonight
when I finish running errands. Miss you lots. Xoxoxo

Then she pushed send, officially burying her mistake. She'd learned from it. It would never again be repeated.

She tried to take comfort in her decision, but solace would not come, only regret. Physically and mentally exhausted, Jaden shut her eyes and clung to the bear made of beautiful moments from a happy time in her life. She imagined a Miami Beach sunset decorating the sky with red and purple. Sitting hand in hand with her on the balcony was Ivan, his hair flowing over his neck and a cigar hanging from the corner of his mouth. They shared a glass of wine as their favorite music played.

Ivan was right. Love is beautiful—when it's not tainted with infidelity.

CHAPTER 17

"Outside"

The air seemed stagnant as the worker bees scurried about setting up cameras and the prep team warmed the burners and prepared the vegetables. Jaden stood with as much confidence as she could muster, which was little to none. She knew any moment now *he* would tromp in and take his place beside her. What on earth was he going to say? Her stomach rolled, a soup of fear, remorse, and regret. She shivered.

"So, how'd it go? I want all the juicy details," a voice called from behind her.

Jaden turned to face Kat, who stood with an eager smile. Of course she'd be dying to know what happened, but this was one conversation Jaden couldn't quite manage just now. It had taken everything she had to relive a version of the evening on the phone with Ivan last night. He'd seemed bewildered by her lack of enthusiasm about the event.

"Really? Just okay, huh? I'd have thought the network would go all out."

"Well, maybe I just wasn't feeling it. Would have been better with you," she'd managed.

"Aw, baby girl, I know you can hold your own," he'd said with a laugh.

Oh, how wrong he was…

"Damn, girl!" Kat exclaimed, drawing her back to the present. "Have you been crying all night or something? Your eyes are all puffy and red." She reached into her oversized makeup bag and fished out a silver tin of loose powder. "You must've been a party *animal* this weekend. No worries. Just sit here. I'll have you fixed up in a jiffy!"

Jaden sighed and closed her eyes, taking a seat and tilting her head back to let Kat work her magic. "I guess I'm just overtired."

"So? How was the party? Did you have fun? Any gossip, hook-ups? Oh, how did Damian look? Was he a prick or tolerable for once?" Kat lowered her voice and continued. "Was Queen Cougar on the prowl?"

Jaden squeezed her eyes shut and fought back a rush of uneasiness. "Damian was, well, Damian. It was mostly a bunch of drunken businessmen and actors."

"Including you?" Kat asked.

"I had a few but…" Jaden trailed off, sensing someone approaching. She opened her eyes to find Damian wearing a hideous smirk.

"A few?" he laughed. "You were a regular sorority sister, Jade. You polished off every drop of alcohol in sight." His look grew even more smug. "Seems to me you were running away from something — or maybe to someone?"

"Looks like we have a comedian in the crowd, folks," she scoffed, sitting up straight. She turned to face him, her fear now morphing into rage. Oh yes, she was going to enjoy laying into this asshole. "Kat, would you please excuse us for a minute?"

"Actually, you're all done, boss," Kat said, not seeming to notice the vehemence in Jaden's voice. In an instant she disappeared.

She spoke so only Damian could hear. "Listen here, you fucking asshole. I've had just about enough of your shit. The other night was a mistake, and I'm disgusted with myself for — "

"Disgusted? Do you really think your Prince Charming isn't sticking his dick in every wannabe model in South Beach? You should be thanking me."

"Thank you? For what? For taking advantage of me when I was drunk?"

"Oh, come on! You wanted to get laid. Don't lie. You kissed me! You should consider yourself lucky. Women would kill to be in your situation." He grinned with his eyebrows, and Jaden felt her blood boil.

"One minute to go. Are you guys ready?" the segment producer called.

"Yes!" Damian barked while Jaden screamed, *"No!"*

The producer just grunted. "You have one minute," he said again.

Leaning over, Damian lowered his voice to match Jaden's. "Don't worry. I'm not going to tell anyone what happened or how freaky you are in bed. I'm gonna keep that juicy little piece of gossip to myself. Or maybe I won't."

She felt sick. She'd risked everything she had with Ivan over someone who thought of her as nothing more than a sexual conquest. Everything was a game to Damian, including her, and she'd allowed him to win. "I can promise you this," she hissed. "If you breathe one word of this to anyone, and I mean *anyone*, I'll make sure every woman here knows you're hung like a light switch."

"Good luck with that," he said with a shrug. "I've fucked half the staff, including my co-host." He turned on his heel and stalked toward the set, leaving her to hurry after him.

"Three...two...one...Action!"

"Hello, I'm Damian Gris, and this is my co-host Jaden Thorne," he began smoothly before she could get to her place. "I hope you're ready for *One Hot Kitchen* because we've got one hot show for you!"

Wait, did she just hear that right? Did he just take charge of the intro and call her his co-host? It was bad enough that he'd ruined her personal life. Now, to make her despair complete, he was making a play to steal the show. Jaden went numb. With movements merely mechanical, she could think of nothing to do but go with the flow.

As they continued to film, Damian interrupted her, joking loudly, and stepped all over her demonstrations. She knew what he was doing. He was displaying his dominance, a dominance she had forfeited to him when she'd succumbed to his touch. She hated herself.

Hours later, which seemed like days, the cameraman called, "That's a wrap for today."

"Yes, yes it is." Damian shot her a cocky look, solidifying his victory.

Jaden left him to review the take alone. She was tired of fighting. She hung her head as she headed for her dressing room, but not low enough to avoid Stacey.

"Hey!" she demanded. "You okay? What happened to you on Friday? Adam was a wreck trying to find you. How on earth did you get home?"

Jaden broke into a cold sweat. What did Stacey know about Damian? She prayed the woman wouldn't catch her in a lie. "I had a bit too much to drink, and I couldn't find Adam. I took a cab home."

"Oh, okay. I just wanted to make sure everything was all right."

Relief washed over her. "Yeah, it is." Jaden forced a smile. "Thanks for your concern." She stood frozen for a moment as Stacey strolled off.

With a heavy heart and a splitting headache, Jaden continued to her dressing room. As she changed out of her kitchen whites, her eyes fell on the calendar on the wall beside the vanity. She'd drawn large red Xs to mark off the days leading up to the Colorado trip—a trip she could no longer look forward to with her whole heart. But she needed to. She had to. This trip could be just the thing to help her move forward with Ivan and put Damian Gris out of her mind for good. Turning on her phone, she found an unread message.

Just thinking about you, baby girl, and can't wait for Colorado!!!

Me neither, she thought. *Let's just get there.*

CHAPTER 18

"Don't Let Me Down"

Looking out the penthouse window of his new office, which now sat atop one of the beach's staple boutique hotels, Ivan lounged behind his desk. The fresh smell of pine, with a twist of lemon and lavender, washed over him as he lost himself in thought.

Should I? I totally should. Hell yeah, I should.

His life and the decisions he made had always been calculated, but they often teetered on the sharp edge of risky. The rush of pursuing the unattainable or, even better, claiming the big prizes in life were what thrilled him most. His entrepreneurial spirit and most recent career change were testament to that. Practicing at his own medical spa before he hit thirty? Not bad.

Hell, even the way he'd chased after Jaden reflected this attitude. She'd been one shot in a million. But what he was considering now—the next big step—seemed like an easy one. It had to be low risk and high return, didn't it? His instincts blazed green lights, and yet a small part of him wondered. She'd sounded strange on the phone when they spoke after the gala. At times he felt so close to her—as if their souls had connected—and other times he couldn't quite get a read. *Ah, women,* he told himself with a silent chuckle. *But what if she said—*

"Dr. Rusilko, you have a walk-in. Can you see him?"

Startled, he turned to find his very petite and very beautiful blonde receptionist in the doorway. "Umm, ahh…" he stuttered, trying to find the heart to say no as he looked at his watch.

"Don't worry, doctor. I'll say you're busy," she said with a rather unprofessional but undeniably captivating wink. "The things I would do to you."

His eyebrows rose in surprise.

"I mean *for* you! The things I'd do *for* you!" She blushed bright red and continued with her retraction. "I, ah…I didn't mean—oh, God. I'm so embarrassed. Can you forget that last part, please? I'll just do you—*No!* What I'm saying is I'll just tell the patient—"

"You're a peach, Liz. Thank you for bailing me out," he interrupted, throwing the girl a lifeline. "Why don't you see if you can schedule him tomorrow morning?"

She smiled and nodded and apologized once more before she turned to go. He couldn't help but admire her as she went. *If I was single…Jesus, she would be worth the lawsuit.* Shaking the lusty visions from his mind, his thoughts returned a much more meaningful place: the task at hand.

He grabbed his keys, took one last look at the rolling waves below, and headed for the elevator. He swelled with pride as he passed by the elegant exam rooms—bone white tapestries and green-apple accents—on his way to the private elevator they used to usher in the VIPs and very VIPs that frequented his new establishment. The elevator descended to the ground floor, and he popped out into the opulent lobby. But when he pushed open the door to the outside, he found something even more beautiful: a seventy-five degree mid-afternoon.

"Fuck it. I'm walking," he mumbled to himself. The colors were neon bright around him, and the beach bustled with sound. The world seemed almost spotless. He was confident and excited and couldn't help but strut down Collins Avenue as he covered the fifteen or so blocks on his way to meet Micky.

He window-shopped a little as he entered the shopping district. "What a fucking clown," he said aloud, shaking his head as he passed a particularly over-the-top boutique. Miami was full of wannabes—even on Collins Avenue. And in this case, not even a swanky address could save them. He turned his attention to the day once again, ignoring the rest of the storefronts that dotted his route. He didn't rush, but he walked with purpose, anticipating the meeting with every step. When he reached Mina D's, he found his friend already inside perusing the goods.

"You looking or buying?" Ivan asked as he entered the store.

"How about that one?" Micky replied not even acknowledging his joke.

"Nah, she doesn't like yellow gold."

"Okay, then, how about this one?" He pointed to an oval-cut diamond beneath the glass.

Ivan looked where he pointed and shook his head. "Ovals are nice, but not for an engagement ring. Look for something square, not round."

"What about this one?"

"That looks like the first one you showed me. Shit!"

"Jesus, Ivan!" Micky walked to a second display case. "This one?"

He lifted his head to look. "It's fucking pink, man. What planet are you from?"

"Perfectionist, are we?"

"When it comes to Jaden, yes." He shot him a glare.

Micky laughed and raised his hands in defeat. "All I'm saying is this is the fifth jewelry store we've been to. Tasha may start to think we're secretly dating or something. I can only make so many excuses to keep coming on these little shopping adventures with you. Why can't we just tell her?"

He glared at him once more and raised an eyebrow. "You know that's not a good idea."

"Fair enough," Micky conceded and returned to browsing.

Then, as he shifted his gaze back to the display case in front of him, it happened. He found the One. Sitting above the others on a small pedestal was the most spectacular ring he'd ever laid eyes on. The perfect Asscher-cut stone burst the light into prismatic flames. He couldn't look away. "This is it."

Micky moved in for a look from across the store, and he too became entranced in the spectacle of dancing colors.

Within moments, a salesman sauntered over. "Hi there. I'm Paul. Can I help you gentlemen with something?"

"I'll take that one!" Ivan blurted.

"Whoa," Micky said under his breath.

But it wasn't just the ring decision that swelled Ivan with confidence, it was his decision to propose to Jaden. This beautiful diamond brought him one step closer.

A series of serendipitous events had led him to this point. He'd made a bold decision to step out of his comfort zone and talk to the woman who stopped his heart one wine-filled evening. He'd traced her to her restaurant to demand an explanation for her sudden disappearance. He'd spent nights of passion with her and come to know her in a way he didn't realize was possible. His family had loved the small town Colorado girl who could shoot guns and drink wine with the best of them, and perhaps most amazingly, he'd been brave enough to break his promise about never pursuing a long-distance relationship again.

He felt certain his decision to propose was right. Jaden was the woman he envisioned himself waking up with every morning for the rest of his life. He could trust her with his most intimate thoughts and feelings. Just like the ring sitting before him, she was the One.

"Excellent choice, sir." Paul the salesman plucked the maroon box from the case and slid it across the counter.

Ivan pulled the ring from the box and held it up to the light. A shot of nerves raced through him. A spectrum of bright, colorful flares danced as he twirled it between his fingers. Fine etching adorned the sides of the platinum band, along with a trickle of smaller diamonds. The setting gripped the diamond the same way Jaden gripped his heart: delicately, but with fierce strength. It was spectacular.

"This is the—" Paul began.

"An Asscher-cut diamond, colorless and flawless, about one and a half carats with…" Ivan leaned closer for a better look. "I'd say about another half carat running down the side of a platinum setting that had better not wear *or* tear."

"When the hell did you become a jeweler?" Micky asked.

"This isn't the first time I've visited numerous jewelry stores. But thankfully last time I didn't buy."

"And what is the lucky lady's size?" the salesman asked.

"Damnit!" Ivan cursed. "I don't think she's ever mentioned it."

"Mr. Know-It-All doesn't know the size of his girlfriend's ring finger?"

"Blow me!"

"She's a size six," Micky replied. "Jaden was harassing me on the phone about proposing to Tasha one time, and she just happened to mention that she and Tasha were both a size six. So unless Jaden has gained sixty pounds since the last time I saw her, I'd say six is a safe bet."

"About time you became useful!" Ivan laughed and slapped him on the shoulder. "Well, there you go, Paul. She's a six."

The salesman returned the ring to the box and gestured to the back of the store. "If you'll follow me, we can get started on the paperwork."

"I'd also like to have the inside of the band engraved. Do you do that here?"

"Yes, sir." Paul sat at a small wooden desk and motioned for Ivan and Micky to sit across from him. After a few keystrokes, the printer behind him hummed to life. He gathered the papers from the tray and slid them across the desk to Ivan. "At the bottom of page three there's a spot for you to write out your inscription."

With quick strokes of the pen against the paper, he wrote the message.

"What did you put?" Micky asked, leaning over his shoulder.

"Something from the heart."

"You aren't going to tell me?"

"Nope." Ivan handed the paper back to the salesman.

When Paul finished filling out the last of the paperwork, he returned it to Ivan to sign.

"Aren't you even going to ask how much it costs?" Micky asked.

"Nope. Don't want to know, and I don't care."

"Sir, all together, the ring will cost—" Paul began, but Ivan cut him off.

"I really don't want to know. Here's my credit card. Charge whatever you need to charge me to have it ready by a week from Wednesday. Is that doable?"

"For you, anything, sir," Paul replied. He ran the card through the machine, and Ivan scribbled a signature and stuffed the receipt into his pocket. Then the salesman showed the men back to the front of the shop, leaving them with a warm handshake.

"That was amazing," Micky said as they stepped out into the muggy Miami Beach air.

"I agree," said Ivan. "Wanna grab a drink?"

"No can do. I have to get back before the better half gets too pissy."

Ivan snickered. He was fond of Tasha, but Micky was right. She could get pissy. "All right, next time then. Thanks so much for your help with this—and everything else. It means a lot."

"No worries, man. If everything continues to go the way it has been, you'll be doing the same thing for me soon."

Ivan winked and slapped him on the shoulder, "Anytime, man, anytime."

"Later," Micky called as he turned the corner and disappeared.

Ivan turned toward the beach and began walking. He needed a bit more time, some time alone with his thoughts. There were still so many details to be hammered out before he could pop the question—the biggest one being the six-foot obstacle named Lee that stood in Colorado waiting to meet him. Time to get a game plan. Nerves swirled within him as he anticipated the trip ahead.

CHAPTER 19

"Demons"

Tick tock. Tick tock.

At an agonizing pace, seconds turned into minutes and minutes into hours. The hands on Jaden's wristwatch scuttled by, and the plane finally started its descent into Denver International Airport. Two torturous weeks of nervous phone calls, awkward moments at work, menacing guilt, and a maddening inability to remember *any details whatsoever* from her damned evening with Damian came to a head when the pilot's voice demanded that all passengers secure their seat belts and prepare for landing. Jaden secured her seatbelt and wished she could just disappear.

She'd spent every waking moment since The Day After reminding herself she'd made the right decision in burying the whole stupid incident. It was behind her, and nothing she could do or say now would make a difference. Telling Ivan would lead to heartbreak for both of them. Damian was in the past. She and Ivan were the future.

But it had been a month since she'd seen him. How would she react when they met face to face? Their last few phone calls had certainly felt strained. Would she break down and cry out her confession? Would she act awkwardly enough to alert him that something was bothering her? Or would she see him smile, smell his alluring scent, and be swept back into his arms as if nothing had ever happened? She prayed for the latter.

The ground drew closer and the buildings more discernible. Tiny cars and trucks sped along the freeway beneath them. The plane dipped and so did her stomach. Ivan's flight was scheduled to land an hour ahead of hers, which meant he was already in the airport waiting for her, likely with flowers in hand and a grin splayed across his face. Would her mother, who hadn't seen her in months, know instinctively that something was off? *Oh shit!* She hadn't thought of that. And now it terrified her.

Then the plane began to bank to the left and the mountains came into view through the portal window. Immediately she smiled and felt a wave of peace wash over her. It had been far too long since she'd seen her family. The sight of the mountains reminded her who she was, where she came from. Feeling more grounded, Jaden found renewed hope that everything would be okay. She'd work to make sure it was. Yes, the biggest mistake of her life had taken her show hostage, and she was about to face the man she loved, not to mention her family, while doing her utmost to keep it together, but she could do it. She had to. She forced herself to focus on Ivan, only Ivan. *I love him, and he loves me. Our love is stronger than anything Damian or anyone else can throw at us. It will work. It will!*

The plane slid to a grinding halt and moments later was docked at the gate. Tension crept back into her shoulders. This was it: truth or dare time. Truth? She was a cheating liar. Dare? Put all this behind her and make it work with the man she loved. Jaden felt her stomach rise into her throat and tried to ignore the voices.

> *She needs to tell him now.*
> *She's only hurting him.*

She isn't hurting anyone.
It was a mistake.

> *Mistake or not, it was still wrong.*

But should they both have to suffer?
Give her time to get over it.

> *Time will just make it worse.*

Only if he finds out, and he won't.

> *Isn't he worth more than a lie?*

Isn't their happiness worth more
than a drunken mistake?

We deserve to be happy, Jaden told herself as she stood and retrieved her bag from the overhead compartment. For God's sake, she couldn't even remember her night with Damian. It meant nothing. Just a terrible mistake. Confident once again, she exited the plane and headed into the terminal.

She burst through the doors and past security, where she was certain Ivan would be waiting for her with flowers in hand, a box of chocolates, or some other little token of affection. She prepared herself to react naturally when she saw him, but she looked around and was greeted by...no one? No flowers, no chocolate, and no Ivan anywhere to be seen. Fear crept up her spine. Did he find out and decide not to come? Oh, God. Why else would he not be here? Terrified, Jaden froze, blocking the way of the exiting travelers behind her as a million different scenarios ran through her mind. There had to be something, anything that could explain his absence besides the most obvious explanation. *He knows!*

Your phone, you idiot! Snatching it from her purse, she switched it on and waited for the connection to reset. Once it did, the phone buzzed violently in the palm of her hand: missed calls, text messages, and emails, but none were from Ivan. He had to know. Tears clouded her vision and sadness overwhelmed her. After collecting herself for a moment, she wiped her face and turned her attention back to her phone. Skimming through the messages again, she found one from her mother and opened it:

We're at the baggage claim. Can't wait to see you!

Jesus! What am I going to tell them? Her mother had brought her sister along? Not that she didn't want to see Magan, but it was bad enough that she was going to have to lie to her mother's face. Now her sister's too? She'd just tell them he got sick, or maybe that something came up at the last minute and he had to stay in Miami. Yes! That's it. Ivan was a workaholic, so her telling them he had business to attend to wasn't a complete lie, was it?

Maybe he doesn't know. There could always be some other explanation, and what had Ivan said about making assumptions? He'd lost his phone. Yes, that's it. He'd lost it three times before, so he'd probably done it again. Or wait! Maybe his flight is delayed. Running to the arrivals board, she scanned it, only to discover his flight had arrived nineteen minutes early. *Damn!*

As she stepped onto the descending escalator, she began to assess herself. *Who am I? What the hell am I doing? I'm not only ruining my life, but Ivan's as well. I'm not a liar. I've never lied to my family before, especially my mom. I'll just have to tell her. She'll understand and help me through this—they all will.*

But no sooner had she come to this conclusion than the escalator dropped her off in a bright space decorated with spinning conveyor belts, colorful luggage, and jetlagged passengers. She found her mother, Diane, standing a mere fifty yards away and laughing with a six-foot tall Tarzan look-alike holding a box of chocolates.

Once more, she stood in disbelief, creating a bottleneck of annoyed passengers behind her. The "we" her mother had texted about was her and *Ivan*, and apparently they were having the time of their life. At the sight of him, Jaden's resolve to tell the truth faltered. She felt a panicky wave of love for the beautiful man who stood just yards away, and she'd fight with all she had to hold on.

She snuck over to a column and concealed herself behind it to study their interaction. Ivan, in his typical travel garb of cargo shorts and fatigued shirt, flexed his muscles and sent striations rippling up each of his arms—thick, powerful arms that seemed even more defined than the last time she'd seen him. His skin looked more bronzed as well and glistened in the fluorescent light of the baggage claim. Large diamond-shaped bulges formed on the backs of his legs as he rocked back and forth on his heels. Her mother laughed and smiled at whatever tale he was telling her. They'd just met! She loved that they'd forged a connection so quickly and loved even more that they'd done it on their own, without her having to facilitate it.

How could she have doubted Ivan's love for her? His place in her life? She knew she was meant to be with him forever, even if it meant burying her deepest, darkest skeleton and carrying it always. Watching her mother laugh again, she smiled. Excitement began sweeping her conscience to the side. Her mother pulled out her phone to type again, and seconds later Jaden's phone buzzed with an incoming message.

Are you here yet?

Jaden pulled herself behind the column and typed a response.

I just got off the escalator. Where are you?

She waited a couple moments and then stepped out from behind the column to make her entrance. She came up behind them. "I'm right here."

At the sound of her voice, they turned, and what she saw warmed her heart. Their faces were alight with excitement and love—a mother's for her daughter, and a lover's for the woman who made him complete. Dropping her bags, Jaden rushed forward and grabbed her mother in a Rusilko-style bear hug.

"Easy, baby, you're gonna crush this old lady," her mother gasped.

Jaden nodded to Ivan. "Well, you can thank him for teaching me that one."

When the women parted, Ivan moved in. His arms encircled her, and he kissed her on the cheek. "Finally, I'm whole again," he whispered.

"So am I." She brought her lips to his for a lingering kiss.

"Ahem," her mother interjected. "We have somewhere to be. Your father has been running around all day—cleaning the yard, setting up the deck, preparing the food. He just won't relax."

"Why is dad the one setting up? It's his party! Shouldn't Magan and Justin be doing all the work?"

"Magan is helping, but Justin is working."

"Working? You've got to be joking, right? Since when does he do anything other than play video games?"

"He's changed a lot since you left. This job is good for him."

Longing tugged at Jaden's heart—a longing for the family she didn't see nearly enough and for a simpler time when everything was easy and right with her and Ivan. Ignoring the remorse that once again threatened to blossom in her chest, she looked from Ivan to her mother and asked, "So, did you guys have a good chat?"

"It was...enlightening." Her mother looked at Ivan, and they shared a secretive laugh. "Let's grab your luggage and start home. We've got a long drive, and your father is probably half in the bag by now."

"Yep, sounds like dad." Jaden took Ivan's hand as they wove through the crowd toward the baggage carousel. She loved the way his warm skin enveloped hers.

Her large, red bag appeared at the end of the belt, and as it rounded the corner, Ivan grabbed the handle and tugged. With luggage in hand, the trio left the airport and piled into her mother's SUV.

CHAPTER 20

"I'm Coming Home"

"You sit in the front."

"No, you," Ivan insisted. "You haven't seen your mom in months. I'm sure she'd much rather talk to you than me."

"Maybe so," Jaden countered. "But I want her to get to know you better. Please, sit in the front and talk to her."

He stowed the last piece of luggage and closed the back door of the silver SUV. "Fine, but it's not your mother I'm worried about. Meeting your dad? That will be a trip."

"Don't worry. I put in a good word for you."

"Well, now, aren't you clever?" He offered his hand and helped her into the backseat before sliding in up front.

As her mom started the car, Heart's "Crazy On You" burst from the speakers, startling everyone. A blush colored her face, and she jabbed at the knob, trying to turn it off. But before she could, Ivan joined in, singing at the top of his lungs in a high-pitched, feminine voice. She and her mother couldn't help but laugh.

"You were rockin' out, weren't you?" he observed when the song came to an end.

"What can I say? This old lady loves her old lady music."

"Well, this young guy loves his old lady music. That's one of my mom's favorite bands too!"

"She sounds like a smart woman. I'd love to meet her one day." Her mom giggled and glanced over her shoulder at Jaden.

"Hopefully one day soon," Ivan replied with a boyish smile, glancing at Jaden as well.

She managed to meet both their eyes with what she hoped was a genuine smile. It felt a little frozen in place. Thankfully they both focused their attention forward as her mom eased the SUV onto the highway for their journey to Estes Park.

Once she'd joined the flow of traffic, the questions began. "So, honey, how are you doing with work? I watch the show as much as I can. I loved the tuna with mint thing you did. Your dad didn't like it though. Said he wants his fish cooked the whole way through."

"Work is good," Jaden said, feeling a bit unsteady. "But we're almost finished with the season, and I'll be so happy when it's over." An understatement.

"How about that co-host of yours? Damian? He's one hot little number, eh?"

Hearing her mother speak his name made Jaden's heart beat wildly—almost as if Damien were in the car with them. "Ahh…He's not the nicest person in the world," she managed.

Her mother just laughed. "What do you think, Ivan? You trust my daughter working with him?"

Jaden wondered if she might throw up.

"I trust her with all my heart." He looked back at her and smiled.

Jaden looked down, so thankful, but disgusted with herself all over again.

"Besides, if she wanted that kinda guy, I wouldn't be sitting here now anyway!" He and her mother laughed, and Jaden managed to join them, reaching up to squeeze the back of Ivan's neck.

"So, Ivan, are you ready to meet our family? They are quite the handful," her mother prattled on.

"I think I grew up in a handful," he told her. "So I hope that means I'm prepared."

As the front seat continued their banter, Jaden took in the familiar landscape outside the car. She let the natural beauty relax her and reassured herself she was the happiest girl in the world. Her lover sat two feet away from her, talking with her mother as if they were old friends. How could she not be thrilled? How could she have ever doubted? Had she just imagined the distance she'd felt between them this last month or so?

Finally the SUV turned onto a one-lane road that snaked through the mountains. Evergreen trees dotted the landscape, along with massive boulders that shot out of the ground. A bright blue sky towered over the mountains on each side of the road. They rose to heights far greater than any building in Miami or LA. The river that paralleled the road sparkled in the sun as the occasional fisherman tried to land a trout. She noticed Ivan's eyes drawn to the fishermen and bet he wished they could stop the car. Carly Simon's mellow voice now filled her ears, and Jaden began to feel safe. Here, in the place she'd come from, she'd do everything she could to return to the person she truly was. This weekend she'd forge ahead with Ivan as her future. There was no other choice.

As they descended into her hometown, she began to feel a little excitement. Her heart jumped as they passed the familiar lookout where tourists stopped to take pictures of the mountains and lake, and the gigantic rock with ESTES PARK carved in it. They drove through town and she absorbed every detail: bed and breakfasts, candy shops, and old country craft stores. Remembering all the nooks and crannies made her feel like a child again. Knowing her childhood home was a minute away augmented this feeling.

"You ready for this, Ivan?" her mom asked as she made the turn down the long driveway, which seemed like a tunnel with the tree branches looming over it.

"Well, I'm halfway there," he replied as the two started giggling.

"You're more than halfway there," Jaden chimed in, not quite sure what was so funny. "We're here!" The white house she'd grown up in appeared through the trees, and the SUV came to a stop amidst a fleet of other vehicles. "The party already started?"

Her mother laughed. "Yes, dear. Surprise! Time to have some fun."

As they piled out, Jaden ran around to give her mom a hug and a kiss. "It's been too long."

"I know it won't happen again," her mother said with a smile. Then she turned to stop Ivan as he headed for the back of the car. "No, no, no. We can get those later. You have family to meet."

Jaden smiled as Ivan swallowed hard. Taking his hand, she reassured him. "Don't worry. I won't leave you alone."

"Good. I can't go home with anyone else here anyway," he said, eyeing the crowd and laughing.

Jaden's heart lurched, but she took a deep breath as he squeezed her hand and looked into her eyes.

"This means the world to me," he said. "Thank you."

She smiled and breathed in the fresh mountain air as she prepared herself for the next few days.

Sounds of boisterous laughter rose to greet them as they headed toward the house. Managing to think beyond herself, Jaden knew Ivan had to be nervous. Though she hoped things would go just as smoothly with her father, Ivan seemed out of his element—not so *Miami Vice* at the moment. She grabbed his hand and pulled him to the door. Her mom led the way, smiling all the time. Jaden had never seen her so happy.

"You ready for this? It's a thorny crowd," Diane jabbed as she led them through the wooden door and toward the growing racket.

"Mom, leave him alone. He's nervous enough as it is." Jaden patted his back.

"You two are a couple of comedians, aren't you?" he countered.

As they reached the sliding door that led to the back deck, Jaden squeezed Ivan's now-sweaty hand. "They'll love you, just like I do." She snuck a kiss for confidence.

Then the door flew open and fifteen faces swung around to identify the disturbance.

"Is that my beautiful baby come back home to the back country to see us simple folk?" Her father's voice, in his best hillbilly accent, rang clear and true above the crowd.

Dropping her guard and Ivan's hand, she ran across the deck to greet her father. "Daddy!"

As she jumped into his arms and was wrapped in his Denver Broncos jersey, she felt home. He swung her around as if she were six years old, and she relished the moment. She was his little princess. But once she came to rest, she gave him one more hug and turned toward Ivan at the door.

Her mom placed a reassuring hand on his back and whispered something that made him smile. She watched as confidence flowed over him, and he stepped forward. The aunts, uncles, neighbors, and friends who looked on now witnessed something like the weigh in of Tyson and Holyfield. New Man versus Old Man, both vying for the attention of Ms. Jaden Thorne.

As Ivan came closer, Jaden could feel her father draw himself to his full height. He cleared his throat. "And this must be the man who's occupying so much of my daughter's time and attention. Professional hunter, right?" Her dad struck the first blow.

Oh my God. He went there.

Seeming unfazed, Ivan responded with a gigantic smile. "Yes, sir. Yes, it is. And you must be the man who helped create such a beautiful daughter. Lucky for her—and for me—she got her mom's looks." A daring uppercut.

Jaden couldn't do anything but laugh. Her dad just looked at Ivan for a moment.

"Well played, young man," he said as he leaned in to give him a hug.

"Happy retirement, sir."

So far, so good. She felt a bit giddy with relief. See? Everything was going fine. Everything would be fine.

"What'll you have?" her dad asked Ivan.

"Oh, a beer would be great," he replied.

"Sonny, get this man a beer," her dad hollered to a stout fellow hovering over a red cooler. "And where's my glass? Fill up my cabernet. It's a party!"

Jaden snorted a laugh when she saw the look on Ivan's face.

"And get my girl a martini, please," he added.

"Let's celebrate!" she exclaimed as she came to Ivan's side. "Beer? You hate beer."

"I know, but I didn't want to look like a douche asking for wine."

Laughing, she elbowed him in the ribs. "Pussy."

"Ahhhhhh! Jaden!" a voice shrieked behind them.

Jaden's face lit up. "Magan!" She enveloped her sister.

Magan, younger by one year, looked almost identical to her, with eyes the same shade of emerald green. After a prolonged hug, she began firing off questions. "So, how's the television lifestyle, big star? How's life with Mr. Perfect?" She nodded in Ivan's direction, and Jaden realized he'd wandered over to strike up a conversation with one of the neighbors.

"Ah, it's…it's amazing," she said with a smile, feeling less unsettled this time.

Magan just rolled her eyes. "What did you guys tell Mom that got her all giddy? She's on cloud nine. Or maybe she's drunk."

"I don't know. She's been acting like that since the airport. I love it! How's Justin?"

"He's good. He's kind of in the restaurant biz these days."

Jaden raised her eyebrows.

"He's a bartender," Magan explained. "And he really seems to like it. He works all the time, and when he's not doing that he's rehearsing with his band. He's even working tonight. That didn't make Dad too happy, but he and Mom certainly want him to keep the job."

The smell of meat on the grill wafted over, capturing their attention.

"Smells good, Dad," Magan called as he flipped the meat.

He raised his glass to her, doing a little dance, and she strolled over to join him at the grill.

As each familiar face caught her eye, Jaden made her way through the group that had gathered to celebrate her dad. She told stories of TV mishaps, Miami restaurants, and Hollywood craziness—each listener more interested than the last. When she explained it just the right way, her life was fabulous. The knot remained in her stomach, but as she sipped her drink and smiled at the people who'd known her all her life, she could feel it loosen. And she made sure to know where Ivan was at all times. Right now he was working the other side of the party, looking quite at home indeed. She smiled. Somehow he was always okay.

Finally she circled back around to find her sister, who was ready with a whole new barrage of questions. "How about that Damian?" she began.

Feeling a slap with just the mention of his name, Jaden shrieked her response. "*What?*"

"How about Damian, girl? How is it working out with him?" Magan asked again.

"Oh, you know. It's fine…Whatever. Hey, who needs a drink?"

"I'll take a martini." She heard Ivan's smooth voice and felt his arms slide around her at the same moment. "Hello, you must be Magan. It's so nice to meet you in person. The genes in this family are outstanding," he added loudly enough that their mother could hear.

"Such a smooth talker," Magan replied. "I see why my sister is head over heels for you. It's nice to meet you, too."

"Let's eat," Jaden suggested. "We'll get more drinks in a minute. It's getting late."

They joined the line and loaded their plates with grilled meat and steaming vegetables. Then selecting their places at the extended picnic table, Ivan and Jaden took turns answering questions about Miami, Hollywood, and various celebrities. Ivan fit in at the dinner table as if he'd always been there—a carefully placed dirty joke here and a quirky one-liner there—and he hit it off with her family like no one had before.

Once everyone had eaten their fill of dinner, as well as the gigantic cake that had appeared, the guests began to filter out into the night. Finally it was just family left sitting amongst a gigantic cleanup job and a lot of alcohol still needing to be consumed.

"So how's the long-distance situation working out?" her father suddenly asked.

Jaden felt her ass clench. Fortunately, Ivan grabbed her hand and began to speak.

"It hasn't been an issue," he said. "I miss her like crazy, but we trust each other, and we're making it work...so far." He laughed.

She knew he was expecting her to chime in with a funny comment, but she was too busy reminding herself that she *had* to lie to both her love and her family.

"Maybe not…" Ivan said cutting through the awkward silence.

She forced a smile and plunged into the deep end, laughing loudly. "Yes, of course we're making it work," she said. "We have to."

"I'm so happy to have you home, and you too, Ivan." Magan beamed at them. "Okay, now I'm going to get this cleaned up. Don't want the wildlife paying a visit tonight."

"Good idea," her father agreed.

"I'll help too." Ivan stood.

Jaden prepared to help gather dirty dishes, but her mother put her hand on her arm. "So, young lady, are you happy?"

"Extremely," she said with a smile. "It's wonderful to be home and see all of you. Well, all except Ben, but I assume he'll show up at some point."

"I'm not talking about that. Are you happy with work, with life, with love?" She nodded toward Ivan, who was fumbling with Magan and her father at the door.

Thoughts of waking up in an unfamiliar bed crept to the back of her mind, but she squashed them. "Mom, work is great. I'm getting to do things I never thought I would. I have to pinch myself occasionally to make sure I'm not dreaming." She paused for a moment. "And I couldn't be happier with Ivan. He makes me feel complete in a world that constantly tries to tear you apart."

"That's all I wanted to hear," her mother said, sounding a bit teary. She scooped Jaden into a hug.

"Love you, mom."

"All done," three alcohol-laden voices sang as the cleanup crew made their way back to the table.

Her mom dried her eyes with a napkin, but even a little tanked, Jaden's dad sensed something was up. "All okay?"

"Yes. We just had a little a mother-daughter moment," her mom said. "It's been too damn long." She smiled as she raised her glass in toast, her eyes lingering again on Jaden. "All right, ladies and gentleman, I think it's time for bed," she added as she finished the last gulp of her wine.

Five in the afternoon had turned into eleven thirty at night, and Jaden was glad when they all agreed.

"You're the boss," her father quipped, draining his glass as well.

The family Thorne hugged their long lost Jaden and bid her beau goodnight.

"Thank you again for the invite, Lee." Ivan shook her father's hand.

"Thanks for taking such great care of my daughter."

"Thanks for raising such a good daughter."

With that, her family shuffled inside and off to various bedrooms for the night.

Relieved to be finished with the party, but not quite ready for the night to end, Jaden suggested she and Ivan go sit by the pond.

"Yes, ma'am." He kissed her on the cheek. "Thank you for this," he whispered as he took her hand and followed her toward the moonlit pond.

The water glistened as they settled into a wicker chair on the wooden deck. Crickets sang an endless song, accented by the occasional splash of a fish jumping. She rested her head on Ivan's chest and listened to the steady beat of his heart.

"Your family is amazing," he said, fingering her hair.

"I didn't know how much I missed them."

"Your dad is a trip, and so is your sister. And your mom—that woman is phenomenal. I love chatting with her."

"Yeah, she's taken quite the shine to you, hasn't she? You must've sweet talked her while you were waiting for me at the airport."

"Well, what's not to like?" Ivan said, earning an elbow in the ribs. "We did have a great chat before you found us." He kissed her on the top of the head.

"It's beautiful out tonight, isn't it?" Jaden willed herself to *be* in the moment, be present with Ivan. Move forward.

"It's magical."

"I could stay here forever," she added, wondering for a moment if that might be possible. Then she sighed. "So, I believe you said something about a surprise coming up. I did let them know I'd be gone a couple extra days."

"It's just something I wanted to share with you. It's a first for me, and I love experiencing things for the first time with the one I love."

Feeling overwhelmed and unworthy, she decided offense was the only way to play this. The only way to keep herself together. "What—are we going to get another girl and have a threesome?"

Ivan said nothing, but she could feel his dick harden against her back. "That would be a first for sure," he finally said.

"Is that right?" She repositioned herself and grabbed a handful of his growing excitement. She worked his erection through his pants. "So my boyfriend would like to have himself a threesome...maybe."

"Well, I would definitely entertain the idea."

His dick lengthened as she worked him even more vigorously. "So you want me to be with another woman in front of you?"

"In front, on top, under. All of the above."

"Blonde or brunette?"

"With you? Blonde."

"Big boobs?"

"Mmmm...Same type of body as yours...with an ass till Tuesday."

"Hmm…" For a moment she considered paying him back for leaving her all worked up with nowhere to go in Meadville, but that seemed so long ago now. Love wasn't a game. Instead, he needed to know just how devoted she was. She would do anything. Stopping abruptly, she stood before him, holding his eyes for a moment before she dropped to her knees.

"Hey! I mean, I'm not complaining, but—hey…" He seemed to lose his train of thought as she resumed her work on his cock. She used her mouth this time, and his pants were no longer a barrier. The squeak of the wicker chair and the song of the crickets filled her ears, and she willed them to fill her mind, forcing the revulsion of that lost night away.

Ivan's hands came to the back of her head and twisted in her hair. She let him guide her, taking him in to impossible depths and relishing the taste of him. With a sharp intake of breath, a hushed gasp, he tensed and came, clearly doing his best to be quiet. She stayed with him until the end, drinking the last drop of him, then buried her head in his lap.

"Baby girl, I think it's been too long," he said after his breathing had slowed. "That had to be a world record. And you didn't give me a chance to reciprocate!"

"I just wanted to do something for you," she said, looking up at him after a moment. "I'm so glad you're here."

"Me too, babe. But there's nothing I can do for you?" He trailed his fingers along her jaw and down her neck, dipping them beneath her shirt.

"Just stay with me a little longer," she said, settling back into his lap.

"Of course, my love."

With his warm, strong arms around her under the starry Colorado sky, she could almost feel at peace. But when they both began to shiver, she knew it was time to go inside. Taking one last look at the surreal pond, they started back to the house.

"Where am I sleeping?" he asked as they crested the front door.

"With me in my old room."

"Bahahahaha! No way. We've already risked enough this evening. That couch looks fantastic, and I will crash there."

"Really?"

"Yes."

"Seriously?"

"Yes, dear. I don't want Lee thinking I have the balls to fool around with his princess right under his roof."

"Okay, okay. Fine." She pulled a spare pillow and sheets from the linen closet.

"Thank you, darling," he said, leaning in for a goodnight kiss.

"Absolutely," she replied, kissing him with all she had.

CHAPTER 21

"Fool in the Rain"

The faintest hint of morning streaked through the windows in the family room where Ivan had turned the couch into a bed. He snapped his eyelids open. "Fuck sakes…even on vacation I can't sleep in," he mumbled in a zombie-like haze. He sat up a bit and noticed Lee monkeying around with a trailer attached to his SUV outside. The chainsaws and axes indicated plans for a morning of cutting and splitting wood.

He perked up. This would be the perfect opportunity to ask a man he barely knew the second-most important question of his life. Forcing the lazy side of himself quiet, he hopped up to find some clothing and, he hoped, join Lee in the woods.

"Jesus," he gasped as he noticed his erection. Morning wood knew no boundaries.

With few resources to solve his predicament, he settled for securing it to his abdomen with the waistband of his boxer briefs. Then he covered everything with his shirt and headed to the restroom to alleviate the issue with a carefully aimed piss. *Carefully aimed* being the key.

Tiptoeing toward the kitchen, he was startled to find Diane in his path to the bathroom. A hot cup of joe in hand, she sat reading on a stool at the island. *Fuck. Play it cool.*

"Morning, Ivan," she called.

He couldn't miss the startled look in her eyes when she realized he wore nothing more than briefs and a tight white shirt. Her gaze moved from his crotch back to her magazine in one swift motion. He knew what she'd seen.

"Gooood morning," he replied, swinging his hands in front to cover his fifth appendage. "What are you doing up so early?"

Turning her attention to her coffee, Diane said, "Lee always cuts wood in the morning. Jaden's brother Justin usually helps him, but he stayed with a friend last night, so I'm up making his coffee." She was cool as a cucumber.

"Oh, I see," he said as he slipped into another seat at the island, still hard as all hell.

"Maybe since you're up you can go with him? Help him out and chat. Get to know each other more." She glanced up from her steaming cup with a smile.

"That sounds like a perfect idea." And it was also the perfect thought to deflate his erection with nervous energy. "Well, I'd better go change. Looks like he's ready to go."

"He isn't going anywhere yet. I have his coffee," she said with a smile. "I'll make sure he doesn't leave without you. Jaden will be in bed for a while longer, I'm guessing, so enjoy your man time."

He thanked her, dashed back into the living room, and realized he had no idea where his clothes were. They'd never brought the luggage in from the car.

"Oh!" Diane called. "I believe you'll find your suitcase by the front door. Lee brought it in this morning."

"Perfect. Thanks!"

He dug through his bag, then trotted back through the kitchen, this time all the way over to the bathroom, still feeling a bit awkward about being minimally clothed in front of Jaden's mom. He closed the door and splashed what seemed to be the coldest, freshest water he'd ever experienced on his face. He looked deep into his own eyes in the mirror. This was it. The moment he'd been waiting for. *Crush it!* "Let's do it," he murmured.

He changed into a pair of dark jeans and a blue T-shirt with sneakers. Reappearing in the kitchen, he snagged Lee's coffee from Diane, along with one she'd made for him. She also gave him a big hug and a wink.

"Wish me luck," he said.

"I think you'll be fine."

When he stepped outside, he noticed the sky was a bitter gray that hinted at showers. Birds taunted each other as they twittered in the trees. He found Lee struggling to pack the trailer.

"Coffee, sir?" he said, apparently startling the man half to death.

"Ivan!" Lee barked. "What the hell are you doing up?"

"It's nine-thirty Miami time, so I've been awake for quite a while." A little white lie couldn't hurt. "Cutting some wood, are ya?"

"Yep. It's my exercise on the weekend. Plus it doubles as my therapy."

"Would you like some help?"

"You don't have to. I'm not even sure how long it this weather is going to hold anyway."

"I want to help, if that's okay. I grew up cutting and splitting wood, so I'd love to say I got to do it in Colorado."

A smile snuck across Lee's face. "Okay, then. We aren't going too far. Just to the end of the driveway. I have some pines I want to clear out."

"Groovy." *Whew! Step one accomplished: get him alone.*

"All right, hop in."

Lee took the driver side as Ivan jumped in the front seat of the SUV.

The two set off, but then came to a stop again not more than a hundred yards from the house. *Damn! Needed a little more chat time than that.* Ivan exited the vehicle, nerves and all. He began plotting his next move, but as they unloaded the chainsaws and axes, Lee broke the ice.

"Fucking A. Nothing like getting out early in the morning and getting your hands dirty."

Step two: Establish rapport. Check! "Damn right," Ivan agreed loudly. *Shit! Too eager!* "Not too many people appreciate the benefits of real work anymore." *Good recovery,* he assured himself.

Grabbing his belt and gloves, Lee continued. "So now, you're a doctor who does what exactly? I've looked at your stuff online. Weight loss, wellness, physical enhancement, and sexual health? Hormones, supplements, and vitamins I get. But sexual health?"

Laughing a little at the very general synopsis of his current life, he formulated his response. "Yeah, it's basically making people feel good, look better, and—" He stopped himself from completing his usual tag line, which ended with *fuck like a rockstar.*

"And?"

"And have a better sex."

"Feel good, look better, and fuck like a rock star, you mean?" Ivan found himself speechless for the first time in a long time.

"I read an interview or two you did," Lee said, laughing. "Quite the job description. Rather impressive for someone your age."

Ivan exhaled as steps three and four checked themselves off: *Make a joke and explain your job.* "It's fun to help people feel their best. Finding your essence is like finding the fountain of youth, in my opinion."

Lee nodded as he handed him the chainsaw and retrieved the ax. They turned to the pine trees that were about to get it. After setting the equipment on the ground, both men did a half-assed stretch to prepare. Just then it started to sprinkle.

"Well, what do you say we get this party started?" Lee called as he pulled on his gloves and positioned his earplugs. He waded into a group of semi-mature pines and began to cut. Ivan found the aroma of pine in the air intoxicating, and it took him back to his childhood days of helping his father with this same task. One by one the trees fell, and he helped clear them from Lee's path of destruction. Then, as abruptly as he'd begun, Lee stopped cutting, his tree lust satisfied. He clicked off the chainsaw and set it down.

Ivan removed his earplugs and straightened up to stretch his back. "Not bad."

"Mission accomplished. Now, time to cut them into firewood."

"Perfect." Ivan began building up to the inevitable question. "Your family is great. You guys seem like you just fit together. Thank you so much for allowing me to join the celebration last night."

"It was our pleasure. We love to have fun together, that's for sure. So what's your family like? You're from Pennsylvania, right?"

Okay, good. He took the bait. Step five: Confirm family values. "Yep. My family is amazing. I consider us educated hillbillies. We work hard, play hard, and enjoy life. I am a lucky man to have such a great support system."

"Educated hillbillies, eh?" Lee laughed. "I hear you there. Your parents still together?"

"Thirty-five years and counting. My mom is a saint—she has to be to deal with my dad's antics."

"Yeah, so's Diane."

Both men laughed and then Lee added, "So values are important in your family."

"They're essential," Ivan replied.

"Good. You ever been married or have kids?"

Jesus. I thought I'd be asking the questions. "Negative on the marriage, but I got close once. And no. No kids that I know about." He shut his eyes as soon as it was out of his mouth. He would've slapped the back of his own head if it wouldn't have made him look even stupider.

"So you get around, then?" Lee's eyes narrowed.

"Ahh, no. It was a joke. I mean, I didn't mean it. Wow. That was rather poor joke selection on my part," Ivan said, embarrassed.

"Haha! I'm just kidding you. I grew up in the Woodstock era, remember?" Lee winked. "Why close but never married?"

Ivan choose his words carefully this time. "Some things just aren't meant to be. It wasn't the right time for us, and it turned out she wasn't ready."

Lee stood silently for a moment, then adjusted his belt as he bent down to fill the gas tank of the chainsaw. "So what's your five-year plan? Where do you want to be in five years?"

Each question upped the stakes and fanned Ivan's nerves to flame. This wasn't one of the steps! *He's throwing bonus questions in here. He's cheating!* "Well, I just opened my own medical wellness center, and I couldn't be happier. It's more like a medical spa for the rich and famous. Eventually I'd like to franchise it into a brand and move it out globally—so fingers crossed. The money is good now, and the security is too, but I always say, the second you settle for normalcy you lose humanity. Maybe I'll try writing a book someday. Who knows."

"Quite the entrepreneur," Lee said, looking up at him from a bent knee.

Jesus, is he going to propose? "I try…" Ivan managed. *Express financial stability: done. And that means all done. Just the big one left.* He took a deep breath.

"And where does Jaden fit in the equation?" Lee asked, beating him to the punch.

Wow. Shit. Fuck. Umm. Ivan's chest began to burn and freeze all at once. He swallowed hard. This was the opportunity he'd waited for. To ask this man the question every father expects and dreads at the same time. The one that involves handing over his daughter to some kid who thinks he can make her happy. Nervousness wasn't a big enough word to describe the feeling now running rampant in his body.

A shiver passed through him, and his palms grew slick with sweat. His heart raced. *How are you going to answer this? You're good at this — use that quirky shit. You've been interviewed in front of all sorts of crowds. You've played this out in your mind time and time again. Use the love analogy. No, use the life speech. No, try the "One" analogy.* And then, in a moment of clarity, his heart screamed, *"Shut the fuck up and speak from me!"*

As a bird chirped in the distance and the sound of rain danced through the tree branches, Ivan settled his thoughts, focused his heart, and calmly said what he needed to say. "Sir, I would love to see Jaden as the center of my universe in five, ten, and twenty years — for the rest of my life."

Lee stopped fumbling but kept his gaze down as the rain began to pick up speed.

"Your daughter has shown me what the meaning of life really is. It isn't cars, it isn't fame, and it isn't money. It's an essence. The essence of complete and utter admiration for another being. In her I've found the essence I never thought existed. Your daughter is more a part of who I am than I can explain. She gives me meaning." Like a love-drunk fool in the rain, Ivan stood looking down at Lee, who continued to study the grass. "God willing and with your blessing, sir, I'd like to ask her to join me in marriage."

The elephant that had been sitting on his chest for the past three weeks stood up and shook his hand. He felt liberated and thrilled that he'd fulfilled his commitment to ask the question.

Lee stood, his face a blank. Then Ivan felt him look directly into his soul. "Jaden is my very first baby. She's my world. She means more to me than one person could possibly comprehend, but I know she's madly in love with you. I know my wife is madly in love with you," he paused and looked at the ground.

Ivan felt he might burst with anticipation.

"If I have to forfeit the portion of my heart that belongs to her for anyone, I'm honored to have it be you. I look forward to welcoming you into our family, son." He offered his hand and his poker face transformed into a look of respect—something Ivan could never have asked for but appreciated beyond belief.

With rain now beating down he accepted the outstretched hand and shook it firmly. "Thank you, sir. Thank you so much." Inside his emotions ran wild.

As they released their grip, Lee added, "You're lucky you won Diane over at the airport. That was a ballsy move asking her for her blessing first. You'll learn quickly that Thorne women can't keep a damn thing secret—especially not a mother. She told me last night before bed." He laughed. "My mind was made up, but I wanted to make you squirm a bit."

Ivan shook his head and just laughed, the nervousness flowing out of him. "Well played, sir. Well played. Yes, lesson learned there."

"Now, I say let's scrap this project and come back to it later…or not. I'm drenched, and we made a pretty good dent."

Noticing he was soaked as well, Ivan conceded his ambition to chop Colorado wood. His true task had been completed, and perhaps Jaden was awake by now. "Agreed," he said with a smile. As if he'd been injected with some wonderful drug, he happily snatched up the tools and headed to the car. A smile tattooed his face and love tattooed his soul. *One more question,* he thought. *Just one more question to ask.*

CHAPTER 22

"Color Blind"

"Really, Daddy? Putting Ivan to work on his vacation in this weather?" Jaden waved as she ran out with an umbrella to greet the men returning from their backwoods man session. She tried to see the expressions on their faces. Had their time together gone well?

"I didn't put a gun to his head," her father joked as she snuggled into Ivan's arms and pecked him on the cheek. She could feel his heart thumping, but they were both all smiles. Last night's friendliness seemed to have continued. *Whew.*

"It was my idea. I wanted to get outside," Ivan said returning a peck to her temple.

"I hope you didn't get natured out, 'cause I made lunch, and I thought I'd take you and your camera into the mountains once the rain lets up."

"Perfect. I could never get natured out. As long as you're there with me, I'm happy," he added softly. "Let me help your dad finish here, and I'll be right in."

"Okay, sweetie," she called as she headed back to the house.

"Quite the charmer, aren't ya?" She could hear her father teasing Ivan as she walked away. *Amazing.*

Traipsing in from the now-slowing rain, Jaden tossed her umbrella in the corner and joined her mother and sister in the kitchen, where they chatted secretively. They smiled and grew silent as she approached.

"He's gonna change clothes, and I think I'll take him to the trails at Rocky Mountain National Park."

"Yes, that sounds good. I was watching the weather, and it looks like the rain is pretty much done," her mom reported. "Scattered showers."

"What were you two gabbing about?" Jaden asked.

"Nothing, darling. Did you pack lunch?"

"You know I did. You helped me pack it!"

"Yes, sorry. This old mind of mine must be slipping." Her mother laughed.

"You guys are terrible at keeping secrets—especially you, Mom."

"I haven't said anything!" Magan protested.

"You need anything else for your picnic date?"

"Mom, I'm not ten."

"Sorry. You guys are growing up so fast. I forget sometimes that you're both beautiful young women."

"Aww, Mom!" Jaden hugged her mother and grabbed her sister as well.

"I love you guys," her mother said.

"We love you too," the sisters replied in unison.

"Heads up, Ivan! The estrogen is thick in here right now." Her father's joke ended their moment as the men rumbled back inside.

"Thanks, Dad!" Magan hollered as she rolled her eyes.

"You about ready?" Jaden asked Ivan.

"Aren't I always, baby girl?"

"Baby girl! Did you hear that? Lee, do you remember when you used to call me that in college? Your father used to be quite the charmer himself—a million years ago. I wonder where that man went?"

"He got married. See what happens when you get married, Ivan? You run out of one liners. Luckily my wife is an angel who doesn't need to be serenaded every day." He sidled over and gave her a kiss on the neck.

"You see what I have to deal with since you left, Jaden?"

"We're out of here before it gets too weird," she said, laughing as she grabbed her bag. "Ivan, quick! Go change."

"I'm on it," he said, disappearing into the living room for a moment, then passing back through to the bathroom.

"You got any wine in there?" her father asked, eyeing the bag she'd packed. "Let me grab you a bottle."

"Thanks, Daddy. I'm going to grab the camera too." She dashed up the stairs as her father headed for the basement, and she returned a few minutes later to find Ivan wearing fresh clothes and chatting once again with her mother in the kitchen.

"I owe you," he told her mom as Jaden approached.

"For what?" Jaden asked.

"Oh, well…" Ivan began, but his attention was soon commanded by her dad.

"Okay, Ivan, I think you'll appreciate this one," he announced as he returned to the kitchen. "It's one of my new favorites. It's an Australian shiraz with a great finish."

What he pulled from behind his back couldn't have been more perfect. In his hand was a black velvet bag with silver embroidery. Serendipity had made her grand entrance.

"Now I'm more of a dry red kinda guy but —"

"Dad, it's perfect," Jaden said. Amazed yet again.

Her father smiled, but looked confused.

"That's Ivan's favorite — his favorite wine and his favorite winery. Mollydooker. And it's come to be one of my favorites too," she added, giving Ivan a squeeze.

"You're full of surprises aren't you, son?" he exclaimed.

"It's a damn fine wine. I can attest to that," Ivan said. "Thank you."

"Well, I hope you two enjoy."

"Thank you, Daddy." Jaden took the bottle and snuck in a hug. She added it to her bag, along with two wine glasses, and zipped it up. "Ready?"

"Yes, ma'am."

"Here, you take the camera."

After a quick round of goodbyes, they headed for the door, and Jaden practically ran to her father's SUV, the anticipation of a long afternoon in the woods alone with Ivan getting the better of her. The acceptance of her family? The perfect bottle of wine? She and Ivan were clearly meant to move forward.

"So what did you and my dad do?" she asked as they sped down the driveway.

"Well, we chatted and cut some wood. Man stuff. A woman, such as yourself, wouldn't understand." He laughed.

"Oh, really? Well, this little lady has chopped her fair share of wood, and I'm fully adept with a chainsaw, mister."

"Teasing, girl! When it started to rain we had to stop, but we got a fair amount done."

"Good. I'm glad you got out there with him. He can be intimidating sometimes."

"Naw, he's a teddy bear."

"Liar."

As the car cut though the beautiful little town, Ivan played sightseer, marveling aloud at the way wildlife marched through the streets as a part of the community. Elk laid in people's front yards, and bighorn sheep trotted down the side streets. When they approached the entrance to the park, with its fields of goldenrod, he scrambled for the camera.

"This is nothing," Jaden said as they passed Beaver Meadows Visitors Center. "Wait till we get into the real park."

They turned on to Trail Ridge Road, and the SUV began to ascend. They picked their way through the picturesque scenery, stopping to run out and snap pictures of each other with backdrops of trees, rock formations, and wildlife. The road seemed to be their own private highway with not another vehicle in sight. Perfect. As they came to a marker indicating them to be halfway up the trail, Jaden pulled the car to the side of the road. "Let's go for a hike and eat."

Ivan followed her along a small trail cut between a field of sage brush and budding wildflowers. She heard him whistle appreciatively from behind and looked to see what natural wonder he'd sighted. But he had eyes only for her.

"Lookin' good, baby," was all he said to her questioning look. "You put the landscape to shame."

They left the field and turned onto a smaller and tighter path through a thicket, which tore at their bags and clothing. "Almost there," she said, offering her hand. She thrilled at the warmth and electricity that surged through her when he took it.

Finally the forest opened up, and they stood on a cliff overlooking the landscape they'd been traversing for the past forty-five minutes.

Snowcapped mountains sheltered a spring-fed valley that harbored every beautiful form of life one could imagine. The trees scattered themselves around monstrous rock formations and between trickling natural turquoise lakes. Eagles flew above, enjoying the same view she was now thrilled to share with Ivan. She could tell he was in awe, as he said nothing and seemed to have forgotten about the camera. He just stood, taking it all in and breathing the crisp, fresh air.

She set the bag down and turned to him with a smile. "Well, doctor, what do you think?"

"Its beauty is surpassed only by yours, Ms. Thorne."

"I thought you'd like it. I came here while growing up to think and relax."

"It's perfect, baby. Simply perfect."

She wrapped her arms around his neck and looked into his eyes. "Thank you again for coming. I can't tell you how much I needed you to be here."

"I needed to be here too. Thank you so much for inviting me. I love everything about you," he added after a moment.

That sentiment brought tears to her eyes. If only she could love everything about herself. She pressed her lips and hips to his, hoping to lose herself in the moment and recover. "I think we both need something right now," she whispered.

She knelt, made quick work of his fly, and took his cock out of his pants. Grasping it at the base she spit on its head and began to swallow him inch by inch. She worked her hand up and down his shaft as her tongue teased the tip of his dick, only to retract as she forced more of him down her wanting throat. Longing to overwhelm him with pleasure, she took his balls into her mouth and sucked them in the most sensual of ways. He looked down at her, eyes filled with lust, and took the liberty of removing his shirt. She followed suit and removed hers, making sure not to interrupt her rhythmic motions.

Suddenly he pulled her to her feet and turned her to face the valley in front of them. He bit her neck like a savage animal, and she quivered in ecstasy as he unbuttoned her pants and tore them from her body before also removing his.

"What do you want me to do to you?" he growled.

"I want you to use me for your own pleasure," she responded, the love in her heart swelling to push the guilt aside.

With a rush of breath, Ivan began his assault. He bent her forward to rest her hands on an overturned stump, then lowered himself to taste her pussy. He licked and teased her as she felt herself go wild, shaking her hips and pressing back against his mouth. He licked every centimeter of her, then she felt him trail his way up to her ass. A momentary jolt went through her, and she tensed, but then he began working her clit with his free hand, and she willed herself to relax. This was for Ivan, yet she moaned in excitement and pleasure. "Fuck. Ahhhhhh, God...That feels...Fuck!"

Her moans turned to screams as she stood bent over in the wilderness with a finger in her pussy and his tongue in her ass. Her orgasm built to a climax with uncontrollable speed, and she burst forth, drenching Ivan's hand as he continued to utilize both sexual centers. "Oh God, Ivan, that feels so fucking good. Don't stop!"

"You like that?"

"Fuck, yeah."

Slipping another and another finger into her wanting pussy, he continued to use his tongue and worked another orgasm from her depths. When she'd recovered enough to stop screaming, she tried to protest. "Ivan...I said...for *your* pleasure..."

"Trust me," he told her as he lifted her leg and braced her foot against a rock. "This *is* for my pleasure."

Grabbing her hips for leverage, his slammed his dick into her with mind-altering force. "Ahhh, yes!" They screamed together as his cock invaded her core, and his balls hit her clit. She had never been so wet. But halting him in his tracks, she turned and took him in her mouth once more, leaving a trail of saliva along his entire length. Then, with a wicked smile, she assumed a position of submission. "Take it," she said, offering her ass. "It's yours."

Without a word, he repositioned himself. Jaden felt the pressure of the head of Ivan's cock butting up against her last remaining virginity. *But wait...*

"Wait!" She moved before he went any further and reached for the knapsack on the ground. Rummaging through it, she pulled out a first aid kit. She unzipped the bag and handed a small container to Ivan.

"Vaseline?" He looked knowingly at Jaden.

"It's better than nothing."

"Are you always this prepared?" he inquired as he coated his dick with a thick layer of lubrication.

When he'd finished he turned her around and placed her arms and legs in the appropriate positions. Then he guided the head of his cock to her ass and pressed it against the taut ring of muscles. With a steady, firm motion he began to slide himself in, deeper and deeper into her darkest, untainted intimacy, pausing when she gasped out loud.

"Are you okay, babe?"

"Yeah," she replied and let out a long, slow breath. "Go ahead."

He began to rock back and forth, taking more and more liberty in his penetrating strokes.

When Jaden could no longer differentiate between pain and pleasure, she pushed back against him. "More," she screamed.

He didn't hesitate as he replaced his small, firm strokes with one powerful push that sent a lightning bolt through her body and out of her mouth.

"Yesssss!" echoed down the valley and probably back into town.

Back and forth he worked her ass, and the harder he thrust, the more she wanted. Stroke after stroke filled her as she fingered her clit to increase the mind-bending sensations. "I'm gonna come, baby! Keep going! Keep going! Fuck me, doctor!"

With a rush of breath and a guttural grunt she'd never heard before, Ivan came into her with an unprecedented force. The feeling of him filling her in a way she'd never experienced, her body taking all of him, toppled her over the edge as well. Without warning, her body rewarded her in a whole new way. Her legs shook as her pussy clenched around his finger and her ass around his dick, and she came harder than she'd ever known she could. Her mind went blank and the world went dark in a moment no words could define.

Ivan supported her and eased them to the ground. Naked, they lay speechless, just looking at each other until a chilly breeze caused a riot of shivering and goose bumps. "Let's clean off real quick," he suggested, looking over at a spring-fed pond.

It was clear as glass — and cold as ice, Jaden knew, but she allowed him to lead her, and hand in hand they jumped in. The second the water touched her skin, she knew they needed to get out.

"Holy shit," she screamed as she ran back up the bank, followed by Ivan. Grabbing the picnic blanket, they huddled under its warmth to dry.

"Bad idea," he observed after a moment.

"At least we're awake and clean now."

Once they began to warm, Ivan reached into the bag and retrieved the bottle of wine and glasses. "Let's get a bit warmer." He poured them each a glass. "To the most precious thing in my life. You make my soul smile."

After touching his glass with hers, she sipped the velvety wine—the wine that had sparked their lust and solidified their love. She leaned against him, feeling much more comfortable in her skin, and stroked his dick back and forth. "God, that was great."

"Yeah, I'm pretty sure one of these mountains moved for me."

Lying naked on a slab of rock overlooking nature at its finest, they drank their wine, ate their lunch, and enjoyed this rare moment of being alone together.

"I wish we had more time here," she finally said. "There's so much to show you that I know you would love."

"I'm sure we'll be back here sometime soon. I love your family, by the way."

"Yes, I noticed, and they love you, which is funny. I've never seen them won over so fast."

"All I had to say was that I loved their daughter. It was easy enough."

"Okay, you already got what you wanted out here in the wilderness, so you can stop the smooth talk, doctor."

"I believe I was following your instructions," he noted. "And don't act like you didn't like it. I've never seen you go off like that. It was hot."

"It was definitely different—and hot, I must admit." She was quiet for a moment, amazed all over again at what Ivan could do to her. She'd set out to please *him* and had ended up more satisfied than ever before. How could she have even considered testing their perfect bond?

He squeezed her hand, and she could tell he was wondering what she was thinking. She steered the conversation another way. "So no hint on what the surprise is?"

"Nope…Well, I will tell you we're going to Miami for it."

"Yay! What time is the flight tomorrow? I should tell my mom."

"It's at eight-thirty, so we've got an early morning."

"Really? Ugh…yes, a very early morning." She took another sip of wine. "Well, I'm already excited."

"Me too!"

Crack! The two naked lovers sprang to attention at the sound of a rather large branch breaking. Following the rustling sounds in the thicket, Jaden spotted some large shadows lumbering through. She looked over at Ivan and mouthed the word *elk*. Motioning for him to grab the stuff, she pointed to their escape route and tried to convey with her eyes that it was time to go. *Now.* Seeming to understand the gravity of the situation, he grabbed their clothes and bag and followed her to make their escape, still naked as all hell.

Sneaking through the brush, she couldn't help but laugh at the ridiculous situation. They crouched in the most un-sexy positions to avoid antagonizing the huge, and hugely dangerous animals. Adrenaline ran high, and the visual had to be priceless. Thankfully Ivan was laughing — silently. Once they'd cleared the brush, their sneak became a sprint. And only when she was sure they were out of range of any charging elk did she stop so they could catch their breath. They leaned against the rocks, just a stone's throw from the path they'd driven in on.

"Damn, girl! You can move!"

"Well, I'm not a pussy," she said between breaths. "I had to save your life!"

Just then a rumbling of a different sort echoed up through the trees, and they both hit the deck. They looked up from the ground to see a minivan drive by — with a camera poked out the passenger window. *So much for having the mountain to ourselves*, Jaden thought, beginning to laugh all over again.

"Why didn't you stand up?" she asked Ivan when the car had passed. "You could've *really* given them something worthy of a picture!"

"Ha! Well, didn't want to risk frightening the wildlife — or causing an accident," he added. "That was quite the adventure."

"Yes, it was. And we still have to get out of here."

Smiling, they sorted through their hastily grabbed things to find their clothes and got dressed.

"Let's get back and spend some time with your family," Ivan suggested.

Relishing the memories they'd made, she sauntered over and kissed his ear. "I hope you had a good time. I did."

"Hell yeah, girl. This was awesome—including the elk."

Hand in hand, they retraced their steps to the SUV and headed back down the mountain for their last night in Colorado.

CHAPTER 23

"Two Tickets to Paradise"

Jaden and Ivan spent their last night in Colorado enjoying a feast of roasted meat and sautéed vegetables, followed by delectable desserts. She continued to marvel at the free-flowing laughter and friendly exchange of opinions and ideas. She caught Ivan telling her father a hunting story at one point—and her dad was captivated, even asking a question or two.

And the time she'd spent with Ivan, the much-needed opportunity to connect, had nearly erased the guilty black mark on her soul. Damian had been a terrible mistake, but he was *her* mistake. For Ivan, this was something she would bear. Gazing at him in the firelight, she admired how he fit into her life and her family. Like some majestic puzzle piece, he linked seamlessly with her. The night wound down with her father wishing them a safe trip, her sister giving them her best, and her mother reminding them they'd better be grateful she was waking up in…*four* hours to drive them to Denver to catch their flight. The only thing she missed was getting to see Justin. But he'd always been this way—coming and going as he pleased. At least it was work keeping him so busy now.

After a round of hugs and thank yous, the family trickled upstairs, leaving Jaden and Ivan with a table full of dirty dishes and Shiraz-stained wine glasses.

"Well…did I do okay? I didn't embarrass you, did I?" Ivan asked as he began to clear the table.

"You? No. Seems like you and my dad really hit it off. You hit it off with all of them."

"It was fun getting to know them in person. They're great. Hopefully I'll get to meet your brother soon, too."

"Yeah, maybe. He can be difficult, and evidently he's working all the time, but I do love him," she said, following him into the kitchen with a stack of plates. "So what should I bring for this little getaway? Any hints?"

"Just yourself and a smile. That's all you need." He put the dishes in the sink and turned to face her. "That's all *I* need too, come to think of it."

"Oh, come on, no hints? You suck."

"Okay, if I tell you, you promise you won't say a word?"

She had no idea what she was promising, but she nodded and crossed a quick finger across her heart.

"I was sworn to secrecy, so do *not* rat me out," he said. "There's a fancy charity event in Miami, and Micky's going to propose to Tasha while we're there."

She felt a rock form in her stomach, though she kept a smile on her face. And she was ashamed at her disappointment. *What did you expect?* she asked herself accusingly. Tasha deserved this. She was going to be someone's fiancé—but not Jaden. Not yet.

"What? That's amazing!" she exclaimed, trying to sound enthusiastic as she busied herself with the dishes.

"Now, don't you say anything!"

She nodded and stuffed down her disappointment and resurging guilt. *You don't deserve a proposal right now.* Then she focused on Tasha and Micky and summoned some true excitement for her best friend's happiness.

"Oh my God! I want details! Where's it going to be? When?"

"Quite the snoop, aren't you? What are you willing to do to find out?" Ivan asked with a raised eyebrow.

She slapped at him with a soapy hand. "Quite the pervert, aren't you? Sexual extortionist? That's a whole new low, doctor!"

"Okay, okay. I'm just kidding. But I am serious about keeping quiet. You can't say anything!"

"I won't!"

"The event is at the Bath Club the day after we get back to Miami. It's a posh little dinner with a singer — the perfect atmosphere. It'll be a beautiful, intimate setting with a bunch of fancy Miami Beachers. I pulled some strings to get us all a table."

"Wow! That's so amazing! What's the charity?"

"The Naked Foundation."

"Oh, of course. You've done lots of work with them." She loaded the last of the dishes into the dishwasher and wiped her hands. "Well, this all sounds great. How can I help? I want to be involved too! Tasha's my best friend." She turned to him with a pouty look, which she could tell turned him on.

"Okay, well, I'd love to get a woman's opinion." He uncorked what was left of the wine and poured them each a drink.

She leaned against the counter. "Happy to help."

"That's my girl." He hopped up on the kitchen island and clinked his wineglass against hers. His eyes held a mischievous spark. "So what flowers would you suggest?"

"Well, roses, of course, but they must be deep red. White belongs at weddings, but deep red means love and passion — thornless if it was love at first sight."

"Interesting formula," he said. "Yours?"

"This is an important day in a girl's life, so we do research." She winked.

"Good to know. What about music?"

"Well, for me it would definitely be Frank Sinatra."

"No kidding."

"Yeah, not a hard guess. For Tasha, I think more modern music."

"Food?"

"Hmm…if I'm cooking—"

"*No!*"

Jaden gave him the eye and continued. "Okay then. I'm *not* cooking. For me, something light and not too filling—like a chicken dish with steamed vegetables. But, you know, Tasha is more of a meat and potatoes girl. She's not a big foodie, though. Pizza would work just fine for her."

"Good Lord. Well, I can assure you *that* will not be on the menu."

"Excellent."

"Drinks?"

"I'd go with wine, and you know which kind, of course. But Tasha? Shots."

"Jesus."

"Yeah, she's a little…well, you know. She's a party girl."

"Yeah, I know," he said with a low laugh.

"So who's coming? Will we know anyone else?"

"Not a big crowd. I know Micky invited a mix of friends so it's a good time. Pretty much everybody important, I guess. And then the paying customers at the event, of course."

"That's so sweet of him. I'm so excited!"

"You'd just better not say anything!" He poised his glass at his lips as he glared at her over the rim.

"Or what?"

"Or I get to do what we did in the woods today when we get back to Miami."

A flash of heat shot through her body. "You might want to consider a different form of punishment," she purred. "Maybe something I didn't enjoy."

"Oh *reallllllly?*"

She winked and drained the last of the wine from her glass, letting her eyes linger at his crotch. He finished his wine in one big gulp and set the glass aside. He smiled at her but didn't make a move.

She set her empty glass down behind her and pushed off the counter. She put her hands on his thighs and pushed his knees apart to snuggle between his legs.

"You're so lucky we're in your parents' house tonight," he said, his voice low and thick.

She leaned in close and squeezed his firm cock. "Why does that matter?"

He gasped, but couldn't seem to come up with a thing to say. She kept her eyes on him as she unzipped his pants and grasped his dick in her hand. She kissed him slowly as she worked him up and down. He groaned into her kiss but pulled away, looking over his shoulder.

Before he had a chance to protest further, Jaden swallowed him whole. Back and forth she moved, her hair draped over his lap. She knew he loved watching her, and she loved the thrill of knowing that at any second someone could turn the corner and catch them. Blowing Ivan on the kitchen counter in her childhood home was even more of a turn on than miniature golf.

She grew more and more wet as his groans deepened and his guard dropped.

"Ohh, fuck, Jaden…Oh…"

Creeeeeeeeeeeak.

Her head came to an abrupt stop halfway down his shaft, and his groans cut off mid-breath. Her eyes slid toward the hallway.

"Whoops," a male voice called from the shadows.

"Shit!" Jaden cursed as she scrambled to cover Ivan. She squinted to make out the figure who'd just caught them. Too scrawny to be her dad—thank God. "Justin? Is that you?"

"Well, I wish it wasn't."

She sighed in relief.

"I take it you're Ivan," he asked, stepping out the shadows.

"Yep. Uh…hey, man, er…I'm so—" Ivan stuttered.

"Don't mention it. I didn't see anything, and I'm going to bed." Justin sounded a little annoyed, but he hugged her, albeit loosely when she approached him. His caution seemed justified considering the current state of affairs.

"It's so great to see you! Do you want some wine?"

"It's too late, and I'm too tired. I need some sleep. Plus I don't want to interrupt. You looked a little busy."

"Oh, Justin," she sighed. "I'm sorry."

"Have a good night," he called, already across the room. He offered an informal salute and disappeared up the stairs.

"That went well," Ivan exclaimed when Justin's footsteps had faded. "Three out of four ain't bad, right?"

"Don't worry. That's how he always is. He's just a mellow dude."

"And you aren't embarrassed? Your baby brother just caught you with a mouthful of me!"

"Of course I am!" Jaden felt her face heat up. "But it is what it is. I'm sure he's done much worse in here."

"I hope not. That's a health code violation for sure!"

"I did enjoy that taste of you," she said, moving closer. "In Miami I want the whole thing, doctor."

"And you'll get it, Ms. Thorne."

She stifled a yawn.

"We now have *three* hours before we gotta get moving. How about you get to bed. I'll finish this up." He gestured to the last of the mess in the kitchen.

"No, absolutely not." She silenced him with a kiss.

He kissed her back and hopped down off the island. He tucked away his still-erect dick and buttoned up. "Yes. You should get some rest. We have a long couple days coming up, and I want you at your best to help me pull off this proposal without a hitch."

"Deal, babe." She hugged him, breathing his addictive scent. "I love you."

"And I love you."

She smiled as she retreated to her room. Her best friend's engagement. It just seemed perfect. She took a deep breath and realized she was finally happy again.

CHAPTER 24

"Wildflowers"

The screech of tires hitting the runway served as Ivan's alarm clock when the nonstop flight from Denver to Miami touched down. He noticed Jaden stirring as well, and he joined her in stretching arms and legs, shaking off the fitful hours of in-flight sleep.

"Ugh, I am so tired."

"Didn't you sleep well last night?" she asked, eyes concerned.

"I just need a few more hours." He groaned as he retrieved his phone.

"Ah, poor baby," she teased. "Too much jet-setting lifestyle."

"Aren't you funny."

"Well, you can sleep in the cab."

"And you can give me a back massage while I do."

Rolling her eyes, Jaden laughed and stood up to retrieve her bag from the overhead bin. "We'll see."

Soon they were strolling hand in hand through the all-too-familiar Miami airport. The way it was supposed to be. He smiled as he looked over at her. Normally so put together in public, she hid today behind oversized sunglasses and a pajama-like outfit she'd hastily chosen that morning. She still looked beautiful.

Cresting the opposite side of the security gate, he checked his phone again.

"What the hell are you doing?"

"Will you quit your snooping?"

"Always a workaholic. I know you do have ADD, but you also have your girl in town, so just relax," she commanded sweetly.

"Who said it was work? You're the queen of assumptions!"

Her smartass grin faded into sheer excitement as she looked toward the exit and saw someone — someone who came running toward her, squealing all the way.

"Jadeeeeeeen!"

"Tashaaaaa!" She dropped her luggage at his feet and ran. They nearly knocked each other over.

"I'm so excited to see you!" Jaden hugged her friend tight.

"Me too, Ms. Superstar. Wow, you're in phenomenal shape."

"Oh, stop! I love your hair!"

"Yeah? They cut it shorter than I wanted to, but I think I love it now too."

More incomprehensible woman chatter ensued as Ivan scooted past the gabbing girls to Micky. "Women," the two muttered simultaneously. Shaking their heads, they left the ladies behind and began loading the suitcases into Micky's silver Grand Cherokee.

"She have any clue?"

"No, I told her you were proposing to Tasha."

"What! Why the hell would you do that?" Micky nearly yelled, panic in his voice.

"So she'll be extra careful not to meddle or get suspicious."

"God, I hope she doesn't tell Tasha anything."

Ivan laughed. "What, you couldn't handle her?"

"Oh, I can handle her all right. You have everything set up?"

"Fuck, I spent all last night emailing every contact I have to make this thing the way she wants it. Didn't sleep a wink."

"How do you know how she wants it?"

"When you're good, you're good, man." He slapped Micky on the back.

"Well, fingers crossed for you. It would be a shame to see that rock go to waste."

"No shit." Ivan rolled his eyes.

"What are you going to do if she says no?"

Ivan glanced over at Jaden, still talking a mile a minute in her pajamas. He couldn't help but smile. "If she says no, it will be the first time in my life I haven't had any idea what to do…Of course then I suppose I'll go on a rogue mission of mindless, nameless, faceless sex and depravity. Never done that…But don't they say the best way to get over someone is to get under someone?"

They burst into laughter, and Micky added, "Or behind someone."

"Now you're speaking my language, my friend."

"How was her parents' place? You survive that okay?" Micky asked, shifting gears.

"Yeah, it went amazing, actually. Not a problem at all. I got that much-needed stamp of approval from both parents, so I'm more relaxed now. Hopefully they were the hard ones to convince," Ivan said with a laugh.

"One girl the rest of your life? You ready for that?"

Without hesitation Ivan smiled. "Absolutely."

"And her? She's ready for one dick for the rest of her life?"

"Jesus, no cuff," Ivan laughed. "I hope so."

"What's up with her co-host, by the way? Tasha says he's kind of a douche."

"Ehh, he's harmless. Fucking pretty boy Casanova wannabe. There aren't too many people in this world that irk me, but that little shitstain does."

"Wow, does he irritate Jaden that much too?"

"You know, he did at first, but she hasn't said much about him at all lately. Things must have settled down. I'm sure she's got him whipped into shape."

"Well, that's good," Micky said. "Yo, ladies! This taxi is leaving with or without you."

Tasha and Jaden shot over a pair of dirty looks, but they did begin making their way to the "taxi."

"She'll say yes," Micky said softly. "And if not, at least you have a free-range sexual mission to look forward to."

Ivan snickered.

"What are you two talking about?" Tasha inquired.

"Totally irresponsible bareback sex with a slew of random beautiful women. Usual guy stuff, no big deal," Ivan deadpanned.

Two pairs of unpleasant eyebrows aimed in his direction.

"Oh *reeeeallly?*" Jaden asked.

"Actually we were talking about a lovely dinner tonight at your old stomping ground," Micky said.

She smiled and greeted him with a big hug. "You're such a gentleman, Micky." She winked at Ivan over his shoulder. "You should take notes."

"I'll give you notes…" he teased.

"Stop it! I'm busy being indignant."

"All right, let's get this show on the road." Micky exclaimed.

They hopped into the SUV and headed back across the causeway to Miami Beach. In no time, Ivan's building rose up in front of them, and Micky pulled to a stop out front.

"Ah, home sweet home. Ready for that back rub?" Ivan asked, wiggling his eyebrows at Jaden.

"Why, yes, I am! My shoulders are killing me."

"Very funny." He pulled their luggage out of the back with Micky's help. "So we'll catch you guys tonight, right?"

"Oh yeah! You're buying, right?" Micky teased.

"For sure. It's the least I can do for the most accommodating car service in Miami Beach." Ivan shut the car door and snagged the luggage from the sidewalk as the SUV drove away.

A bag slung over her shoulder, Jaden followed him through the lobby, past the doorman, who called out a pleasant hello, and down the hallway to the elevator bank. They entered the elevator and Ivan pressed twelve. He turned to find a huge grin on Jaden's face.

"What are you giggle-pussin' about?"

"Tasha. She has no clue. She's going to be so happy. I'm excited for her."

"Me too. Micky seems good. Excited, but not too anxious."

"As long as he's confident, he'll be fine," she said.

Ping! The doors opened, and she continued to smile as she backed out of the elevator.

Ivan dropped the bags in front of his door and fished his keys out of his pocket.

After a moment Jaden stepped across the threshold and took a deep breath.

"Air conditioning ASAP!" he called from behind her.

"Okay, okay! Hold your horses." She trotted to the thermostat. "What is this? Good Lord."

"That's Bob the bear," he explained, chuckling. "I sleep with him every night. You have BoBo, and I have Bob."

"BoBo is a twelve-inch stuffed animal. This is a full-fledged, six-foot bearskin rug."

"Yeah, but he's good company, and he reminds me of you."

"Are you saying I'm hairy?"

"No, baby girl. You're soft and something I love lying on top of."

"Oh, slick willy, huh?"

"Isn't it every woman's dream to make love on a bearskin rug?" he asked with an impish grin.

"Uh, no," she said. "It's every *man's* dream."

"Hmmm, you may be right about that." He stepped behind her and wound his arms around her waist, kissing her neck as she looked out his window across the water at Miami. Between kisses, he yawned.

She ran her hands over his forearms. "You really didn't sleep last night?"

His kisses stopped. "No."

"Why not?"

"Just had a few remaining details for tomorrow night. I promised Micky I'd help."

"Poor baby," she said. "Lay down, and I'll give you that massa—"

Before she could finish, he'd shucked his pants and shirt and dove face down on Bob.

"Okay, that was fast."

He waved his hands impatiently.

Jaden laughed and moved to straddle him. The warmth and weight of her thighs caused him to moan in pleasure.

As she worked every muscle in his back, Ivan felt himself slipping away. Gorgeous woman nearby or no, within minutes it had all faded to black.

CHAPTER 25

"Higher"

The smell of searing chicken drenched in soy sauce tickled Ivan's innermost hunger center and enticed him out of sleep. He rolled out of bed and, as if he were a cartoon character, floated toward the source of such a delectable smell.

When he turned the corner, his appetite for food was replaced with an appetite for sex. Jaden stood in the kitchen wearing the Mario Lemieux jersey she'd worn the first time she spent the night — and seemingly nothing else. Her rhythmic movements were almost sexual as she danced around the kitchen. As she reached for things and turned the chicken, the curves of her ass were blatantly visible, and just perfect.

"Fuck me, you look gorgeous," he said, his voice thick with sleep.

She smiled. "Thank you, baby. Are you hungry?"

"Yes…"

"Hmmm…For food?"

He smiled at her, rubbed his eye with his fist, and shook his head.

"Hold up there, Tiger. You need to eat. This is just a snack because we're late already. We have to be there in twenty-five minutes." '

"You're kidding me. Because you look too good not to fool around with."

"There will be more chances," she said with a wink as she flashed him a shot of her shaved pussy.

"Dammit! Now I'm hard!" He nearly ran into the wall as he retreated to the shower.

"My bad!" she called.

Once in the shower, he flew through a soap and a scrub. He couldn't quite shake the thought of Jaden in his favorite jersey, so his dick remained hard, proving to be quite the inconvenience. He laughed at the spectacle of it all: running around the bathroom with a hard-on, shaving, doing his hair, trying to put his suit on.

"You okay?" Jaden asked, appearing at the bathroom door. She now wore a dress instead of his jersey.

"Don't you start with me, young lady! You're the reason for this," he grumbled, motioning at the bulge tucked away in his dress pants.

"Hmmm…" was all she said as she ducked out. He could hear her laugh as she returned to his bedroom.

A short time later they'd finished getting ready, munched their snack, and rushed out the door. Downstairs they hopped into a waiting taxi and sped off to meet their friends at Bianca.

Ivan could sense the excitement and anxiety swirling around Jaden. This was the first time she'd been back to the restaurant since she left. The taxi pulled up near the massive shrubs outside, and a doorman opened the door for them. Jaden stepped out and looked all around. "Still looks the same," she noted. Once they entered, however, she seemed to notice something new. "New hostess." She snickered. The snooty French maître d had been replaced with a young blonde in pressed white clothing.

"May I help you?"

"Rusilko for four."

"Ah, yes. The other two guests have already been seated at your table."

As they followed her to the table, Ivan watched Jaden's eyes dart around the room. He squeezed her hand and smiled. She quickly returned the gesture.

Tasha and Micky glowered at them as they sat. "Jeez, how late are we?" Jaden asked as the hostess disappeared. "It isn't what you think. He overslept and—"

"Ahh, don't worry. We had a few drinks. Ivan's paying so it's not a problem." Tasha burst into a smile.

"Yes, drink up! Let's have some fun!" Ivan enthused.

Everyone picked up a menu, and Ivan pretended to study it while sneaking glances to see what Jaden's reaction would be.

"Well, I'm getting the tuna," she announced. "I'm curious to see how they make it now."

"Excellent choice." He leaned over to give her a quick kiss.

A dark haired girl approached and asked to take their drink order.

"Excuse me, does Susan still work here? Or Bert?" Jaden asked as they requested a bottle of wine.

"Actually no. Susan moved, and Bert got a job as a chef in downtown Miami."

Jaden smiled. "How fantastic for him. And Geoff?"

"He's in the back. Would you like me to get him?"

"Could you just let him know Jaden is here and would love to say hi?"

"Will do," she replied. "And I'll also get you that wine."

Making up for lost time, the couples laughed, shared stories, and drank. As the main courses arrived, Jaden made sure to study each one and mentally critique it before she allowed anyone to eat. "Okay," she finally announced. "Proceed. But I may need a bite."

Ivan watched as she tasted her tuna and let it sit on her tongue. "Well, what are your thoughts? Satisfactory?"

"It's very good. They did a great job."

He breathed a sigh of relief, and the evening continued. As their dinner wound down, he noticed a man approaching their table from behind Jaden.

Catching Ivan's eye, he winked and tapped her on the shoulder. "Can I interest you in some desserts?"

She shot up and gave him a huge hug and kiss on the cheek.

"How are you, darling? I'm so happy I get to follow your progress each week on TV!"

"I'm doing great. And you look amazing, Geoff! How is everything?"

"Very good. When I heard you were coming, I couldn't help myself." He motioned to the kitchen door, which now opened to display a chocolate soufflé with fiery sparkles dancing around it. "Thank you so much for always being you, Jaden." He hugged her again.

"Geoff, thank you. This is so special."

With a smile, he turned his attention to Ivan. "Thank you for bringing this little lady back home—even if it's only for tonight."

"It's my pleasure. How are you feeling?"

"Like I'm twenty again. Thank you so much!" He extended his hand for a shake.

"Wait," said Jaden. "You're a patient?"

"A very happy one," Geoff said with a smile. "Your boyfriend does wonders. I haven't felt this good in years."

"Why didn't you tell me?"

"That, my lady, is illegal," Ivan noted.

"Well, it was so nice seeing you, but duty calls so I must get back to work." Geoff smiled. "I'm taking care of the check. The tip's on you."

"Thank you," Ivan and Jaden said together as Micky's mouth fell open.

Once Geoff had gone, Ivan smiled back at Micky and winked. "Don't worry. I got it."

"You slick son of a bitch!" Micky said. "You can swim in shit and come out smelling like a rose, can't you?"

He just shrugged.

Jaden hugged him. "Next time you play doctor, it had better be with me," she whispered before turning back to the soufflé.

He gave her a look to let her know he was filing that one away for later.

After topping off their five-star meal with chocolate soufflé and too much wine, eyes all around the table grew heavy and the inevitable time to call it a night swept over them. Ivan pushed away from the table and tossed down the money for the tip before helping Jaden to her feet. "Let's hit it."

They exchanged sleepy hugs, and Tasha and Micky insisted Jaden and Ivan take the first cab available. Snuggled together, they seemed content to wait for another.

As the cab drove them through crowded Miami Beach streets, Ivan watched Jaden, thrilled all over again to have her with him—and back in Miami no less. Her head bobbed and rolled as she fought against the dreaded food coma, with a lack-of-sleep chaser.

"See, you needed a nap too!" He chuckled.

A hum of acknowledgement was all she could muster.

Minutes later, the cab rolled to a stop in the horseshoe drive at his apartment building. He shuffled her upstairs and helped her to bed. She was fast asleep before her head hit the pillow.

Dead tired, he lay down next to her, but sleep wouldn't come. Instead he just looked, admiring her in the dark as she slept. This would be the last time they slept together as boyfriend and girlfriend. He could hardly imagine what tomorrow would bring.

CHAPTER 26

"Crash Into Me"

A Miami Beach sunrise cast rays of light and color across the blue sky, and they bounced off clouds, water, and the distant Miami skyline. Thin beams filtered through the blinds and warmed the room where Jaden and Ivan lay snuggled together in bed.

Jaden blinked as her eyes adjusted to the morning light. Ivan's heavy arm draped over her middle, and his warm body pressed against her backside. She ran her hand over his forearm and snuggled closer into him, matching his posture curve for curve. He was the perfect spooning partner. He was the perfect lover. He was—well, good morning to you too!—completely dependable. Even his morning hard-on was like clockwork. How amazing to wake up and find everything right, everything familiar. She closed her eyes for a moment as the horrid feeling of disorientation and isolating fear from that morning not so long ago shot through her.

Forward, she reminded herself. *Move forward.* Forcing a smile, she wiggled her ass against his erection and stifled a laugh. His breath in her ear told her he was still asleep, but she knew he wouldn't be for long. She glanced around the room and noticed a lab coat hanging from a freestanding mirror in the corner. A very erotic thought came to mind, surprising her.

She rolled over and nudged Ivan awake.

"What?" he mumbled without opening his eyes.

"Explain to me how you treat women's sexual health."

His eyebrows furrowed. "What?"

"What is sexual augmentation? I've never really asked you."

"Better orgasm for a better tomorrow," he quipped.

"Why have you never used it on me?"

He cranked one eye open and studied her for a moment, then closed it again. A smile played on his lips as he pulled her close. "I don't think you need it. You come like a champ."

Giggling, she slapped his shoulder.

"Ow!"

"I want the full consult. *Now.*"

His eyes flew open, and the grin on his face grew wider.

"I'll pay you," she said reaching for what she knew would get his attention.

"Is that right?" he inquired as she stroked his dick. "You want to become my patient? Papers and all? The full shebang?"

"Yes, doctor."

He assessed her for another moment, then smiled. "Well, then, you'd better get dressed. You don't want to miss your appointment."

"Really? You'll do it?" Jaden matched his smile and gave him a quick kiss.

He sat up to glance at his phone. "I just happen to have an opening in my schedule. Twenty minutes in the living room, Ms. Thorne. Don't be late."

She threw back the covers and jumped out of bed, rushing to choose an outfit and get ready for what was sure to be some kinky sex. As she rifled through her belongings she felt him behind her. She turned, and he handed her an iPad with a patient history form open on the screen.

"Please fill this out, Ms. Thorne. The doctor will be with you shortly. And take this." He dropped a small, round greenish pill into her hand.

She gave him a questioning look. "Don't you usually discuss first, prescribe later?"

He shrugged. "You want the full consult, right? Fill out that form and put that under your tongue to dissolve."

"Oookay," she said with a sultry smile. "And if this is the full consult, I want the lab coat on, doctor."

"It's the full consult, Ms. Thorne, I assure you. I only put the lab coat on for VIP clients, so you'd better be paying well," he called as he disappeared.

Settling on black pants, red heels, and a red blouse, she opted for buttoned-up sexy, rather than the lift-my-skirt-up-and-fuck-me-hard attire she knew he liked. This was business, and she meant it. Making a quick pit stop in the bathroom to prepare, she ran a comb through her hair, brushed her teeth, and dabbed on some makeup. Then she grabbed the iPad and headed for the couch, placing the small pill under her tongue as she'd been instructed.

"Mmmmm…kiwi," she said to herself as she began to type.

Name: <u>Jaden Thorne</u>

Sex: <u>Hard and deep…I mean, female</u>

Age: <u>27</u>

Birthday: <u>September 11</u>

Chief Complaint/Reason For Visit: <u>I want to come harder and more frequently with my boyfriend!</u>

Past Medical History/Past Surgical History: <u>None</u>

Family History: <u>High blood pressure—Mom; High cholesterol—Dad</u>

Tobacco? <u>Fuck no.</u>

Alcohol? <u>When the spirit moves me</u>

She stopped before the next two questions. These needed to be answered in just the right way.

Marital Status: <u>Open to adjustment</u>

Living Arrangement: <u>Alone, unfortunately</u>

Yes, that should do.

Allergies: <u>None</u>

Medications: <u>Birth control, and whatever is currently dissolving under my tongue</u>

REVIEW OF SYSTEMS

After scanning the next batch of questions, she decided to click "normal" after each one. At present, there wasn't much of anything wrong that couldn't be fixed by her boyfriend living closer.

General, Psych, Cardio, Pulmonary, and GI all received normal checkmarks. But she did find a few spots in need of comment.

Breast: <u>Needs fondling</u>

Gyn: <u>Needs exam</u>

Rectal: <u>Already examined</u>

She laughed to herself after this one and got a little turned on. Goodness, the doctor wasn't even in yet.

And then he was. At that moment Ivan emerged from his bedroom and rounded the corner. She swallowed hard. He'd dressed his part tip to toe. All he needed was theme music as he approached her with a whole new aura — one she hadn't seen before. He was in professional mode, and yet also dripping with raw, sexual power.

His hair hung around his collar, and he'd shaved. His dress shirt was open at the neck, exposing a bit of his smooth chest, and the whole package was wrapped in that gorgeous white coat. The stethoscope around his neck drove her even more wild. *I hope he uses that.* She wanted to jump off the couch and fuck him on the spot, but that would break character, and she wasn't about to ruin her own fantasy.

"Good morning, doctor," she said in a sultry voice.

"Morning, Ms. Thorne. How are you today?" He took a seat in front of her and crossed his legs. A wave of his cologne washed over her, and she grew even more damp. He picked up the tablet and began reading. After a moment he stifled a laugh.

"What?" she asked innocently.

"Well, I want to thank you for filling out your paperwork so thoroughly. Your suggestions are quite helpful."

She smiled.

"Let's see…So you want more, and more explosive, orgasms, and it seems you need some examining."

"Yes. That's correct."

"Well, let's get you checked out and see if we can't move you toward your goals immediately."

As he came closer, she began to feel oddly on edge, excited and a bit flushed all over. *What is this?* she thought. *Is role playing my thing?*

Ivan took a seat beside her, and they exchanged smiles. "Sit up straight and unbutton the top of your blouse," he instructed.

Once she'd complied, he slipped the stethoscope from his neck and placed it against her chest through the open neck of her shirt. The cold steel felt exhilarating on her skin, particularly in contrast to his warm, firm hand on her back. She felt herself flush with him so near. It was as if he had her under some intoxicating spell.

"You're tachycardic," he said in a low, authoritative tone.

Her breath hitched a little. "And what does that mean?" She looked into his eyes.

"It can mean a few things. Maybe you're overweight and need to increase your heart rate to pump more blood to your massive body."

She laughed out loud.

"Yes, I can see that isn't the case. Maybe you don't have enough blood in your system, but that is also unlikely. This could be a side effect of too much alcohol, caffeine, or medication, but those are also unlikely considering the timing and your answers. An electrical problem could cause your heart to beat frantically for no reason, but you're healthy with no cardiac history. Hmmm…" He paused for a moment, and his hands crept toward her already hard nipples. "The only reasonable conclusion I can draw is that you're sexually aroused and anxious to maximize your orgasmic potential. We'll have to test a few things."

Jaden knew this consult was about to take a dirty turn. "And what test will confirm that?"

"I'll have to do an in-depth pelvic exam, along with a sexual enhancement challenge where I cause you to orgasm and gauge its intensity," he explained calmly. "Do you consent to such a procedure?"

"I insist." Just the thought of him inside her made her slippery wet.

"First you must sign this." He grabbed a paper and pen from the table and handed them to her.

"Okay." She scribbled *Jaden Elizabeth Thorne* across the paper.

"We'll begin with a full-body exam. I'll need you to stand up for me and remove your pants and blouse," he explained in that same authoritative voice. "Slowly."

Without hesitation she stood and began to remove her clothing, watching him as he watched her undress. She let her pants slide down, exposing her frilly white boy shorts. When she bent to remove her heels, he stopped her. "Leave the shoes on. Everything else should be taken off immediately."

She arched her eyebrows, then slowly unbuttoned her shirt. She could tell he was hard by the way he was sitting. *I fucking love this so much.*

When the last button came undone, she let her shirt fall off her back and onto the floor. She stood in front of him in nothing but boy shorts and high heels, enjoying the way his eyes drifted over her body.

"Turn around so I can check for any signs of scoliosis."

Doing a one-eighty, she turned and stuck out the ass he loved for inspection. He placed his hand on her back, and she gasped as a new shot of lust flushed warm on her skin. He ran a finger up and down her spine, checking every vertebra. Every touch was a jolt of pleasure that ran through her nervous system like brush fire.

His thumbs came to rest on her hips, and she felt him dig into the two dimples just above the crack of her ass. "Checking for symmetry," he murmured. "Bend over." It wasn't a request.

"Yes, doctor." She bent to touch the floor. She felt his firm cock brush the side of her hip. *Oh, I want that.*

"Come back up slowly."

She stood and straightened her spine once more.

"All right, Ms. Thorne. Please lay on the floor. On your back."

Jaden arranged herself on the plush carpet. He knelt beside her.

"Cross your arms." He rolled her toward him, cupped one hand around her spine, and lowered her back to the floor with his hand under her. "Do you trust me?"

Absorbed in the moment, she just nodded.

"Then breathe in…and out," he instructed, placing his other hand on her crossed arms.

As she exhaled he drove the full force of his weight directly though her and into the floor, eliciting a string of cracks and crunches from her spine. Shots of ecstasy burst through her body as she nearly came at the sensation of her back orgasming in such a way. "Holy shit!"

Ivan didn't say a word, but a smile played on his lips as he repositioned himself near her head.

"That was—"

"Shhh…we aren't done yet."

God, she wanted him.

He placed his hands around her neck, and Jaden was surprised that no fear or inhibition bubbled up in her. She just laid there—topless in high heels—and let her personal physician do his work. Taking her head in one hand and her neck in another, he transitioned her neck to the left, bent her head right, then rotated everything left. "Relax and breathe in…and out."

As she did so he gave another quick thrust that, as with her back, yielded cracks and crunches and felt like an orgasm in her neck. "Oh my God! I love that."

He set up the same position on the opposite side.

Crack-crunch, crack-crunch. Again her neck orgasmed.

"Fuck!"

He bit back a smile and held out his hand to help her stand. "It's time for your pelvic exam. I need you to remove your panties and sit on the side of the couch."

She hitched her thumbs into the elastic and began to shimmy them down.

"Slowly," he demanded. "You must do it slowly."

In slow motion, she moved to the couch and pulled her boy shorts down, exposing everything she had. She leaned back on her elbows and spread her legs wide, inviting him to do his job.

After a moment he sauntered over and knelt in front of his patient. "Are you ready for your pelvic exam, Ms. Thorne?"

Sucking on her fingers, she nodded.

He reached under her hips and pulled her to lie on her back. He hooked her legs around his elbows and inched her closer and closer to the edge of the couch until her hips teetered at the precipice. Then he went to work.

"Let's see here. Your labium major is smooth and soft. Good start," he said, stroking the outside of her pussy with his fingers.

The second he touched her, her heart raced in anticipation.

Then he spreading her outer lips and moved deeper. "Your labia minor is extremely wet, indicating you are primed for sexual activity. Your clitoris is becoming engorged with blood and is much more sensitive thanks to the nitric oxide in your system." He leaned in and licked her fully exposed clit, just about causing her to come on the spot, and her legs nearly crushed his head. Without a word he returned to his kneeling position and continued his exam.

"This physiological reaction is due to chemical responses in the brain and adrenal system," he explained as he inserted his finger into her vagina and fucked her with it, driving her insane. "Your testosterone level has peaked, and your sexual desire is obviously high. The choline released by your brain right now is stimulating your urethral glands to produce lubrication. Couple this with the increased pressure of your vaginal wall, which forces lubricating plasma through your capillaries and onto its surface, and you have the reason you're dripping wet. And your estrogen is making sure these processes run smoothly and without hesitation. It's beautiful. Just beautiful."

She loved the way he appreciated the human body and even more the way he particularly appreciated hers. She could see the infatuation in his eyes as his fingers began to move more quickly and explore her. She squirmed and rocked into her doctor's touch. She gasped and dug her fingers into her thighs.

"Now the feeling you have right there—"

"Fuck!"

"That feeling of a pleasurable reward is dopamine being released in your brain, which is telling you this is good and not to not let me stop until you come—your ultimate reward."

"Fuck! Don't stop, doctor. Please don't stop!" she said, finding it hard to keep her eyes in focus. *What is going on?* Being fingered had never felt so goddamn good.

"Now your vagina is relaxing and elongating in hopes of being penetrated with something more than just a finger."

"Do it, then! God, yes! Do it."

"In time," he said as he repositioned the angle and motion of his hand. "Now for the actual orgasm. Are you ready for your evaluation?"

"God! Fuck! Ahhh!"

"I'll take that as a yes," he said, increasing his speed once again.

"The sensation you feel building right now—the one that promises something better with each stroke? That's a result of oxytocin building in your system and wreaking sexual havoc on your mind and body."

Jaden now writhed under his touch and raised her legs even higher to give him more access.

"It is the number one orgasm neurotransmitter in your body, and this, Ms. Thorne, is the answer to your question. This is the center of my sexual enhancement treatment."

Her climax drew closer and closer and promised to be one of the biggest of her life. She bounced herself back and forth against his hands, which worked her into a bliss she hadn't felt before.

"It's the little green pill you took just before your exam, and it's the reason for what you are about to feel. Are you ready, Ms. Thorne?" His voice rang in her ears and throughout her body.

"Oh, God! Yes! Yes!"

He leaned into her and curled his hand in a way that sent her soaring. Her body quivered as she rocked back and forth, kicking and flailing her arms against the sofa. She even kicked his fingers out of her as she came in a way she'd never come before. Her orgasmic screams filled the room as come ran down her thighs and her mind shut off. She was transported to a place she'd never been, but now wished she could live—a place without inhibitions, rules, jobs, or worries. A place of unity and earth-shattering orgasm.

As she came down from her high, a feeling of peace and trust settled over her. Eventually she was able to focus on her stunned doctor, who still knelt before her.

"I knew it worked great, but damn! I should charge more," he said with a smile.

She laughed. Wearing nothing but her heels, she looked down at him from between her legs. "Wow, that's a first," she said, a bit embarrassed as she noticed her juices covering the couch, the floor, and—oh yes—his fabulous doctor coat.

"Now I know how you must feel," he joked as he removed the jacket and curled up beside her on the couch.

"I hope that isn't how all your exams go."

"No, if they squirt like that, I charge them extra."

Laughing, she kissed him. "That was fucking hot."

"Yes. Yes, it was, baby girl."

CHAPTER 27

"In the Air Tonight"

The air remained chilled after the mid-afternoon showers that had swept through Miami Beach. Gazing across the bay from Ivan's balcony, Jaden drank in the oranges and yellows and pinks that painted the Miami skyline as the sun set. She leaned against the railing and breathed in the smell of ocean, willing away the sense of worry that was her near-constant companion these days, always lingering just below the surface. Convincing herself again that she'd chosen the right path forward, she tried to focus on the beauty of the sunset.

In the background, Phil Collins sang of something in the air, and she took a sip of the wine Ivan had poured her. The bouquet of flavors danced across her tongue and rolled down the back of her throat, raising goose bumps on her arms and under the silky green dress that hugged her body tight.

As she scanned the islands scattered throughout the bay, marked by flickering lights, and listened to the crowd at the pool twelve stories below her, she remembered why Miami was such a magical place. And tonight was the night she'd get to watch her lifelong friend's dream come true.

With a smile, she thought about all the times she and Tasha had imagined their weddings and their dream men. From gabbing over juice boxes to sipping cocktails, they'd long envisioned the day when just the right man would slip a diamond on their finger and they'd say yes. Jaden began to sway to the music and couldn't help but feel a bit jealous. But surely her day would come. She and Ivan were on firm ground with a wonderful future ahead. It was just a matter of getting there. For now, she'd be content with being happy for her best friend.

She glanced inside to find Ivan scurrying around half naked, talking on the phone and texting as he tried to get the rest of his suit on. *Wow, he's pretty stressed.* Helping to organize such an important moment was a big deal, but this was the first time she'd been ready before him in their entire relationship. She watched as he paced back and forth: black shoes, black pants, and a black shirt, unbuttoned with shirttails fluttering at his sides. His open shirt exposed his abs and chest in just the right way to get a girl hot and bothered—not to mention wet.

As she watched him, she knew he'd given her the greatest happiness she'd ever known. This was the man she wanted to wake up next to every morning. This was the man she'd confide in and trust with her most intimate self. He knew her better than she knew herself sometimes. Why hadn't it always been clear? When she was with Ivan, nothing was missing, and she was missing nothing. If he were to ask her, she'd have nothing to say but yes. And she'd make sure he asked her. No more mistakes. No more doubts. She was his.

"You okay?" he called from the living room.

"More than you know," she said with a smile. "You look stressed. Come join me and have some wine."

He checked his reflection in the mirror and ran a quick hand through his hair. "That's an excellent idea." He turned his attention to her and stepped onto the balcony, smiling all the way.

He grabbed the wine glass he'd abandoned earlier when balcony sex had been the priority. After taking a sip, he gathered her into his arms and embraced her as if he might never let go. She felt him breathe her in as she did the same. She ran her hands up his back and under his shirt, taking comfort in his warmth.

"You mean the world to me," he whispered as his arms tightened around her.

She squeezed him in return.

He relaxed his embrace and stepped back just enough to raise his glass in toast. "Here's to a night where words make wishes come true…a night when fate dictates an eternity."

She smiled as they clinked glasses and turned toward the Miami skyline. It had provided the backdrop to so many of their nights together.

"Beautiful, eh?"

"Yes, it is. I miss it so much. But it's moments like these that make it all worthwhile." She took his hand in hers.

He smiled. "You never have to leave if you don't want to."

She nuzzled her head against his shoulder and sighed. "One of these times, I may not."

He put his arm around her, and she felt exhilarated at the thought of spending the rest of her days in this moment with him. It was perfect—the sights, the smells, the sensations, the romance, the man.

"Well, I hope tonight goes off without a hitch," he finally said.

"It will. I know Tasha's going to say yes, and I know you've made sure it will be quite the show. I wonder how Micky's feeling right now."

"Nervous, scared, anxious, happy, overwhelmed…I'm guessing, of course. Just a shot in the dark, really." He took a large gulp of wine.

"What are you nervous about? I'm sure everything is perfect. You should relax. Have fun. After all, you aren't the one proposing."

He laughed. "Yeah, well, I have to be sure my girl will say yes first."

"You'll never know if you never ask," she replied.

"Hmmm…well, after tonight I should be able to gauge where and when that question might pop up."

With that he pulled her close and kissed her. She tasted his lips and tried to ignore the shot of nervous electricity racing through her.

"You ready to get going?"

"Yes." She gave him one more quick kiss and hugged him before heading back into the apartment. She gathered her purse, found her shoes, and was surprised to find him still on the balcony when she returned. "You coming?" she called.

He took one last massive chug of his wine and smiled. "Yes, dear! But first I've got to finish getting dressed. I can't go anywhere like this."

CHAPTER 28

"Sail"

"Are we stopping in the lobby?" Jaden asked as she watched the elevator's descent.

"What?"

"Are we not taking Betty?"

"Oh! Nope. No Betty tonight," Ivan said with a laugh. "I decided to class it up a bit."

"I like the tie, doctor! We match." She straightened and smoothed his tie, which glimmered with hints of green.

"Well, isn't that a coinkydink?" He grabbed her waist.

Ding! The elevator doors opened and a couple that looked to be in their early hundreds exchanged places with them. They smiled at each other as they passed. Ivan took her hand and towed her along toward the front of the building.

"Could you handle me for that long?" he asked.

"I'd probably trade you in around seventy for a newer model."

"Isn't it supposed to be the other way around? It's the guy who usually upgrades his partner, isn't it?"

"Trade-in maybe, but upgrade? Could you do better than me?" She smiled as she motioned to the way her dress hugged her curves, but she felt a quick stab of conscience within.

Ivan turned and stopped her. He held up their clasped hands and turned her slowly so he could check her out.

"No way in hell," he concluded. "Perfection, baby."

"You just want to get into these panties again."

"Guilty. But also spoken from the heart, *mi amore*." He pulled her in for a soft kiss that was interrupted by a screeching cackle.

"Will you two knock it off? We have places to go and people to see," Tasha called from the end of the corridor.

Jaden looked up to find her friend standing with Micky, both of them dressed to an elegant perfection.

"Yeah, yeah, yeah. Can't a man show affection these days without being ridiculed?"

"As long as he doesn't keep his friends and the limo waiting!" Micky said.

"Limo?" she whispered.

"Well, a guy only gets to propose once, so I wanted to make sure it was perfect."

"Ahh, that's so nice, Ivan."

"You seem surprised. Jeez." He laughed as they joined their waiting posse.

"Everything go okay? Was the limo there on time?" Ivan asked Micky as the men shared a handshake and the girls a hug.

"Yes, sir. Right on time."

She felt her excitement brimming close to the surface. *Oh, if she only knew...* "You look gorgeous, Tasha," she gushed. "And you too, Micky. So nice!"

"We match," he said proudly as he adjusted his black and blue striped tie, which coordinated with Tasha's blue dress.

Jaden bit back a laugh and cut her eyes over to Ivan. "What a coinkydink."

He just smiled as he motioned to the black Chrysler 300 stretch limo parked outside the doors. "All right, let's get a move on. I'm starving and ready for a drink."

"Well there's a copious amount of champagne and booze in there, so I think we can get this party started on the drive over," Tasha said as she started to the door.

"Sounds like someone may have *already* started!" Jaden called.

With a nod over his shoulder, Micky confirmed her suspicion.

Outside they were greeted by a large, bouncer-type fellow dressed in black. "Hello, Dr. Rusilko. It's been too long."

"Yes, it has, Terrell." He stopped to chat with the driver and motioned for the other three to get in the car.

Jaden sat across from Tasha and Micky, reveling in their obvious natural connection. She wanted more than anything to jump across the seat and congratulate them, but she restrained herself.

When Ivan joined them, Micky pulled out a bottle of chilled sparkling Shiraz and poured four glasses. As the elongated car started its four-mile journey across Miami Beach, he took it upon himself to toast the group.

"To beautiful experiences with beautiful friends and making lasting memories," Micky said.

"Here, here!"

"Cheers!"

"Salud!"

After a collective sip, likely the first of many toasts to come this evening, Tasha leaned back in the seat. "So what is this event?"

"It's a fundraising dinner for a local charity—the Naked Foundation. They raise awareness and donate condoms to prevent HIV and STDs. And it's at The Bath Club," he added, taking another sip of wine.

Tasha nodded approvingly. "Thanks for getting us in!"

"Absolutely. I do a lot of work with them, so they owe me," he said with a laugh. "Should be a great event with amazing food and music. Think of those underground clubs where you knock on the door and a little panel slides opens and then shuts before they let you in...or not. 'Speakeasy cool' is the best way to describe it. They put a lot of work into the production."

"Sounds like it's gonna be fun!" Micky exclaimed, shooting Ivan a grin.

"Is it a red carpet thing? Are there gonna be a lot of people there?" Tasha asked. Jaden could see her celebrity radar preparing to spring into action.

"No, no, no. This will be very intimate. It's a sit-down dinner where people pay a lot of money to support the charity and enjoy the venue and the show. It's going to be a very special performance too."

She felt Ivan's hand grow damp with sweat. "Don't worry, babe, it'll be great. They'll love it," she whispered.

Ivan smiled and winked at her before downing some more bubbly.

"We're here, sir," the driver called. They all turned to see exactly where "here" was.

The car had stopped in front of a large set of wooden doors. The surrounding stones were covered in vines and illuminated by a soft, golden glow. Theirs was the only car in sight.

"You sure it's tonight?" Tasha asked. "Doesn't look like anyone's home."

"Positive."

The driver opened the door, and Tasha and Micky climbed out.

Before she got out, Jaden turned to Ivan, held his face in her hands, and kissed his lips. "I love you."

He smiled back at her, and before her hands slipped from his face, he leaned in and kissed her again.

After he helped her from the car, Ivan thanked the driver and led the crew to the massive, medieval-style wood and iron doors.

Knocking on the door elicited an unseen brusque voice. "Name on reservation?"

"Hey, darling. It's Ivan."

Darling? Jaden thought. *What the hell?*

"Hi, Ivan! One second."

The enormous doors creaked open and a gorgeous little blonde in a very tight black dress emerged.

"You look so much better than you sound on the other side of that door," he teased, giving her a friendly hug and kiss on the cheek. "Liz, this is my table for the evening."

"This must be Jaden, right?" she asked, completely unconcerned with Micky or Tasha.

"The one and only."

"Wow, you are *gorgeous*."

"Ah, thank you," Jaden said, a bit uncomfortable.

"So nice to meet you! I hope you all have fun," she said, smiling big as she directed them through the door.

"Thanks, Liz."

"Sure thing, doc."

Micky and Tasha went on ahead, and Jaden walked more slowly with Ivan as they entered the club.

"She was…nice."

"She's great. I tell everyone about you. Is that a bad thing?" Ivan smiled and squeezed her hand.

"No. Of course not. Just takes me by surprise sometimes."

"Oh! This way," Ivan called as he stepped ahead to direct the group out on to the patio for cocktails.

Jaden admired the beautiful space. Perfectly placed lighting created a magical glow, and an assortment of lounge furniture waited at the ready, along with an hors d'oeuvres table and a large wine bar. She smiled as she looked around. Every man in attendance was dressed in black, except for a tie to complement his date's ensemble.

The group helped themselves to the vino and bites and then found a spot to relax.

"I have to take care of some things, so I'll leave you guys to mix and mingle. Is that okay?" Ivan asked.

"Yes, of course, baby," she replied around a mouthful of food. "You do what you need to do. We're fine."

"Love you," he sang as he scurried off.

Jaden sipped her wine and turned her attention to the crowd. She felt at home as she noticed that many of the people she knew in Miami were here. She spotted Bert and Geoff in the crowd and excused herself to greet them. She was thrilled to catch up on Bert's new gig and talk further with Geoff about what was happening at Bianca. They were deep into a discussion of the new chef when she remembered Tasha and Micky. But a quick scan revealed them to be perfectly at ease and off making new friends. Tasha gestured broadly as they chatted with another well-dressed pair. Being with old friends back in Miami and seeing Tasha and Micky so happy was like heaven on earth. Jaden felt like herself again. No chance creepy Damian was going to pop up out of nowhere to ruin this. *It's going to be a great night.*

After a few minutes, Ivan reappeared with a boyish grin and a lot of extra energy.

"What's up?" she asked.

"Nothing. Just having fun!" he exclaimed. "You okay?"

"Yes! Why do you keep asking me that? This is amazing, baby." She gave him a quick kiss.

"Well, hopefully you feel the same way after dinner." He laughed and motioned toward the ballroom. Inside the dimly lit room, she could see a grouping of perfectly set tables, each with gorgeous linens, crystal glasses, and sparkling place settings.

"Is that where he's gonna do it?"

"Yep, that's where a poor sucker's going to pour his heart out."

She smacked him playfully. "It's a big deal to ask someone to marry you! Have some respect, eh?"

"I was teasing, baby! I can imagine just how big a deal it is." He squeezed her hand. "Let's grab a drink and find our table. They're starting dinner in five minutes."

"Okay, sounds like a plan. I'm so excited for them!"

Ivan scooped up two glasses of vino, followed by Tasha and Micky, and led them into the ballroom for dinner. They wound their way through the room to what had to be the best table in the house—right in front of the stage—where two velvet-wrapped bottles of wine flanked a beautiful floral centerpiece. Jaden glanced around at the other tables. No one else had little black velvet bags of deliciousness. Ivan had done this. It was the wine he loved and had shared with her. Even in the midst of helping Micky plan, he'd thought of her—of them. A pang of guilt stabbed her heart even as she smiled at the gesture.

As the others started to chatter about the venue and who was who among the attendees, Jaden looked around the elegant setting and the dark red roses featured at every table. At a closer look she confirmed her suspicion: they were all thornless.

"The menu looks good," Tasha mused as she reviewed the card set atop her plate. "Rosemary chicken with lime-infused steamed vegetables or filet mignon with garlic mashed potatoes and asparagus. Hmm…I think the meat and potatoes for me."

"I'll second that," Micky chimed in.

"And I think we'll counter that with the exact opposite," Ivan said with a chuckle.

"You guys are way too healthy," Tasha asserted as she finished off her wine. "What's in the bag?"

"More wine, my dear. It's a special night. Let's have some fun!" Ivan reached for one of the bottles and began to unwrap it. He motioned for a waiter to assist with the opening and pouring, and they raised their glasses for yet another toast.

"To friends!" Ivan announced.

Clink, clink, clink, clink!

"I don't know where you're going or where I'm going," he added, turning to Jaden. "But wherever that is, I hope we'll be there together. I love you."

Before she could speak, a voice boomed over the sound system.

"Hello, everyone, and welcome! I hope you're all having fantastic evening here at Behind Closed Doors, The Bath Club's charity event for the Naked Foundation."

The crowd erupted in applause, but she and Ivan just looked at each other: invincible, inseparable, and impossibly in love. It was magic.

The enthusiastic voice continued. "I'm Max, your hostess for this fabulous evening, and as we begin I want to give a special thanks to Dr. Ivan Rusilko. He has long been a supporter of the Naked Foundation, and he worked tirelessly to help make this event a success."

She gestured toward Ivan, and Jaden's eyes widened. "That's you, baby! Better give the people what they want."

He smiled and might have even blushed a bit as he took to the stage and accepted the microphone. "Everyone give it up for such a beautiful hostess!" he began, seeming instantly at ease. "My thanks to everyone here, as you've made a vital commitment to creating a better community and a better, healthier world. Tonight's Behind Closed Doors event is particularly special for me. And I'm sure we can all agree that this is truly magical, right?"

Enthusiastic applause sparked up around the room.

"It is an honor to support the Naked Foundation this evening and ensure that their important work around the world in the fight against HIV and other sexually transmitted diseases can continue," he added once he could be heard again. "I hope you'll join me in showing your appreciation and enthusiasm for such a noble cause. And by appreciation and enthusiasm, I mean penning some fat checks." He paused for a round of laughs from the crowd.

Jaden loved watching him work a crowd. Among his many other talents, he seemed to have a gift for improv. He could think on his feet with no problem, but she giggled as she recalled how reading lines was another story. He'd helped her get comfortable with her scripts in the early days of *One Hot Kitchen*. He'd fumble through them over the phone and get so pissed at himself, but she'd loved it.

"We're about to enjoy a delicious dinner, and we also have a great show for you this evening: the magnificent stylings of ALFIO, straight out of Australia and just for you, Miami Beach." The crowd greeted this news with yet another round of applause. "Before you dive into your meals, I want to welcome to the stage the president of entertainment for the Bath Club and our true host for the night, Gary Pallaria."

As the crowd clapped yet again Tasha turned around in her seat. "You having fun, girl? Ivan looks great up there."

"Yes, it's so nice to be back—" She stopped short at the sight of the man crossing the stage to join Ivan. Why did he look so familiar? The closer got to Ivan, the closer she came to recognition, but she still couldn't quite place him. Did she know him from Miami? Maybe it was someone Ivan had introduced her to before? That was probably it—he knew everyone.

As the two men shook hands, Ivan handed over the microphone, and the man addressed the crowd. "Hello! I want to welcome you to the beautiful Bath Club. Thanks for coming out tonight to support such a great cause!"

His accent…what is that? *Oh shit. Boston!* A feeling of complete and utter fear raced through her body and settled in her stomach, sending waves of nausea through her. She clasped her hand over her open mouth. "Oh my God," she muttered. *What have I done?*

CHAPTER 29

"Send in the Clowns"

"Are you okay?" Tasha asked. "What happened?"

Jaden wondered how horrible she must look. "I'm fine. Sorry, it must be the heat." *I am. I'm fine. Am I fine? No, I'm not. I am not fine!*

That Boston accent had dropped everything into place. Once Gary spoke, she remembered meeting him on that cursed night she'd tried so hard to forget. He'd been at the network gala in LA—the night she went home with Damian. *Oh, fuck. Fuck. Fuck.* Her careful plan to move forward, leaving past mistakes behind, began to unravel as the feelings she'd suppressed and forced into remission—kept there by the latest intimacies and explorations she'd shared with Ivan, his unbelievable connection with her family, and their renewed bond of love—now roared to the surface in a flurry of angst and turmoil.

How dare she try to conceal this?
How could she do this to the man
who's given her everything?

What's the big deal? It was a one
night thing, an accident.
She doesn't even remember.

Accident. Accident? Bullshit.
That's a bullshit excuse.

He's probably done the same thing.
You saw how the girl at the door
fucked him with her eyes.

He's never given any inkling
of infidelity. He's treated Jaden
like a queen.

But why has he been so nice? Is he
making up for something, just as
she's been doing with him—giving
her everything she wants to make
sure she's happy?

"Jaden? Jaden!"

She snapped out of the war zone and looked at Tasha, who seemed a little annoyed. "He needs your order. Do you want the chicken or beef?"

She looked up to find the waiter with an equally annoyed look on his face.

"Umm...chicken, please. Sorry."

She grabbed her glass of wine and tried to center herself—or at least tune out the torment. She couldn't decide which would be better.

"You okay, Jaden?" Micky asked. "You look a bit pale."

"I'm fine. Sorry...ah...just had a girl moment." She rolled her eyes, which seemed to confuse both Micky and Tasha.

"Okaaaay," Tasha replied.

Her eyes darted around the room, looking for Gary. *Was he talking to Ivan? Had he seen her and Damian getting friendly and leaving together? He certainly could have. He must have. Why did I ever think I could hide this? So stupid!* Frantically she searched the room and found Gary chatting with a sound engineer and pointing at various speakers that loomed above the crowd. Then a short time later she found Ivan on the opposite side of the room chatting with Max and a few other guests.

She blew out a relieved breath she hadn't realized she was holding. She breathed for a second and then began to convince herself everything was going to be fine. If Gary and Ivan just stayed on opposite sides of the room all night, everything would be okay. Her stomach tossed and turned.

Jaden glanced across the table at Tasha and Micky, now lost in themselves again. Their over-the-top affection could usually make her smile, but tonight it just made her even more sick. This was supposed to be their big evening, and all she wanted to do was curl up in a ball somewhere alone. *I would do anything to put that night behind me.* She took another sip of wine and watched as Ivan excused himself from the small group he'd been chatting with and headed across the room toward Gary. *Shit, shit, shit! No, no, no! What's he doing?*

Oh, she's screwed. Karma!

No, she isn't. She didn't do anything.
It was an accident.

*Yes, she is. She probably fucked another
man, certainly lied about it, and has
been acting like nothing's wrong.*

People do it all the time. She's young,
and they aren't married.

*She's leading him on. Living a lie just
to keep her dirty little secret.*

He's happy, so who cares?
Again, they aren't married.

*So what if they were?
What would happen then?*

Doesn't matter. They aren't, and they
won't be for a while. Time heals all.

That's bullshit.

"Here you go, ma'am." A waitress interrupted round two of Jaden's inner battle to place a caprese salad in front of her. The smell of food, even food this good, only kicked up her nausea.

"Delicious," Tasha called from across the table with a mouth full of tomato.

Jaden managed a smile she hoped seemed enthusiastic as she cut the tiniest bite possible from a piece of mozzarella. As she put it in her mouth, willing it to stay down, she leaned over to look past Tasha. She watched as Ivan and Gary shared another handshake. Gary pointed out various places around the room and motioned to what looked like a spotlight in the far corner. The another man joined them. The singer? They had to be getting ready for the show. Good. As long as they were busy with logistics, Gary wouldn't be making any small talk. At least she hoped not. And maybe he didn't know. Maybe he left early. Maybe he hadn't paid that much attention to her. Was she nervous for no reason?

Continuing to watch them as she moved her salad around on her plate, she noticed their attention now seemed to fall squarely on their table. But why? The hand gestures and animated conversation made her anxiety worse.

Oh! Micky! This was how he was going to ask Tasha—during the show. *How sweet.* But that meant all eyes would be on their table, including Gary's. Should she, could she excuse herself when the show started? What was better: missing the most important moment of her best friend's life or risking the chance she'd be identified and her relationship with Ivan ruined? How could she explain why she'd hidden this from him? Round three started up where it left off.

She's nervous. She knows she's doing something wrong.

She isn't nervous, and she's moving on with her life.

Wrong is hiding something from your lover.

Wrong is ruining a wonderful relationship. She was experiencing life.

Experiencing life…but hurting someone else.

So there's no need to hurt him more. She's learned from her mistake.

Love is about trust. If she disregards
this, she's disregarding love.

He won't find out. Relax.

He needs to find out.

Swishhhhh… The lights faded and a spotlight cast a radiant glow on the evening's hostess. Max's black dress shimmered. "Ladies and gentleman, for your entertainment I am pleased to introduce a story of love, lust, and a beginning tonight. Put your hands together for the sweet serenades of ALFIO!"

Fuck! There's no graceful way of getting out of this now. Jaden watched Micky and Tasha's faces light up when the spotlight fell on the only man in the room not dressed in black. His gray suit seemed to glow softly under the illumination. He was seated at a baby grand piano. A soft string of notes poured out of the instrument and in-stantly soothed Jaden's warring mind—at least for a moment. ALFIO leaned in to the microphone, and his beautiful voice filled the room. His rendition of the Ave Maria silenced the crowd in an instant.

Where is Ivan? she thought, noticing the goose bumps that had raised on her arms. She needed him. His touch would silence all her doubt. She was doing it for him. She would never again hurt him or what they had. *No need to put him through your mistake as well.*

Her eyes returned to ALFIO's hands, which seemed to float over the keys. As she hummed along with the familiar tune, she felt a bit more comfortable. It was beautiful. When the Ave Maria came to an end, ALFIO stood and came to center stage for a well-deserved ovation.

"Thank you all for coming tonight to support such a great cause," he told the audience. "It's an honor to be here, and I'm so happy to share such a lovely experience with such lovely people. This next song goes out to a friend in the audience tonight. Good luck, my friend."

How does Micky know this guy? Jaden wondered. Perhaps Ivan had introduced them. What a prelude this was going to be! In spite of her panic, she felt a flicker of excitement for Tasha as well. The audi-ence *oohed* and *aaahed* when a second spotlight revealed a group of musicians —a full big band orchestra— behind ALFIO on the stage.

But as the music began, Jaden's heart froze. The notes linked themselves into the unmistakable start of the song that had been the theme for a wine-soaked tryst. As ALFIO's voice joined the piano and horns, a story unfolded in her mind—one she cherished above all else and would do anything not to lose. As her and Ivan's song echoed through the ballroom, she closed her eyes. Before her flashed their very first dance in the garden, their sea turtle-watching escapade, their night in the Pennsylvania forest, the sight of him at Bianca when he'd tracked her down, the faces of his family—and hers. Soaking through it all was his unmistakable, delectable smell. The scent that kept her grounded and had thrilled her since their first embrace. She could almost smell him now…and it wasn't faint or subtle. It was almost overpowering. As if he were right—

A flash of light burst through her eyelids as the music faded to silence. She opened her eyes to find herself bathed in the spotlight—not Micky, not Tasha. She sat as the centerpiece to something above and beyond her. She sat with nothing but her thoughts and the intoxicating scent she would forever associate with love.

Slowly she turned in her seat to find not a doctor, not a model, not a player on the Miami scene, but just a humble man in a black suit. Ivan knelt on one knee with his heart on his sleeve, a smile on his face, and his soul on the line. He held a box with a ring that she knew was so much more than a stone. It was a commitment. A commitment to love her for the rest of her life.

She felt numb, paralyzed. There were no voices now to tell her yes or no. She was alone. She looked into his eyes. She loved everything about him. He treated her like no one ever had. He was the man she'd dreamed of meeting her entire life. He was perfect for her.

And so she couldn't sell him short. She took a moment and breathed him into her heart and soul for what might be the last time.

"I don't deserve you, Ivan…I am so sorry."

She stood with tears blinding her and turned away from the only man she'd ever love. And then she began to run.

Hushed whispers echoed through the crowd, and all eyes focused on Ivan as the evening came to an abrupt halt. Tasha sat astonished as Jaden disappeared out the door, and he appeared unable to move from his position on the ground. Slowly he looked around, and when his eyes fell on hers, she tried to think of something to say, some way to explain. But she had no idea and no words. He smiled strangely at her, clearly hiding a wall of emotions about to burst forth. She tried her best to smile back and squeezed Micky's hand desperately. Then he stood and walked out of the room, leaving through an entirely different door than Jaden had.

Tasha waited until the door closed behind him before leaping from her chair and running after Jaden. She searched the ladies room, and finding it empty, she rushed to the parking lot. She spotted a slender figure dressed in green collapsed on a bench. As she drew closer, she could hear her friend sobbing into the night. *Oh, Jaden.* Tasha gathered up her skirt and ran. "What's going on?" she asked as she sat next to her on the bench. "What happened? Are you okay?"

Jaden said nothing, but she turned and fell into Tasha's opened arms. Her words were a jumbled mess as she tried to speak through her tears. "I...I can't live like this. He deserves the truth. *I* deserve the truth. I just need to know. I...I have to go back."

"What are you talking about? What do you need to know, Jaden?" She tried to make her voice soft and comforting, rather than simply confused.

"I just need to get back," Jaden repeated, starting a fresh wave of tears.

"Babe, calm down. It's okay if you're not ready to get married. That was unexpected and a lot to take in — maybe too much. Take some deep breaths and relax. I'm sure Ivan will understand if you tell him you need more time."

"That's not it!" Jaden yelled. "I want nothing more than to marry Ivan."

Tasha bit her tongue and took some deep breaths herself. "Then what's the problem?"

"I went home with Damian," Jaden screamed, her voice full of anguish.

As Tasha composed her next words, trying to get them just right, she looked out into the night and froze. Jaden must have felt her stiffen, because she too looked up. And saw Ivan standing there.

Instantly her demeanor changed. She wiped her eyes and stood, as if ready to accept whatever lay ahead. "Ivan, I'm so sorry. I should have explained this long ago, and now I'm not sure where to begin. I just missed you, and I was confused, and I don't even really know for sure what—"

Ivan raised a hand, stopping her, and he shook his head, a look of heartbreak on his face. Tasha watched in horror as he turned on his heel and stalked off into the night. Would Jaden go after him? She looked over at her, but found her firmly planted on the bench, her face mirroring the heartbreak Ivan's had shown moments before.

As the first drops of rain began to fall, Tasha knew she needed to take action. Noting the line of taxis near the building, she gathered Jaden in her arms and pulled her to her feet. "Come on, Jaden. Let's go home."

Once inside the cab, Jaden laid across the back seat, sobbing. Tasha stroked her hair and offered comforting words that seemed to do nothing to soothe the pain.

CHAPTER 30

"If You Could Read My Mind"

Ivan stared at the rising sun as it crested the horizon. Facing an ocean once full of dreams and promise, he sat alone in the sand, still wearing the suit his heart had been broken in.

Wave after wave rolled in, mimicking the sadness that swept over him, taking a piece of his heart away with it each time. Even the smell of the ocean was different now. No longer beautiful and vibrant, it now smelled of something spoiled and decomposing. And the colors the sun painted across the sky seemed pale, as if someone had removed pigment from their usually glorious palette.

He stumbled through his thoughts, unable to process his next move. How could she do this? Had her love always been a lie? No... What they'd had was real — wasn't it? He just couldn't bear to hear her try to explain it away. What he'd heard was enough. She'd been with someone else. That was it. Deal with it. Move on.

So why was it so hard to breathe?

"What now?" he asked aloud as the beach began to come to life.

He didn't know the answer. He didn't *want* to know the answer. He didn't want to know a life without her. Without them. He dropped his head into his hands. *Had she been worth it?*

As he shifted in the sand he felt a sharp pinch against his hip. He reached into his pocket and found the small black box that contained the commitment he'd offered Jaden. A commitment she'd refused. He turned the little box over in his hands, and tears welled up inside him for the first time, threatening to breach the perimeter he'd stubbornly held for hours.

He opened the box and stared at the ring through blurry eyes. It was nothing more than a bit of metal and stone—nothing precious about it now. Its carat size and purity rating didn't mean anything. They never had. He snapped the box shut, squeezed a fist around it, and dropped his chin to his chest. Broken and defeated, he let the tears fall. And the weakness he felt in this surrender made him feel more alone. He'd lost something precious, his chances of finding it again were next to impossible, and that hurt. He'd lost his miracle. And perhaps worse than that, for all he knew it had been a lie all along.

You'll find a way through this, said a voice inside him. He didn't believe it, but he was desperate to find even the smallest measure of comfort. After all, it was in the wake of a romantic rock bottom where he'd found her in the first place. He looked up at the nearly colorless sky above him and blew out a ragged breath. He wiped his eyes with the back of his hand, turned his attention back to the foamy water that ebbed and flowed in front of him, and wished like hell for a resolve that never came.

After the sun had climbed into the sky, he tucked the black box into his jacket pocket and stood to find himself exhausted. He made a half-assed effort to brush the sand from his clothes and began the walk home.

When he'd cleared the sand and stepped onto the paved walk, he heard a raspy voice.

"Hey, man. Hey, man. You look beat up, man."

He glanced around, trying to identify the source of such a dead-on assessment. A disheveled man with a long beard and even longer hair, which had matted into what looked like a helmet, sat on the seawall.

"Hey, man, was she worth it?"

"What's that?"

"Was she worth it, man? Ain't nobody gonna ruin clothes like that for no reason."

Ivan looked down at his suit and breathed out a sad laugh. It was ruined. Jaden hadn't laid a finger on him, but she'd managed to destroy another suit. This time she'd destroyed his heart too.

"It's gotta be. Gotta be a woman to cause that kind of foolishness," the man added with an animated nod.

"Impressive," Ivan conceded. "You're quite observant, aren't you?" He'd walked a few steps down the path when he heard the voice again.

"You didn't answer my question, man. Was she worth it?"

He shoved his hands into the shallow pockets of his jacket, rocked on his heels, and dropped his head. As his hand brushed the rounded edges of the black box, he realized he hadn't answered that question for himself, let alone this guy. He pulled out the box and held it in the palm of his hand.

Images of vineyards and mountains, cabins and beaches, airports and balconies, parties and kitchens played out like a movie in his mind and ended with the face of the woman who'd taught him that real love is a privilege only a few ever enjoy. How long it lasts is inconsequential. It's what you do with the time when this feeling is shared that makes it special.

He closed his hand around the box, closed his eyes, and asked himself one last time. *Was she worth this heart-wrenching emptiness?* Exhaling his decision, he turned to the man and smiled. He tossed him the box that once had contained a commitment and now held just a ring.

"Yeah, man, she was. Love...love *is* worth the fall."

CHAPTER 31

"Love is Worth the Fall"

The smell of the Los Angeles airport hit her like a wall as she stepped off the overcrowded plane. Her eyes, rubbed raw from nonstop crying the night before, now hid behind a pair of oversized Jackie O sunglasses she'd borrowed from Tasha. Looking down at herself in the clothes she'd also borrowed from Tasha, Jaden felt ugly. Not because of what she was wearing—she didn't care about that. The ugliness she felt came from the inside out. Everything was a mess, and it was all her fault.

Thank God for Tasha, she thought and remained amazed by the fact that her friend hadn't asked one question or made any accusations as she consoled her throughout the night. She was lucky to have her.

As she made her way through the terminal, she dodged the early morning buzz of tourists scurrying about getting ready for their flights. Their happy faces rubbed salt in the gaping wound she'd inflicted on herself less than twelve hours ago. She wished she could go back to the time when she and Ivan had traveled with similar looks on their faces. At the thought of their trip to visit his family in Meadville, instinct and emotion dictated more crying, but she couldn't. She had no more tears to cry.

As the exit doors parted, the mellow warmth of California greeted her, followed quickly by the smell of exhaust and the sounds of horns and buses, which beat down on her already cluttered mind. She felt guilty as hell asking Adam to drive her on a day she knew he reserved for his family, but she also knew he'd help her if he could. Her knotted stomach and killer headache only amped up her anxiety. At least now she wouldn't have to do this on her own.

Today she would face her most colossal mistake. She would look into the eyes of her real-life demon and get the answer to a question she wished she didn't have to ask. She'd given up the love of her life because of an indiscretion she couldn't recall, and suddenly, immediately, she needed the truth. She owed it to herself, and she owed it to Ivan.

"Where the hell is he? He's always right here," she muttered seconds before Adam's familiar town car swung to a stop at the curb.

He came running around the car to make sure she got in all right, but instead of sliding in, she collapsed against his shoulders. "Thank you, Adam, for picking me up. I'm so sorry to have called but —"

"Jaden, stop. You've been nothing but kind since the day I met you, and I consider you family. Of course I want to help."

Even in the fog of emotion, she noticed he'd called her by her first name. She wiped away her tears with a quick hand and managed a smile.

"Now, let's get you home and —"

"No. No!" She pushed away from his guiding hand, leaving him a bit flustered. "No, I don't want to go home. I want you to take me to *his* house right now." A seed of anger began to flourish inside her.

"To...to Mr. Damian's?" Adam asked, his eyes searching hers.

"Yes," she said through gritted teeth.

"Yes, ma'am." He nodded and moved to the driver's seat.

As she settled into the backseat, she could feel the adrenaline building. The image of Ivan's face when she'd refused him no longer evoked tears, but a rage focused on Damian. Whatever had happened, she hadn't done it alone, and the emotions she'd spent weeks fighting now forced her into action. No more hiding and avoiding. She was ready to fight.

*She's got to find out exactly
what happened.*

This guy ruined her life.

This guy ruined Ivan's life.

This guy ruined their love.

He took advantage of her.

He took advantage of the situation.

Look at what she's lost.

If what he said before was true,
why doesn't she remember?

She can't leave till she gets an answer.

He owes her.

Fuck him.

Fuck him.

"Almost there Ms. — I mean, Jaden. Are you sure you're okay?"

Almost there? She looked at her watch. What seemed like moments had been a thirty-five minute ride. "Yes, Adam. Thank you," she said confidently.

That confidence was shaken as the car rolled to a stop at the scene of the romantic homicide that had taken place a little over two weeks ago. Neither occupant of the Town Car moved as Jaden finalized her thoughts and worked to bolster her courage. Minutes passed as they sat. Finally Adam spoke.

"Jaden…It will be all right. You don't—"

"Thank you, Adam," she interrupted, not letting him give her the option of not going in. Every muscle in her body tensed, but the most important one flexed hard and gave her the strength to forge on: her heart.

She stepped out of the car, and the world seemed to move in slow motion. The sun danced off the concrete sidewalk, and shadows crept along the ground, forming shapes only the birds flying high above could decipher. The scent of cut grass filled the air, and her heart beat in her ears. Her feet carried her up the steps to stand before the wooden door, and in one fluid motion, she knocked.

Bam. Bam. Bam.

Part of her wanted to turn and run, but she couldn't. She wouldn't. She needed this.

Fuck him.

Fuck him.

Anticipation and anger coursed through her body as she heard him approaching within. The doorknob rattled and shook, as did her knees, and the deadbolt released. When the door swung open, the demon stepped into her narrowed line of sight.

"Jade Thorne. I always knew you'd come back someday. What can I do for you? Another go?" His words raked over her, along with his eyes. "Jesus, you look terrible."

His insults fed her fire, and the look on his face unleashed her inner beast. This man had fucked her world, her career, and her relationship in one fell swoop. An eerie calm swept over her.

"What happened that night?"

A smile crept across his face. "Curious, are we?"

"What happened that night?"

"I told you already. What do you *think* happened?"

"What happened that night?" she asked a third time. She clenched her jaw and stood her ground, unmoved. She'd shut him down by not reacting. This was a game he wouldn't win.

Frustration furrowed his plucked brow. "You know, this is why I can't stand chicks like you. You're so fucking enamored with idea of perfect relationships and cuddling and *feelings* and puppy dogs and ice cream—always looking for that fucking prince charming. News flash: He doesn't exist."

Still receiving no reaction, he continued. "You were a fucking game, Jade. I saw how amazing you thought you were with that ass-hole boyfriend of yours. The perfect couple. A storybook romance, right? Wrong. You're just like every-fucking-body else out there. Welcome to the club! The grass is greener on the other side, right?"

She could feel the heat rising within her, but willed herself to keep still.

"Your problem is you got too goddamn drunk to do anything, let alone remember it. We got back here, and you started sobbing and crying about how much you missed Ivan. *I love Ivan. I can't do this cause I wanna marry Ivan.* Boo hoo! You passed out on the bed in your bra and panties like a college slut. So disappointing. I would have loved to hit that—loved to get my dick wet and prove you aren't as perfect as you thought you were. Well, fuck you and your ridiculous boyfriend. I think I proved my point any—

Pop! Her clenched fist, without considering the ramifications of such a primal reaction, had connected with Damian's face, splattering a trail of spit and blood on his door. She'd taken a piece of herself back and learned the truth about that horrible night. She'd always loved Ivan, and this proved it. In her most drunken state, in the presence of temptation, she had ultimately made the right choice. However lonely or confused she'd been in the moment, she'd held true to the man she loved, her soulmate.

Nevertheless, she soon realized, no matter how right she'd made *her* situation, *their* situation remained lost. Though she'd technically remained true, she'd wronged Ivan in so many ways. The moment she'd started down this path with Damian, and the longer she concealed it, she'd been careless with his heart. Then when he'd offered it to her, she'd refused him with no real way to explain why.

Without a word, she left Damian whimpering and cursing on his porch and ran for the town car. She prayed she could run fast enough to catch what she'd left behind.

I'm coming, Ivan, she told him silently. *I have the answers now. You have to listen.*

Would he forgive her? She could only hope.

Acknowledgments

Dr. Ivan Rusilko

What is hope?

Is it the ambition of discovering for the first time what the carnal definition of physical love is without understanding the concept of true passion? Or is it imagination running wild and free fueled by the dream that tonight will last forever and tomorrows will always come as you are blinded by the brilliance of another's smile?

Is it a theory of inevitability that relies on fate or destiny bringing two souls together for their one shot at true and unbridled happiness? Or is it plea to erase a past that used to hold the potential for limitless smiles and endless laughs.

I define hope as a narcotic.

It courses through our veins, igniting ideas and feelings and emotions that all work in collaboration to produce a better tomorrow, while leaving today but a distant memory. The essence of its unknown and unseen promise is beautiful and addicting to those who are in need of its satiating grace.

The dependence on the idea of possibility can become a crutch however; an excuse for ignoring the here and now. It can swiftly morph from a therapeutic escape to an addictive obsession that somewhere over the rainbow lies the answer that will make everything right again.

I am thankful to call myself a true addict to hope's mind altering panacea. Its blissful nirvana can seem both inconceivably irrational yet entirely fathomable to anyone lost in a sea of uncertainty. Just as age brings wisdom, experience brings the understanding that no matter what pot of gold lies at the end of your hopeful rainbow, the relief it casts over tragedy and heartache is the power behind its true magic.

To the hope that resides in the depths of my being, thank you.

ACKNOWLEDGMENTS

Everly Drummond

When Ivan and I embarked on this little journey of ours over a year and a half ago we had no idea where The Winemaker's Dinner was going to take us. And now, here we are, writing the acknowledgements for book two. We've had the privilege of working with the amazing team at Omnific publishing: Elizabeth Harper, Micha Stone, Traci Olsen, Lisa O'Hara, CJ Creel, and our editor, Jessica Royer Ocken. But what I am most grateful for is the response we're received from you, the reader. Your kind words and thoughtful messages do not go unnoticed or unappreciated. Thank you.

Over the past year I've also had the privilege of working with and talking to some amazing book bloggers, some of which have become close friends. A huge shout out to Delilah Rains at Riverina Romantics, Kathy Womack at Romantic Reading Escapes, Tamie at Bookish Temptations, and all of the other awesome book bloggers that have read, reviewed, and promoted The Winemaker's Dinner. Thank you for taking the time to read our books.

With the help of Lyss Stern, Jen Boudin, Cakes Jagla, and all the other members of Diva Moms, the launch of the series in NYC was a huge success. Thanks for making our time in New York so memorable and for going above and beyond anything I could've ever expected. Y'all are an amazing group of women. And thank you to Sparky and Sarah Marquis and the good folks at Mollydooker Wine for not only allowing us to use the name of Mollydooker in the book, but for being an essential part of the NYC launch.

Thank you to my mom and all of my family and friends. I am truly blessed to be surrounded by so many loving people. Your unfaltering love, support, and encouragement keep me going. And Ivan, what can I say about him that I haven't already said? I'm honored to call you my friend and colleague.

About the Author

Dr. Ivan Rusilko, DO, CSN, PT, is an accomplished weight loss, wellness, physical enhancement and sexual health physician in Miami Beach, where he currently practices international concierge medicine and is the Medical Director and co-founder of Club Essentia, a cutting edge, medical retreat facility specializing in luxury medicine that will debut in early 2013. A certified sports nutritionist, champion bodybuilder, international male fitness model, and former Mr. USA 2008 & 2010, Dr. Ivan graduated from the Lake Erie College of Osteopathic Medicine in 2010 and sits as the national media expert and spokesperson on diet, exercise and sports nutrition for the American Osteopathic Association. In the summer of 2012, he added author to his extensive resume with the release of the fictionalized erotic memoir, *The Winemaker's Dinner: Appetizers*, and is anxiously awaiting the release of the second book *Entrée* and is working on the third and final book in the series, *Dessert*.

About the Author

As a student of the Centennial College Social Service Worker program, and the Trent University Biology program, Everly Drummond had a previous life in administration and transportation before launching her career as a writer. Everly's other writing projects include City of the Damned, a paranormal romance series, and *Blood of the Ancients*, a YA paranormal romance. All four novellas in the City of the Damned series have appeared on the Amazon.com bestseller list. Everly resides in Toronto, Ontario, where she is currently working on the third installment to *The Winemaker's Dinner* with co-author, Ivan Rusilko.

PHOTO BY REDANDALCOM

←----→Young Adult←----→

Shades of Atlantis and *The Ember Series: Ember* and *Iridescent* by Carol Oates
Breaking Point by Jess Bowen
Life, Liberty, and Pursuit by Susan Kaye Quinn
Embrace by Cherie Colyer
Destiny's Fire by Trisha Wolfe
Streamline by Jennifer Lane
Reaping Me Softly by Kate Evangelista

←----→Historical Romance←----→

Cat O' Nine Tails by Patricia Leever
Burning Embers by Hannah Fielding

←----→Erotic Romance←----→

Becoming sage by Kasi Alexander
Saving sunni by Kasi & Reggie Alexander
The Winemaker's Dinner: Appetizers and *Entreé*
by Dr. Ivan Rusilko & Everly Drummond

←----→Anthologies and Singles←----→

A Valentine Anthology including short stories by Alice Clayton, Jennifer DeLucy,
Nicki Elson, Jessica McQuinn, Victoria Michaels, and Alison Oburia

It's Only Kinky the First Time by Kasi Alexander
Learning the Ropes by Kasi & Reggie Alexander
The Winemaker's Dinner: RSVP by Dr. Ivan Rusilko
The Winemaker's Dinner: No Reservations by Everly Drummond
Big Guns by Jessica McQuinn
Concessions by Robin DeJarnett
Starstruck by Lisa Sanchez
New Flame by BJ Thornton
Shackled by Debra Anastasia
Swim Recruit by Jennifer Lane
Sway by Nicki Elson
Full Speed Ahead by Susan Kaye Quinn
The Second Sunrise by Hannah Downing
The Summer Prince by Carol Oates
Whatever it Takes by Sarah M. Glover
Clarity by Patricia Leever
Glimpse of Light by Jennifer DeLucy

CPSIA information can be obtained at www.ICGtesting.com
Printed in the USA
BVOW080228210113

311152BV00001B/10/P